C702381853

SOUTH LANARKSHIRE
Leisure & Culture
www.library.southlanarkshire.gov.uk

## South Lanarkshire Libraries

This book is to be returned on or before
the last date stamped below or may be
renewed by telephone or online.

## Delivering services for South Lanarkshire

| | | |
|---|---|---|
| LN-MOBC | | HF -LN |
| 01. AUG 18 | 27 NOV 2018 | LN- HTH |
| 29 AUG 18 | LN-LN | 26 FEB 2020 |
| CO45 | 22 FEB 2019 | LN C087 |
| 05. NOV 18. | 12 MAR 2019 | LN- HO |
| | COY( | 15 OCT 2020 |
| LN | -4 APR 2019 | 15 JUL 2021 |
| LN -HF | LN-Lm | 23 SEP 2021 |
| | 17 MAY 2019 | |
| H | LN-SV | |
| SMITH, ETHYl | 16 JUN 2019 | |
| DARK TIN | | |

D1420206

First Published in Great Britain in 2017 by
ThunderPoint Publishing Limited
Summit House
4-5 Mitchell Street
Edinburgh
Scotland EH6 7BD

Copyright © Ethyl Smith 2017

The moral right of the author has been asserted.

All rights reserved.

Without limiting the rights under copyright reserved above, no part of this publication may be reproduced, stored in or introduced into a retrieval system, or transmitted in any form or by any means (electronic, mechanical, photocopying, recording or otherwise), without the prior written permission of both the copyright owner and the above publisher of the work.

This book is a work of fiction. Names, places, characters and locations are used fictitiously and any resemblance to actual persons, living or dead, is purely coincidental and a product of the authors' creativity.

Scripture quotation taken from the Holy Bible, New International Version Anglicised Copyright © 1979, 1984, 2011 Biblica. Used by permission of Hodder & Stoughton Ltd, an Hachette UK company. All rights reserved. 'NIV' is a registered trademark of Biblica UK trademark number 1448790.

Cover Image © Ethyl Smith
Cover Design © Huw Francis

ISBN: 978-1-910946-24-4 (Paperback)
ISBN: 978-1-910946-26-8 (eBook)

www.thunderpoint.scot

# Acknowledgements

Doctor Jan Fortune of Cinnamon Press and Seonaid Francis of Thunderpoint cast careful eyes over my words and suggested relevant amendments. Thank you.

I gained insight into this period from James King Hewison *The Covenanters*, John Howie *Scots Worthies*, Robert Watson *Peden: Prophet of the Covenant*, Andrew Murray Scott *Bonnie Dundee*, Magnus Linklater & Christian Hesketh *For King and Conscience*, Charles Sanford Terry *John Graham of Claverhouse*, Dane Love *The Covenanter Encyclopaedia*, David S. Ross *The Killing Time*, Rosalind K. Marshall *The Days of Duchess Anne*, Ian Whyte *Agriculture and Society in Seventeenth Century Scotland*, John Greenshields *Private Papers*, Robert McLeish *Archivist of Lesmahagow Historical Association*, Newsletters *Scottish Covenanter Memorial Association*, Dr. Mark Jardine Jardine's Book of Martyrs, Culpeper *Culpeper's Complete Herbal*, J.H Thomson *The Martyr Graves of Scotland*, Elizabeth Foyster & Christopher A.Whatley *A History of Everyday Life in Scotland 1600-1800*, Ecco *The Laird and Farmer*, Maurice Grant *The Lion of the Covenant*, Maurice Grant *No King But Christ*.

| South Lanarkshire Library Service | |
|---|---|
| **EK** | |
| C702381853 | |
| **Askews & Holts** | |
| H | £9.99 |
| 5734271 | |

# Dedication

For Robert Ferguson Smith

## Thegither

*A feegur breks the brackish muir,*
*stauns heich, preachin, prayin. Here*
*Covenanters gaither oan rimied loam,*
*sombre witness agin a pewter sky. Stern chiels*
*an dairk plaided weemen, worn buits crack*
*ice. Hunners settlin tae ane - a Conventicle.*

*They tak tent, spek wi their God, haud tae Bible*
*an conscience, thegither. Ae lug oan Peden*
*unflinchin in his Lord. The ither lug cockit*
*fir the danger o bridle jangle, the rattle o bit*
*in mooth, the slash o swuird. At the edge,*
*a feegur wi the leuk o Peden, fause faced*

*in laither, locks an teeth. This hare will rin*
*tae lure Redcoated Hounds. Oan the wrunkelt map*
*there's nae trace o bluid skailt by Dragoons.*
*Bracken bodies tak liturgy's comfort. Nae king*
*is awmichtie here. Prayers flee as flaucht*
*frae lips. Gainstaundin.*

Finola Scott 2017

*'There comes a time when one must take a position that is neither safe, nor politic, nor popular, but he must take it because conscience tells him it is right.'*

**Martin Luther King Jr.**

# Chapter 1

*Each one should test their own actions. Then they can take pride in themselves alone, without comparing themselves to someone else, for each one should carry their own load.* **Galatians, Chapter 6, verse 4-5 (NIV)**

## June 1679

A full, mounted platoon galloped up the track towards John Steel's farm at Logan Waterhead minutes after the local curate burst into the courtyard shouting, "John! Soldiers! Ye need tae run."

And he had, slipping round the end wall of his barn like a startled rabbit. Without the little man's warning he'd still be in his own kitchen, about to be captured.

Earlier that day the battle at Bothwell Bridge had turned into a rout. On the losing side, John had escaped when one of the cavalry leaders swung in at the wrong angle, allowing him to counter the attack then gallop from the battlefield. The earl, Airlie by name, proud and vindictive, had made it his business to root out John's name and village. Now he'd arrived to exact revenge.

John ducked into the byre and raced past his cows, lined up, waiting to be milked. In the open again he headed for the vegetable garden, darted between rows of carefully tended beans, then jumped the drystane dyke to put more distance between himself and the troopers.

By the time he reached the end of the garden his gathering speed helped him clear a high fence and land among the sheep. They looked up, but his familiar figure brought no warning bleat or sudden scamper. Each mouth returned to nibble the sweet grass while John half ran, half-crawled among them to reach the gate into the next field.

Beyond there the ground grew rough as it rose toward the small wood of pine trees his father had planted twenty years ago on the edge of the open moor. He pounded up this steep slope, the hard soles of his boots snapping heather roots, brittle from weeks of unusually dry spring weather. Up here was a promise of escape. Here a man on foot had the advantage over a hunter on horseback.

While this was happening Sandy Gillon, curate to the Parish of Lesmahagow, was standing in the farmyard, holding tight to Marion Steel's hand. Only half an hour ago he'd been driving in his horse and trap, enjoying the green fields and twittering birds, trying to pretend he was a happy man, when mounted soldiers had appeared out of nowhere, demanding the whereabouts of John Steel's farm. He'd sent them in the opposite direction. No doubt there would be a price to pay.

Sandy had been in the village for only a few months, but long enough to destroy his illusion of a fine position, away from his previous life in the nearby town of Lanark. There he'd been a mere shoemaker, a tradesman, at everyone's beck and call. To his credit he was a fair scholar, mostly self-educated, but also too naive to realise that something was amiss when the sheriff not only considered his application to become a curate but appointed him with almost indecent haste.

Thrilled with the promise of money, a fine house, and the chance to be somebody, he'd arrived in Lesmahagow to discover closed faces with no sign of welcome. Worst of all, his kirk remained empty Sunday after Sunday.

In desperation he'd written to the sheriff who'd sent soldiers to deal with the problem. Except they'd made matters worse by following their pig-headed lieutenant into a trap. The very men they'd come to threaten had captured the whole platoon and made them a laughing stock in front of the village. The sheriff had been quick to retaliate. The men involved had been rounded up and taken to Lanark, to face a week in the tolbooth with further punishment of a heavy fine before they were released.

After that Sandy and his wife had been left to live like hermits and bicker with each other. They felt guilty over what had happened but could do nothing to make amends. Even worse, they were stuck in this village with no prospect of returning to Lanark. And then a few weeks later, these same villagers had been involved in some kind of battle at a hill beyond Strathaven. Law and order had lost that day, and fired up with victory a good number of them had marched away to face another battle. John Steel had been up front as elected captain, leading them in open rebellion against their lawful king. Mad fools or brave men, many were either dead on Bothwell Moor or captive with a dreaded future in front of them, or running for their life.

John had been one of the few who spoke to Sandy and seemed sympathetic, but not enough to attend the kirk of a Sunday. And yet Sandy had tried to save him by sending the soldiers on a wild goose chase. If only he'd used his head and not his heart they'd have arrived at the farm in time to capture John, or worse, and Sandy would still be driving his horse and trap round the country lanes, enjoying the fine day, instead of standing in the middle of this courtyard with a rebel's wife.

The sight of her had made him stay. Now they both tried to put on a brave face when the grizzled old leader of the troop juddered to a halt in front of them.

"Ye again." He glared at Sandy. "Whaur's Steel? The truth this time."

"I dinna ken," Sandy replied.

"So hoo come ye sent me and ma men on a chase tae the wrang side o the village?"

"Ah must hae misunderstood. Steel's a common name here aboot. Ah didna mean – "

"Ay ye did." The tip of a long sword flicked under Sandy's chin, forced his face up, then up again till he was staring into the grey flecked eyes of an angry man. "I had tae get the richt directions frae somebody else, somebody whae isna feart tae tell the truth; a law abiding somebody. And when I finally arrive here I find yersel in the very yard o the very place I asked aboot."

"John Steel's no here." Marion Steel spoke up for the first time. "Ah'm his wife. He's been awa frae here these past few weeks."

"Ay. Fighting against his king and flouting the law. I'm Jamie Ogilvie, Earl o Airlie and Strathmore, here tae represent law and justice. Yer man wis pairt o the mutinous rag bag we had tae deal wi back at Bothwell." The old man grinned at Marion's horrified expression. "During this wee stramash I happened on Maister Steel. Instead o surrendering he ran awa so I reckon we hae unfeenished business atween us. Rebellion is a hanging offence."

"Luk sir," one of the troopers interrupted. "Up there."

Airlie wheeled round and saw a figure, a man running beyond the second field from the farm, heading up the hill towards the small pine wood at the edge of the moor. Instantly he knew exactly what had happened. In that moment he was back in the thick of battle, charging down on this man, about to run him through as he deserved when everything changed. His saddle straps had been sliced. He'd slipped to the side where an extra whack from the flat of a broadsword had sent him tumbling to the ground among prancing hooves. Even worse, his youngest lieutenant had dared to laugh. That's what Airlie remembered. Not the fact that John Steel had made no attempt to carry through his advantage with a sword thrust, but had simply slipped away and left the great earl with only a few bruises and wounded pride.

And that was the crux of the matter.

"Yon's Steel!" Airlie roared. "Aifter him!"

The earl's huge horse swung round against Sandy. Marion grabbed his coat and pulled him clear of the sharp hooves as the small courtyard rocked with riders trying to turn and head back through the narrow close.

The chase was up.

Marion and Sandy watched the long line of horses gallop across the meadow, intent on the fleeing figure who'd almost reached the wood.

"Better there than onywhaur," Marion whispered.

"But he's on foot. They'll hae him in nae time."     ·

"He kens the ground, they dinna. It's no as bad as it seems."

John swerved and seemed to dive among the trees. The riders certainly believed this. They reached the wood and fanned out to beat a path through the tight packed trees.

There was no way they could know that this particular spot held a secret. Years of heavy rain had washed away much of the top soil and allowed deep channels to form below the dense banks of heather, deep enough to swallow the unwary. One minute a man might be tramping through the heather. Next minute he'd vanish, dropping through layer upon layer of wiry branches and roots to land in a soft, dark space a good six feet below while above him the green and purple tangle closed over as if nothing had happened. This was just what John needed: a fast exit and no evidence of how or where.

John knew the whereabouts of the deepest channels. At the

right spot he simply stepped forward and allowed the heather to swallow him then spring back. Down among the damp leaf mould he crawled further along till he was tight against a small overhang of solid rock. That way if one of the horses stumbled through he might still escape detection.

He pushed hard against the rock and almost stopped breathing as he peered through the spidery pattern of roots to the faint light above. He could hear the soldiers thrashing about, then felt the ground judder as heavy hooves came out of the little wood and picked across the rough, open space towards the edge of his hiding place.

Airlie's temper seemed to have reached boiling point. He pointed back at the wood. "Search again. He canna jist disappear."

His men swept the wood one more time while their master stayed put, unaware that the centre of his wrath was crouched only ten feet beyond him.

The soldiers returned, reported nothing. Airlie glared at them then turned to scan the waving grass and ferns, and many miles of heather. Around them the wind sighed. They could even hear the curlews and moorhens calling and scuttling, but no sign or sound of the fugitive. Airlie was forced to admit he was baffled. "Wheel roond. Back tae the farm."

John heard this order and guessed Marion was about to face the brunt of this terrible man's wrath. He was tempted to call out, to surrender, but the thought of what would follow had him staying put, listening to metal hooves fading back down the slope towards the farm.

Marion and Sandy were still standing in the close mouth when the riders returned.

"Mistress Steel, step furrit and hear this," Airlie ordered. "Under fugitive law I claim this farm and land. Frae this meenit on ye've nae richt tae be here."

"But sir," Sandy dared, "surely. Ah mean. Surely no. This canna be richt."

"Steel's a rebel by his ain admission and actions. I hae every richt and claim it. As for ye, sir." Airlie's sword swung forward again. "Man o the cloth or no my patience has run oot. Stand back till I deal wi this woman."

Marion gripped Sandy's arm.

"Stand back," Airlie snapped, "or I'll whip ye." He leant forward and propelled Sandy against the wall then turned on Marion.

"Surely sir, ye've nae argument wi me."

"Ye're a felon's wife. That's enough. Intae the hoose, and fetch oot yer bairns."

Marion ran into the house to find her two terrified boys huddled behind the big settle, in the darkest corner of the kitchen. When she reappeared she dared to ask, "Whit can ah tak wi me?"

"Yersel. Yer bairns. Naething else."

Marion stared at this stranger who'd arrived out of nowhere to turn her world inside out.

He glared back.

Face white with terror, rage and disbelief, she stumbled out the front door to stand before the earl's great horse. William and Johnnie were beside her, two reminders of how much was at stake.

"Oot ye go, mistress." Airlie pointed through the close mouth. "And keep walking."

Marion clutched her sons' small hands and took the first step of the longest journey she'd ever make.

Slumped against the whitewashed wall Sandy watched the young woman he scarcely knew walk down the farm track with no extra clothes, no food, no money, and probably no idea of where to go or what to do next.

Behind him the Earl of Airlie also watched the slight figure. Probably his heart resented her show of courage. Possibly he also felt the tiniest flicker of shame. But it was only of the moment and then gone.

The platoon captain sat on his chestnut mare and kept his thoughts to himself. Dominic McCann was an experienced and trusted leader of the earl's unit and knew when to speak and when to remain silent. On this occasion he was silent, the picture of the man his master believed him to be. Tall, slim, with a pale, fine-boned face dominated by the darkest of warm brown eyes peering out below his steel helmet. Those eyes were his best feature, capable of winning any woman's heart. Not that he ever wanted to. He was captive to the tremor he felt at the sight of a young, fresh-faced boy. Being Irish and Catholic he tried to repel such an urge yet it never changed nor left him. Many a night he'd slip away from his billet to find some private place to relieve his own tension. Not that it brought much relief, only intensifying his self-loathing.

Always courteous and fair in his decisions he seemed an ideal captain of Airlie's mounted platoon. He certainly looked the part, his uniform clean and well cared for. Today his long, skirted, scarlet coat was mud spattered, as was the officer's scarf knotted round his waist, and his steel corselet had more than one dent from a thrusting sword. It had done its work to protect him during the close fighting of the battle that morning. Sword now looped up for riding, his pistols in their saddle holsters, he sat very still and watched a young woman and two small boys stumble through the narrow close of the farmyard and out to the world beyond.

He glanced at Airlie's hard profile, the sneering look. At that moment he knew he hated this man and everything he stood for, everything he was. He also knew he was a dutiful captain and paid to obey.

Marion stopped at the end of the farm track to look back at her home perched on the last patch of good ground before the open moor. A sturdy, stone built house with wisps of lazy smoke curling up from the chimney; a good-sized byre and outhouses formed a sheltered courtyard. The crops in the fields were growing. Healthy animals grazed the pastures, while a flurry of brown hens scratched and clucked as if all was well.

She peered beyond to the undulating miles of heather and rough grass and focused on the lines of dark trees where John had disappeared. She'd no idea what to do next or even where to go. Less than an hour ago she'd been turning oatcakes and fussing about the griddle being too hot. Every last one would be burnt black by now, and she no longer belonged in the only place she wanted to be. And all because some grand earl had taken ill against John.

"Whaur noo?" Johnnie's eyes were full of tears. "Are we goin tae

Granny? Will she luk after us?"

Jerked into the moment Marion couldn't answer. Waterside Farm and her mother had been her first thought and then others crowded in, warning her. Whit if yon earl gits wind an comes aifter us? Ma brither Gavin will be there. He wis fightin alangside John at Bothwell. Whit if the earl sees him? Whit if he recognises him? He micht. An then whit? Mither has suffered enough wi the loss o faither at Drumclog. Naw, ah canna tak that chance. She stared at the little face and slowly shook her head.

Johnnie burst into tears and stood as if refusing to go any farther.

She knelt beside him and gently kissed the angry brow. "We'll go tae Waterside aifter. But richt noo it's nae safe. Ye dinna want onythin happenin tae Granny dae ye? Ye dinna want yon earl burstin intae her hoose an shoutin at her lik he did at us?"

Johnnie shook his head then stared back at her. "Whaur then?"

"Cousin Bess. Ye like her?"

Johnnie nodded slowly but looked suspicious.

"Weel, she's got plenty space an she's aye pleased tae see us. She'll enjoy oor company fur a day or twa insteid o sittin in her hoose by hersel. Yon earl will nivver guess wur in the village. It's the last place he'll think aboot. An if ye ask nicely cousin Bess will mak yon wee dumplin ye like."

"That's a guid idea Ma." William took his brother's hand. "C'mon, stop wastin time. We canna staund here. Yon awfy man tellt us tae keep walkin." He smiled up at his mother as if well aware of what was happening, suddenly old beyond his years with the terror of it. "C'mon Ma. We'll manage. Jist sae lang as Pa's safe."

"Ay. Ye're richt." She blinked back her own tears and turned towards the road for the village. "A day or twa wi cousin Bess is best. Aifter that we'll see."

They trudged along, the dust sending up tiny clouds that made her cough. More than once her foot slipped into the deep wheel ruts. She was also angry with herself, her selfishness, her keenness to be a rebel, to flout the law, to encourage John in all this awful nonsense, for that's what it was.

Glancing fondly at William's dark, curly head, so like her own, she saw how he bobbed along with an energy she envied. She also guessed his fear and confusion was more than equal to her own. And it wasn't as if he understood why any of this was happening.

Why should he? A bairn should be playing in the yard or running across the fields, not walking this dusty road to nowhere. And John. She hardly dared think about him.

They reached the hump-backed bridge just beyond a row of houses skirting the river Nethan. There was no-one to be seen. Each door was fast shut. Had they heard the soldiers pass? Were they waiting and fearing a knock on their door or were they simply keeping out of sight?

Just past the bridge she stopped and looked through the shady overhang of tall willows skirting both sides of the long, shingly bank where children often played and threw stones into the slow flowing, peaty Nethan. She stopped. "Mony's the time ah've watched ye splash aboot there wi yer heids fu o nonsense an yer claes aw wet. Happy days, eh?"

Two solemn faces nodded but said nothing as she stood there wallowing in her misery. And then a little hand yanked her arm and pulled her over the edge of the steep bank. Next thing she was sliding all the way to the bottom, ending up with her toes in the water. Johnnie and William crouched beside her while the air filled with the sound of metal hooves clattering across the stone bridge then fading up the hill beyond. The children had heard the soldiers approach and decided to hide.

Safe among the green fronds Marion lay and listened to the burn rippling over the stones in its path. Finally she looked up and saw a fat grouse leaning over the bank edge to watch the three, huddled figures. It looked surprised. A little, red-rimmed eye blinked then blinked again. She sat up and smiled at its silly expression. Her movement brought a loud cackle as the round head jerked up. Brown wings flapped desperately till the heavy body managed to defy gravity, clear the bushes, and disappear.

She turned to the boys. "Noo jist suppose we hud a pair o wings."

They grinned and followed their mother up the steep scramble to the road above.

At the top of the bank Johnnie stepped onto the now deserted road. "Whit if we meet thae soldiers again?"

Marion gave him a reassuring squeeze and tried to sound convincing. "They'll be weel awa by noo. Chasin some ither pair soul wi nae thocht for us."

At that moment Airlie and his men were pulling up in the village square and attracting attention. "Listen weel." The great earl glared at the gathering crowd, "I'm James Ogilvie, Earl of Airlie and Strathmore, here tae tell ye that yer so called rebellion is ower for guid and aw. The battle at Bothwell Brig made sure o that. As for John Steel – " he spat out the name. "Yer erstwhile captain led some misguided creatures oot o this village a few weeks ago and noo he's paid the price."

"Wis he killed in the battle?" an old man asked.

"No. Mair's the peety." Airlie gave him a spiteful look. "Steel's on the run. A branded felon. He's lost his lands and ony richt tae bide there. And the same goes for his wife and bairns. If ony o ye are daft enough tae gie them shelter, or food, or dare help them in ony way ye'll be in the tolbooth afore ye ken whit's happening."

The old man drew back.

Airlie smiled. "I've claimed his farm under fugitive law and noo I'm awa tae Lanark tae see the sheriff post up Steel's name wi a thoosand merks written across it. That means a wee word in the richt ear cud mak somebody weel aff. That's aw it taks. Freedom doesna mean much when there's naewhaur left tae go."

The earl wheeled his horse round and left the villagers glancing uneasily at each other. Nothing was said. One by one they scurried away to worry about their husbands, fathers, sons. Whatever had happened at Bothwell Bridge it had shattered any hopes or foolish notions of a few weeks ago when the village platoon marched away behind their brand new, blue banner. Christ and the Covenant had a new meaning now.

As she reached the brow of the hill Marion heard the steady clip, clop of a well-shod horse and metal wheels turning on the gravel behind her. This time she made no attempt to hide but simply stepped aside to wait, and was surprised to see Sandy Gillon.

He stopped the horse and jumped down beside her. "Yon earl's an auld deil. He's awa tae the village tae warn them against giein ye ony help. He's left three men back at the farm so ye canna gang back there either."

"Whit aboot John?" she asked. "Is ther ony sign o him?"

"Nane. That's why the great man's in a temper. Aifter he's been tae the village he's aff tae Lanark tae see that the sheriff posts John's name ootside the garrison wi a thoosand merks against him."

"Does that mean we canna gang tae cousin Bess?" William's voice trembled.

Marion nodded. "It luks lik we're oot on the moor, same as Da."

"No ye'll no," Sandy cut her short. "No if ah can help it. Yon Airlie threatened me within an inch o ma life. But ah'm no havin it. No frae him, an no frae the sheriff."

"But ah thocht ye wur the sheriff's man? Aifter aw, he sent ye here."

"So he did. An comin here wis ma worst mistake ivver. Mibbe this is ma chance tae mak up fur it. Richt noo yer man's safe enough oot there on the moors. Whit aboot yersels?"

"We'll manage."

"Wud a bite tae eat and a proper bed no help?"

"But Airlie's warnin against us."

"An ah'm no listenin. Come tae the manse. It's a big hoose wi plenty room. Ma wife Meg will be mair than pleased tae welcome ye. Come for the nicht then we'll see whit next. We jist need tae be carefu. Ah'll gang on aheid an tell Meg tae expect ye. Bide ootside the village till aifter dark then come on kinda carefu like. When ye reach the manse slip roond by the back door. Naebody'll ever ken." Sandy jumped into the trap again and clicked the horse on.

Marion watched him go and wondered if she dared accept any more help from this strange little man.

# Chapter 2

Airlie left his young lieutenant and two experienced troopers to guard the farm while the rest of the platoon set out for Lanark. These three could hardly believe their luck: a comfortable billet, good food, plenty of it, and virtually nothing to do. Or so they thought till they heard a loud noise from the byre. The two older soldiers had been brought up on a farm and knew what this meant. They grinned at each other. It was a long time since either had done anything like this but within minutes they were in the byre, coats off, sleeves up, squeezing the teats, to relieve the strain on the udders of John Steel's six good milking cows. They even remembered the routine and carried the pails of milk into the little dairy then strained them into milk pans to cool.

Meanwhile the young lieutenant explored the kitchen and pantry beyond. When the other two returned they sniffed the sweet smell of baking potatoes and saw a table spread with hunks of Marion's fresh, baked bread, an ashet of smoked ham, and a huge, creamy cheese. Better food than any military barracks. Best of all, the young lad had found a full barrel of ale. It all seemed too good to be true. At dawn they had been on the field at Bothwell, expected to hack and cut and kill, then help round up hundreds of prisoners before riding ten hard miles behind their angry master, to capture a man who had vanished into thin air. It had been a strange day. To round it off with the best of meals, a warm fire, and no superior officer barking orders felt like heaven.

Supper was a long, enjoyable affair with mug after mug of home brewed ale. By the end of their meal all three men were more than content.

"Guid stuff." Fergus, the oldest soldier, lit his clay pipe and grinned across the table at his companions. "Ken whit, ah cud git used tae this."

"Ay," his friend Gilbert agreed. "Better than chasin tae Lanark ahint his lordship. Whit a fuss he's makin ower ane man."

"It's maistly ma fault," the young lieutenant admitted. "If ah hadna laughed when Steel knocked the maister aff his horse there micht no hae been sic a tantrum."

Gilbert shook his head. "Dear o me Ross. Ye've a lot tae answer for."

"Stop tormentin the lad." Fergus turned to the red-faced lieutenant. "Dinna fash yersel, son. We aw ken whit his lordship's like when he gits a bee in his bunnet. No that we'll ivver catch this Steel. He's mair than fit for auld Airlie."

Gilbert nodded. "Weel he kens it. That's whit the fuss is aboot."

After dark John Steel crept down from his hiding place on the moor and made for the farm. He knew his dog would recognise his step and stay silent. Indeed, he'd every intention of taking his clever collie away with him.

Lamp-light spilled into the dark courtyard. Everything seemed peaceful. So it was. Through the tiny panes of glass in his kitchen window he saw three soldiers lying back on his big settle, shirts undone, boots off, a mug of ale in each hand. All three seemed half-asleep. The fire was blazing, the room must be hot, and they looked as if they'd had more than enough to eat as well as drink.

John edged along the wall to the main door then gently lifted the sneck. It made a tiny squeak. He froze and listened. No movement. No reaction from inside. No one seemed to have heard so he pushed the door open enough to slip into the dark hall. Now a trespasser in his own home he tiptoed to the edge of the open kitchen door and felt the blast of heat from the fire.

The soldiers' conversation slowly rose and fell. Words were slurred. John took a chance. Two quick steps. He was past the open space hurrying further along the narrow passage. A moment later he was in his bedroom, kneeling by the old kist to lift the heavy lid and reach through piles of neatly folded clothes. Searching fingers closed on the leather pouch he was after. He smiled. His precious savings were still there. He'd need these gold coins in the days ahead. One less thing to worry about. His heart sang as he stuffed the bulging bag inside his thick, tweed jacket before digging further through the layers of clothes. This time he pulled out his grandfather's sword. Hours ago he'd dumped his by the kitchen dresser. The minute he arrived home from Bothwell his only thought had been Marion in his arms. There was no way now to retrieve it, but this old sword would serve well enough.

He turned and made to rise when soft footsteps stuttered along the flagstone hall. A moment later he could make out a man's fat shape sway in the doorway. A tired voice called out, "Drink on if ye like, I'm awa tae lie doon."

Bare feet shuffled across the floorboards followed by the sound of a heavy body dropping onto the big bed. There was a loud creak, a long belch, and a blast of sweet smelling ale.

The bed was only a few feet away but the room was so dark John had no way of knowing if the man's eyes were open. All he could do was stay perfectly still and listen. Minutes passed, then he heard a contented sigh. A few more minutes brought the sound of a snore, then another. This trooper was too tired and comfortable to sense or even care about anything, let alone guess that the man he'd been chasing earlier was in the room beside him.

Gradually the snores became a steady rhythm. John slowly stood up, took a step then stopped to listen. No break in the snoring. Now he dared tiptoe to the door and slide into the hall again. The next part was easy. Down the long passage to the outer door.

The two men in the kitchen were lost in a world of their own indulgence. What with the heat from the fire, and the steady tick of the clock on the back wall neither was aware of an intruder sneaking past the kitchen door.

Out in the fresh air, his pouch of gold coins inside his jacket, John clutched the hilt of his grandfather's sword and crept round to the hay-shed. Fly had been shut in since the soldiers arrived at the farm and the dog leapt as the door opened. He licked his master's hand and John ruffled the furry head before leading the happy dog through the darkest shadows in the courtyard and out by the narrow close mouth. After that they kept to the grass bordering the farm track until they reached the same road as Marion had taken earlier that day.

Next morning Fergus woke to the sound of restive cows. He rolled off the comfortable bed and shouted, "Ross, Gilbert. Git up. We need tae feed thae beasts."

He had to shout several times before the other two lifted their heads from the kitchen table and stared bleary-eyed at each other.

"Whit's he on aboot?" Gilbert asked.

"Somethin aboot beasts." Ross's head slumped back down on the table.

Fergus came into the kitchen and grabbed the boy's collar. "Come on. Dae ye no hear thae beasts? Thur needin fed."

Ross and Gilbert swore and stumbled out after Fergus to spread fresh straw and fill the water troughs in the byre. "Noo let's dae this richt." Fergus handed a brush to his two unwilling helpers. "Feenish brushin up an then we'll walk the ladies oot tae the field ahint the farm."

Back in the kitchen they lit the fire. This done Ross began to clear the mess from last night's feast. "We canna leave the place lik this. C'mon. If ye muck in an help ah'll mak breakfast."

They tidied up as best they could then Ross fetched a pot and some oatmeal, went out to the well for fresh water, mixed the meal and water and swung the pot over the rising heat. The mixture bubbled as he stirred. It smelt good. A big bowl of porridge along with creamy milk would set them right after last night's indulgence.

He was reaching for a ladle when Fergus stopped him. "Leave it. Ah can hear horses gallopin up the farm track. The platoon's comin back."

All three buttoned up their tunics and rushed outside to stand at attention before their master arrived.

The platoon juddered to a halt and the first rider grinned at the three rigid figures on the doorstep. "Staund easy lads. The maister's still in Lanark. The sheriff's entertainin him for a day or twa."

"Whit aboot Steel?" Davie asked.

"Onybody's guess. Richt noo ah'm mair interested in some breakfast."

Fergus nodded towards the young lieutenant, "Ross has made the porridge."

"Only a wee drap."

"Nae problem." Fergus grinned. "Fling some extra meal in yon big pot, an there's bound tae be plenty eggs aboot. C'mon lad, ah'll help ye. Cheer up. We hud a guid nicht, an Airlie's still nae here."

Marion's first night away from the farm wouldn't be in the open, under the stars, but in a proper house, between clean sheets, on a comfortable bed. Sandy Gillon had been as good as his word and given her shelter, yet none of it felt right.

He'd warned her to be careful, to come into the village after dark. And she'd done that, slipping past familiar houses like a thief then through the back gate to the manse. Sandy had been there, waiting to pull the three waifs inside, lock the door, and lead them down the long, unlit hall into a safely shuttered kitchen with a warm fire and dancing candlelight. A woman stood by the fire stirring a big, black pot, and the smell of hot soup made all three realise they were hungry. The woman had turned, her round, friendly face smiling as she came forward to give Marion a hug and let her know all was well, at least for the moment. She'd sat them down, filled big bowls of soup, cut hunks of bread and cheese but asked no questions.

Once upstairs the three Steels had been left to snuggle under warm covers. The boys' eyes closed as they lay down. Both were asleep in seconds but Marion's head buzzed with scary sights and sounds, and an overwhelming sense of foreboding. She wished she could think clearly enough to unravel what had happened. Nothing seemed to make sense. She could only feel the hate and the fear. She tried again to think through the sequence of events. It didn't work. Maybe she was too tired, and the soft pillow under her head was suggesting leave it be, just slide away, no need to be brave, let it wait till morning.

Awakening in a strange bed Marion stared up at the high, carved ceiling and studied the delicate tracery of plaster, trying to work out what kind of leaves they were supposed to be. This was a fine room in a fine house, nothing like the low, wooden ceiling in her bedroom. Nothing like the rough, white, plastered walls of her home. This made her sit up. Taking care not to wake the two sleeping children curled up beside her she slipped out of bed and opened the shutters to peer out at a greying dawn. John was out there somewhere. She prayed he was safe.

As for Sandy and Meg, what would happen if that grand old earl found out about their kindness? The world beyond the window was no longer the world she'd known.

Suddenly uneasy she stepped back. Not that it mattered for Gaby, the tinker, had seen three dark figures slip into the manse garden last night, and known only too well who they were. He also knew they'd no business to be there, not after Airlie's announcement in the village square that very afternoon.

Never one to waste an opportunity Gaby was already on his way to Lanark, skipping along, muttering about the chance of a coin or two once he reached the sheriff's ear.

While Marion had been staring out the upstairs bedroom of the manse her cousin Bess was at the back door, whispering to Meg Gillon. She'd seen Gaby listening to the old earl in the square and was sure he'd still been around after dark. She'd also seen Marion and the two boys tiptoe past her house and into the manse garden. Because of the threats she'd heard in the village square that afternoon she hadn't called out, hadn't stepped forward as a good cousin should.

The more she thought about it the more ashamed she felt. Worse than that, she couldn't sleep for thinking about Gaby with his twisted smile and pretence of being helpless. He'd harmed the Steels before, creeping away to the sheriff at Lanark with a tale about John breaking the law. And John had ended up with a heavy fine and a spell in the tollbooth. Maybe this time it was Marion's turn. This worried her enough to be up by first light and across at the manse to wake Meg and share her suspicions.

Minutes later both women were up the stairs, tapping on the bedroom door, telling Marion about Gaby being in the village, reminding her of the harm he'd done before, insisting she must leave the manse at once.

"It's haurly daylicht," Marion protested.

"An naebody likely tae see ye or the boys," Bess suggested. "Ye didna hear that auld earl in the square wi his terrible threats, but ah did. Come wi me in case yon tinker saw ye come here. It'll be safer in ma hoose. Ye can bide a day or twa while we try tae git haud o John. Aifter that we'll work somethin oot. C'mon lass. Ye ken ah'm richt."

Marion crossed to the big bed and woke the boys who found themselves lifted from snug warmth. Half asleep they were marched downstairs, out into a misty morning, then along the lane towards Bess's house at the edge of the square, and not a word spoken.

Meg stood at her back door and watched her overnight visitors disappear along the lane. Bess's words about the old tinker worried her, especially how he could spin a tale, and always to his own advantage.

Airlie was in a better mood this morning. The sheriff had listened to his tale about John Steel, agreed with every word, and then ordered a notice to be posted outside the garrison proclaiming John Steel as a rebel with a thousand merks on his head.

Sheriff Meiklejon had also been a good host, with a generous dinner and the best of wine for his visitor. All very civilised as befit a great lord of the realm, and Airlie enjoyed being given his due respect. And of course the free-flowing wine had helped the two men warm to each other as they sat long into the night planning the best way to capture John Steel, and maybe a few other rebels as well.

Airlie eyed up a full plate of best ham and three perfectly fried eggs then stabbed at the centre of the nearest yolk.

A light, mocking voice cut through his pleasure. His good humour vanished, and he swung round to face the speaker. "It's yersel Clavers. Whit brings ye here?"

The slim figure in the doorway swept off his hat and bowed. "There wis much tae be done aifter ye galloped aff the battlefield yesterday. Yer expertise in organising the prisoners wis sair missed. Monmouth wants them marched tae the capital for their just desserts."

"I had some o my ain tae deal wi." Airlie's tone barely disguised his dislike of John Graham, the Duke of York's current favourite. "So whit are ye daeing oot here if there's aw that tae deal wi?"

"A bit extra rounding up. And naething tae dae wi personal maitters." Clavers' smile broadened.

"Ay weel. Each tae their ain needs." Airlie remembered how he'd met Clavers at the end of the battle and told him how John Steel had whacked him off his horse. He also remembered how Clavers had dismissed his demand for revenge.

"Ah. Claverhoose." The sheriff appeared in the doorway. "It's yersel. Noo this is an unexpected pleasure." He tried to look as if he meant it. "Whit can we dae for ye this mornin?"

"A plateful lik my freend here is enjoying wud dae a treat."

"Nae sooner said, sir." The order was barked downstairs then the sheriff tried again. "Is this an official visit?"

"Ay and no. Since the rebels are weel and truly beaten it's time tae clamp doon on the Kirk truants and mak sure they understaund the meaning o surrender. The king is determined on nae mair rebellion, and the duke has charged me wi making sure the miscreants see the error o their ways."

"I see." The sheriff thought about an earlier quartering of Claverhouse and his platoon in Lanark garrison. "Dare I ask aboot yer accommodation requirements on this occasion?"

"Rest easy." Claverhouse smiled sweetly. "I'm for anither billet. I'm tae set up my headquarters in the Black Bull Inn, at Moffat."

"Is that no a bit far oot?"

"It's a fine billet. But like ye say, no the maist convenient place for patrolling the district. But the duke wants me there, so whae am I tae argue wi the king's ain brither?"

"So ye're jist passin thru?" The sheriff could barely hide his relief.

"In a manner o speaking." Just then the serving girl appeared with a full breakfast plate. Claverhouse took the plate, thanked the astonished girl, and sat down opposite Airlie.

The sheriff stared at Airlie. Airlie stared at the sheriff. They both shrugged and allowed the steady ticking of the wall clock to fill the uneasy silence which was only disturbed by Clavers' champing away at his ham and eggs. After a few minutes he looked up. "No hungry then, Airlie?"

Airlie picked up his own fork and started to eat again.

"Gentlemen. If ye'll excuse me a meenit, I hae things needin attention." The sheriff made his escape and rattled downstairs to his clerk's little room.

Thrum looked up from his writing. Meiklejon pointed up at the ceiling. "Airlie and Clavers are up there eatin a guid breakfast and smilin at each ither as if they're the best o freends. Ah ken they're no. That maks me suspicious for ah also ken they're baith set on causin trouble. Whit if they decide tae poke their noses intae garrison business? Aw I'm sayin is mak sure oor paperwork is up tae date and in order."

"Ye ken fine ah aye dae ma best."

"So ye say. Jist mak sure the garrison accoonts are richt tae the last bawbee or I'll hae yer guts for garters. They twa are trouble and I want nae mair than I've got aready."

Thrum scraped away with his quill.

"Did ye hear whit I said?"

"Ay sir. If yer visitors care tae cast their een ower ivvery scrap o paper in the garrison they'll find naethin amiss. Trust me."

"Trust ye?" The sheriff marched out the room and banged the door shut.

As soon as the sheriff left Claverhouse pushed his plate aside and stared at Airlie. "So whaur's yer fugitive noo?"

"Hiding on the moors. We chased him aw the way tae his hame. Somehoo he got awa. But nivver fear I'll hae him afore lang. In the meantime I've taen ower his farm and put oot his wife and bairns."

"Is that necessary?"

Airlie banged his fist on the table. "The man's family need tae be taught a lesson as weel!"

"If ye say so." In his mind Claverhouse was back at John Steel's farm a few months ago when he'd warned that same man about siding with rebels, even suggesting how someone of his ability might do well to consider the other side.

"Ye said ye kent the man." Airlie frowned at Clavers. "Hoo come?"

"The last time I wis here in Lanark and sat as a magistrate he wis ane o the rascals I fined for rebellious behaviour. In fact, he had the heaviest fine. But then he did deserve it." Claverhouse smiled at Airlie. "Ye're no the first tae tak umbrage at Maister Steel. My ain lieutenant wis sair discomfited by him. A laughing stock if the truth be tellt. Mind ye, Crichton's no the easiest man in the world, and sadly lacking in tact. He wis raither heavy handed wi some lassies he caught coming back frae ane o thae open air prayer meetings that were banned a few months ago."

"I'm sure yer lieutenant wis justified."

"Maister Steel didna think so. He took it upon himsel tae reprimand the lieutenant in a raither special way. Tae put no too fine a point on it, Crichton and his platoon ended up as prisoners, strung up lik chickens. Crichton wis slung across his horse lik a bag o meal. He didna like that. He liked it even less when Steel and his men led the platoon in a procession doon the village main street afore sending them back tae the sheriff. I suspect there micht hae been mair laughs that day than ye've had tae endure. Crichton's dignity wis sair dented on that occasion. Mind ye, I made sure that Maister Steel paid for his nonsense. Aw the same, ye hae tae admit whitever he is, he's a wee bit different."

"Different?" Airlie almost choked. "The man's a threat tae law and order."

"And dignity," Claverhouse teased.

Just then the sheriff burst into the room pulling a raggedy figure behind him. "If yer lordships please," he wheezed, "this tinker has a tale that micht interest ye."

Gaby escaped the sheriff's grip and danced into the middle of the room. "Sam Galbraith, sirs. Gaby as ah'm kent. A travellin man." He gave Airlie a mocking bow. "Ah'm here bringin yer honour a nice wee story." He turned to the sheriff. "Ye can vouch fur me, an whit ah say. It's no that long since ah wis here tellin ye aboot the Lesmahagow villagers darin tae bury thur meenister's wife in the kirkyard withoot ony permission tae dae sic a thing."

"Get on wi it," the sheriff barked.

Gaby looked hopefully at their lordships.

Claverhouse understood and a small silver coin glinted in his fingers. He flicked it towards the tinker. Gaby caught it and pocketed it. Claverhouse turned to Airlie. "Hoo aboot ye, Jamie?"

Airlie shook his head.

"Come on man. It micht be worth yer while."

Airlie reluctantly obliged.

Gaby pocketed a second coin. "Mistress Steel's bidin at the new curate's hoose in Lesmahagow. Ah ken she shudna be ther for ah heard yersel, in the kirk square, threatenin ony whae dared offer help."

"Is she noo?" Airlie stiffened. "Wife seems as bad as the husband. As for that curate..."

"Whit aboot the curate?" The sheriff grabbed Gaby's shoulder.

"The very ane ye sent tae replace yon meenister that wis flung oot his kirk for speakin agin the king. If ye mind sir, the meenister's wife fell aff the cairt when the horse tried tae run awa frae the soldiers. It wis a peety she got hersel killed. No that it wis onythin ither than an accident. But ye ken whit folk are like. Ah think that's why they didna tak tae yer man, an left the kirk empty every Sunday."

"Enough," the sheriff ordered. "Their lordships are no interested in that."

"But whit aboot yer man ignorin yer orders an helpin rebels? Is that no a slap in the teeth?"

The sheriff's face darkened. "Aifter aw the expense and bother he's caused it's mair than a slap, it's a hangin maitter."

The serving girl, who'd been clearing the table, dropped her pile of plates.

The sheriff rounded on her. "Gaither up that mess and awa oot o here!"

The girl lifted the plates and scurried from the room, ran downstairs to the kitchen where she flung the dishes across the big table then headed for the back door.

"Here, here, Jean," the cook called after her, "whit's wrang?"

The girl was already out and away, running up the High Street to the vintner's yard. She raced through the open gate calling, "Geordie! Whaur are ye?"

"Whit's wrang?" Her husband appeared from behind a cart. "Ye luk as if ye've seen a ghost."

"It's oor Sandy."

"Whit's yer brither done noo? Is his fine life as a curate no suitin him?"

"Worse than that. The sheriff's threatenin tae hang him. Somethin aboot breakin the law by helpin rebels."

"Did ah no tell ye his fancy ideas wud end in tears?"

"Wheesht. Ye'll hae tae ride ower tae Lesmahagow afore the sheriff gits there. Ye'll need tae warn him afore it's too late."

"It's a guid ten miles," Geordie protested. "Ah havena a horse. Onyway, ah'm at ma work."

The vintner stepped out from the other side of the cart. "Under the circumstances ah think ye can be excused." He pointed towards his stable. "On ye go. Tak ma black horse."

"Ye mean Jess? She's yer best yin."

"She'll git ye there aw the quicker. Whitever yer brither in law's done ahm sure it disna merit a hangin. Ye canna jist staund there an dae nuthin."

Geordie was still protesting as he found himself bundled into the stable and forced to saddle up. Five minutes later he was at the bottom of Lanark High Street, muttering to himself as he galloped out the town.

Jean turned to the vintner. "Thank ye sir. That wis kindly done."

"Nae bother." The vintner grinned. "The sheriff owes me a tidy sum. He's awfy guid at orderin ma best ale an wine. He enjoys drinkin it but he's no sae keen aboot payin. An it's no as if ah dinna remind him. Jist consider this ma ain wee pay back. Noo, awa back tae yer kitchen. An dinna let on."

"But the cook's sure tae ask," Jean wailed. "Ah banged a pile o dishes doon an ran oot in sic a hurry."

"Ye'll think o somethin. Jist mak sure it's no the truth." With that the vintner got back to loading the cart while Jean crept back to the kitchen where she surprised herself by spinning a ridiculous tale about a child being lost, and a stray dog, and what a worry it was. The cook surprised her even more by appearing to believe every word.

The reluctant messenger stopped outside the manse in Lesmahagow and stared at the grand, sandstone frontage, very different to his own tiny house in one of Lanark's dark vennels. "Sandy, Sandy. Ye and yer high, falootin ideas. Whit on earth did ye think ye were dain?" He tethered his horse to the big, black railings and hurried round to rattle at the back door.

Sandy jerked it open and gaped at his unexpected visitor. "Geordie. Whit brings ye here?"

"The sheriff's comin tae hang ye, that's whit. Ma Jean heard him say so. He's in a fair rant aboot yer defiance. Somethin tae dae wi some rebel's wife."

Meg appeared beside Sandy. "Somebody must hae seen Mistress Steel comin here."

"But she's no here," Sandy insisted. "Her cousin taen her an the bairns awa this mornin."

"But she wis." Meg grabbed hold of his arm.

"Please yersels if ye want tae waste time arguin. But dinna say ah havena warned ye. Ah'm awa. If ah wis ye ah'd dae the same. Yon sheriff's no kent for bein lenient wi onybody that crosses him." Geordie left them glaring at each other, and was down the manse steps, back on his borrowed horse, and away from the village as fast as he could.

# Chapter 3

The sheriff and platoon were about to leave the garrison when his two visitors appeared in the yard. Claverhouse held up his hand. "I'm minded tae come wi ye."

"As ye wish." The sheriff tried not to sound so reluctant. Earlier dealings with John Graham had taught Meiklejon that this man rarely did anything without good reason.

"I'll come as weel," Airlie added. "Time I wis back at Steel's farm tae see whit's happening."

Minutes later a grand, mounted procession clattered down Lanark High street, drawing wary glances as it passed. This pleased the sheriff. Maybe there was some benefit to be had from such esteemed company after all.

The platoon arrived in Lesmahagow about noon and lined up in front of the manse. Four troopers dismounted and marched over to the front door, pushed it open, and disappeared inside. Minutes later Sandy Gillon was dragged out, making no protest, as he was half-hauled, half-marched towards the spreading beech tree in the middle of the village square. Its branches usually sheltered those who cared to sit and talk. Today it looked like taking on a new role when the sheriff ordered a long, hemp rope to be strung over the lowest branch.

Meg could scarce believe what was happening when Sandy disappeared behind a barrier of uniforms. She ran down the manse steps to follow him. A stout line of soldiers stopped her. "No!" She began to scream for help.

House doors opened. The inn and shops emptied as villagers rushed out to find the new curate, the man the law had sent, being led in front of the sheriff like a condemned criminal.

Claverhouse and Airlie sat astride their big horses and watched the sheriff lean forward to confront the prisoner. "So, Maister Gillon. I hear ye've been consorting wi rebels. If that's no treason I dinna ken whit is. And we aw ken whit the law thinks aboot that kinda offence."

Airlie nodded approval. Claverhouse, on the other hand, began to fidget then held up a gloved hand. "A moment please."

The sheriff turned to glare at him. "Sir, I tellt ye afore we came here this is a hangin maitter."

"Indeed ye did." Claverhouse smiled. "But indulge me sir. Alloo a few meenits tae mak sure yer prisoner deserves the hanging ye're set on."

Meiklejon gave a reluctant nod and Sandy was trailed towards the commander.

Claverhouse eyed the tear-stained, bloodied face. "Whit hae ye done that maks the sheriff want tae hang ye?"

Sandy stammered, "I wis only daein my Christian duty by a hameless wummin an her twa bairns."

"Dinna come the pious act," Airlie cut in. "Ye're a renegade pure and simple. When I arrived here the ither day and asked the way tae Steel's farm it wis yersel sent me galloping for miles in the wrang direction. Ah lost ma chance tae capture Maister Steel. Whae's fault wis that?"

Sandy hung his head.

"Is this true?" Claverhouse pursed his lips.

Sandy said nothing.

"Is that no guilt?" Airlie demanded.

"It seems so," Claverhouse agreed.

"The sheriff's in the richt then." Airlie snapped. "The man deserves hanging."

"And whit if he's no hanged? Whit if we alloo him tae see anither day?" Claverhouse leant towards Airlie and lowered his voice, "Think hoo grateful he'll be. Mair than that he'll feel obliged. Wud oor work roond here no benefit frae a guid ear picking up a wee whisper here and there? Whae better than a man accused o breakin the law?"

Airlie's eyebrows rose. "Whit aboot the sheriff?"

"I'm sure he can be persuaded."

Somewhere among the commander's gentle tone Airlie sensed this was exactly what was going to happen. He also sensed it might be unwise to argue.

Sandy stared at the two grand gentlemen, one an imposing sight, in full military uniform, every inch the battle worn soldier, pride and experience oozing out of him, the other a fine-looking gentleman in hunting leather and soft velvet, a delicate lace ruff circling his throat, accenting his almost feminine face, all topped by a large hat with a long white plume waving in the breeze.

These two were very different characters but Sandy knew who was in control for the still, grey eyes of this particular gentleman were the eyes of a man well used to having his own way.

"Are ye feenished?" The sheriff edged his horse closer. "Can I get on?"

"No quite," Claverhouse said evenly. "In fact I'm beginning tae wonder if ye shud think again."

A tiny flicker of hope rose in Sandy's throat.

The sheriff almost choked. "Sir, I tellt ye I wis set on a hangin. I see nae reason tae chainge my mind. And let me remind ye that this business comes under Lanark jurisdiction. I hae the richt."

"I dinna dispute yer richt." Claverhouse waved a hand at the watching crowd. "But hoo will a hanging affect thae villagers?"

"It'll gie them a fricht and mak them unnerstaund whit it means tae break the law."

"And whit aboot a wee act o clemency raither than a hanging withoot a trial?" Claverhouse's voice sharpened.

The sheriff's mouth opened and shut as he tried to control a mixture of emotions, not least the desire to hang John Graham himself.

Claverhouse clicked his horse forward, slid past the sheriff, and cantered across the square to the old beech tree. He grabbed the thick rope and swung it back and forward while the crowd watched and waited. He pointed at the cowering Sandy. "Whit this man did against his king and government wis wrang. Wrang enough for this." He swung the rope again and looked round the crowd. "But human nature is a fickle thing. We aw mak mistakes, some worse than ithers. I suspect this eedjit is mair misguided than maist, allooing himself tae side wi rebels instead o leading his flock in peace and righteousness. I think he kens that noo. Given the chance I think he'd try tae mak amends, mak himsel an example as the sinner returning tae the richt path, tae law and order. My royal maister wud understaund this. He's a generous man, nivver set on retribution for its ain sake. As his representative I'm minded tae spare yer curate, and alloo him tae chainge his ways, tae become the shining example he shud be tae ye aw." With that the commander jumped down from his black horse and walked over

27

to the dumbstruck Sandy, turned him round, then gently led the stumbling figure back across the square, past the crowd of watchers, the waiting soldiers, the red faced sheriff, the scowling earl, up the steps of the manse, and out of sight through his own front door.

Airlie and the sheriff stared after them then Airlie rounded on the crowd. "Mind whit wis said aboot law and order." He jumped off his horse and hurried into the manse with every intention of confronting Claverhouse over his extraordinary performance.

The commander plonked Sandy down on a kitchen chair, called for a bowl of water, a soft muslin cloth, and started to wipe his bloodied nose.

"Why are ye dain this?" Sandy whispered. "I mean nocht tae ye."

Claverhouse smiled. "Ah. But ye will."

"Whit dae ye mean, sir?" Sandy looked sideways at the still, grey eyes studying him with amusement.

"I cud dae wi some help aboot here."

Sandy stiffened.

Claverhouse leant closer. He spoke so softly Sandy only just caught the words. "I'm aifter a bit listening. Mibbe some watching. Nothing serious mind. But nae silly stories either. Jist enough as tae keep me in the picture, and help me understaund whit's happening aroond here. Whae better tae deliver the information than the man least likely tae be suspected?"

Sandy watched the commander dip the cloth in the bowl then lift it out again and slowly squeeze out every drop of water. No words were necessary.

"And mind it's me ye report tae. Naebody else." Claverhouse stood up and patted his shoulder. "Ay. I'm sure ye'll dae fine."

Airlie burst in, ordering everyone from the room.

"Does that include me and my prisoner?" Claverhouse asked as the soldiers hurried to obey.

"It's ye I want a word wi. In private."

Claverhouse patted Sandy's shoulder again. "Awa back tae yer religious duties Maister Gillon. And lik I said, mind hoo ye go."

"Whit are ye up tae, John Graham?" Airlie watched Sandy stumble away.

"Tut, tut, yer lordship. I wis only gieing the curate some guid advice. Noo if ye'll excuse me." Claverhouse winked at Airlie and stepped into the hall. The heels of his boots clicked along the parquet floor, almost in a dance, as if this particular gentleman was enjoying himself.

Once outside he walked over to his horse, took a rolled up poster from his saddle bag, ordered it to be nailed to the would-be hanging tree then positioned himself in the middle of the square again. He looked at the watching faces and called out, "This is a list o rebels frae these pairts. If ye tak a guid luk ye'll find a price alangside each name. The mair ye tell the mair ye'll earn."

This announcement was met with stony silence but his good humour appeared unaffected. He ended with, "Guid day tae ye aw."

He turned to the sheriff. "Richt sir, I think we're feenished here." Claverhouse remounted his horse and smiled at the angry face. "God sakes man, ye canna aye get yer ain way. Stop huffin and puffin ower a wee chainge tae yer plan." He clicked his fingers and signalled for Meiklejon's platoon to line up behind him.

A red faced sheriff joined the commander in front of the line up. Claverhouse gave another signal and the full contingent stepped forward in perfect order.

"I tak it ye're biding," Claverhouse waved to Airlie who stood at the top of the manse steps to watch them leave.

Airlie nodded.

"Oh ay, yer new property will be needing yer attention." Claverhouse doffed his hat to the old earl and trotted off smiling to himself.

"Bloody upstart," Airlie spluttered. "Ower clever by half."


Marion peered out from cousin Bess's attic window and took another look across the village square. The soldiers were gone. The place was deserted, as if there had never been any drama. The only clue was the long, thick rope still dangling from the old beech tree. "Naebody aboot," she whispered. "An nae sign o Maister Gillon. Pair man. It's aw ma fault."

"His heid's still on his shooders," Bess said. "Yon fancy gentleman led him back intae the manse as nice as ye like. The sheriff didna seem ower pleased though."

"Nor that auld earl," Marion added. "He didna catch John so he's takin it oot on me an the bairns. God kens whit he's plannin noo."

"Rest easy." Bess tried to sound confident. "Ye're safe here. Naebody, includin yon auld earl, kens whaur ye are."

"But supposin somebody finds oot?"

"It'll be fine."

"No it'll no. A word in the wrang direction an ye'll end up wi a platoon at yer door. Me an the bairns need tae be somewhaur that disna bring trouble on onybody else. Mibbe the moor. Or the auld birch wood. Aifter aw it's summer. We cud build a wee shelter."

"Dinna talk nonsense."

"So whit if ye git caught wi me in yer hoose?" Marion's eyes glistened. "Think aboot it. As for John…"

"We'd ken if he'd been captured. Yon earl wud be makin a big song an dance an busy organisin a hangin. But they need tae catch him first. An that's no likely tae happen." Bess smiled kindly at the tense, white face. "Noo, leave aff lukin oot that windae. The show's ower."

Marion reluctantly followed her cousin downstairs to the kitchen where the two boys were sitting still and silent by the fire. She held out her arms. They jumped up and ran to her.

The outside door to the scullery opened. Bess heard the tiny click of the sneck. She went white. Her hand flew to her mouth. Marion and the boys slipped into the hall and raced upstairs.

Bess marched towards the scullery to meet the last person she wanted in her house. Gaby stood there grinning, eyeing her up as if he'd every right.

"Whit are ye dain here?" She grabbed her floor brush and thrust it out like a spear. "Naebody invited ye. It's a sad day when an honest hoose is invaded for nae guid reason."

"Honest hoose." Gaby took a step back. "Nae new lodgers then?"

"Whit kinda question is that?"

"Ye're related aren't ye? Ye micht feel obleeged."

He got no further. A strong arm slid round the open door to grab his neck and yank it back before he could squeal or try to resist.

Bessie gaped and almost dropped her brush.

"C'mon ye auld deil. Let's be havin ye." John Steel stepped into the scullery without letting go of his victim. "Ah ken fine whit ye're up tae, sneakin here an there, an then high tailin tae Lanark wi yer stories. Dis the sheriff pay weel?"

Gaby glared up at John.

"Whit did ye say this time that brocht thae grand gentlemen an aw that military tae this wee village?"

"The thocht o yer braw wife," Gaby spat. "But it's yersel thur aifter."

John tightened his grip. "An whit aboot Maister Gillon? Whitivver ye said near had the man hanged."

"Harbourin a felon's wife is a hangin offence. The auld earl said so."

John's grip increased.

"The mistress an the bairns went intae the manse. Ah saw them wi ma ain een."

"Is that so?" John turned to Bess. "Ah think this unwelcome visitor needs tae cool his heels for a wee while. Somewhaur he can think aboot his conscience an feel black, burnin shame for aw the harm he dis wi his lies an tales aboot innocent folk."

Bess led the way to a tiny door at the back of the scullery. She opened it. "Twelve steps doon gies ye the cellar. Even if he shouts naebody can hear him."

"In ye go," John pushed Gaby down the steps. "An tak care lest yer conscience leaps up tae bite ye in the dark." He banged the door shut then pulled the bolt across.

"Whit happens when we let him oot?" Bess looked worried.

"Ah'll deal wi him. Jist gie me time tae think aboot it."

"Ah'm gled ye came at the richt meenit but ye're takin an awfy risk comin intae the village lik this."

"Ah hud tae. Whaur is she? "

Bess pointed. "Upstairs wi the bairns."

John hurried out the kitchen, across the shadowy hall, running upstairs to gather Marion in his arms. "C'mon lass." He lifted her face to kiss her. "C'mon, ah'm fine."

"No ye're no. An we've nae hame. Nae onythin. Naewhaur's safe ony mair."

Gaby landed on the bottom step and crouched there while the cold, damp air of the cellar began to creep through his old coat. He was used to the cold, but this step bothered him in other ways. It reminded him of the step in that first cellar, where it had all begun. He shivered, tried not to think about it or bring on that feeling of being so alone and terrified. He'd been four years old that first time. The first of many. He remembered his father's face, the hard eyes, the mouth like a rat-trap spitting out words no child should ever hear. "Ye can dae naethin richt! Worse than that, ye're bad thru an thru! Nae guid tae man nur beast." He felt the push down the steps to the cellar, imagined the bolt sliding across the door at the top, to leave him shut in total blackness for hours on end. Each time he displeased his father the result was the same. At first the dark isolation was unbearable but gradually it grew familiar, almost comforting in the way it shut out what happened in the world above.

At thirteen he'd enough wit to sneak away. He knew no one would come after him. No one would ask. No one cared. Years later it was still the same. He'd grown used to it, and yet that feeling was still there, could still bother him until he thought about the tiny coins he'd earned from the grand gentlemen. Given the chance he'd have more. Gaby was himself again.

The air grew colder, his skin tingled with the raw dampness and he hunched into a tight ball. He stuck his hands in his pockets. Several hard, smooth, round pebbles lined the seams of his deep pockets. He ran his fingers over them and smiled. These stones, and the sling still slung across his chest, were the answer. John Steel might think he had the best of him, but Gaby knew better. All he had to do was wait.

It would be a long wait. But one thing Gaby had learnt was patience, enough to sit through the night till that door at the top of the steps would open. When it did he'd know what to do.

John had stayed the night in Bess's house. He hadn't taken much persuading when Bess said, "Ye twa can hae ma bedroom. The bairns can cosy up in the kitchen bed. Since the door's shut they'll feel safe an snug. Ah'll tak the spare room an gie ye some time tae yersels."

They'd sat on the bed, staring at each other, arguing, then agreeing before questioning each other as they tried to make sense of the terror facing them. Eventually all that mattered was to hold each other and fall asleep.

Marion and John were still asleep when Bess tiptoed downstairs to light the kitchen fire and start the porridge pot. Determined to look after her visitors she cut some hunks of bread, stuck them in the little side oven to warm, then fetched a new cream cheese from the pantry. That's when she remembered Gaby, still in the cellar. Not that she pitied him. But all the same, a full night in the dark and cold, and nothing to eat or even a sip of water. She took two bannocks, a mug of water, and headed for the locked cellar door. She thought for a moment then pulled back the bolt and slowly pulled the door open. The cellar seemed even darker than before. She hesitated, almost shut the door, then stopped. "Bide whaur ye are while ah lay doon twa bannocks an a wee drink o water on the tap step. Dinna move till ah shut the door again."

"Richt ye are, missus. Thank ye." As he spoke Gaby lifted his sling and placed his heaviest pebble in the little leather cradle. He could see the stout figure outlined against the light at the top of the stairs. That was all he needed. He was able to guess where her face, and more importantly, where her brow might be. He pulled back the thong as far as he could, took aim, and held the strain. When he let go the pebble flew towards the dark shape, and she was an easy target for a man who could drop a running rabbit at more than a hundred yards.

The pebble hit Bess above her right eye. She gasped. Her knees buckled. She tumbled forward, bumping against the edge of each of the twelve steps till she landed beside Gaby.

Her eyes were wide open. Not that she could see anything. Not that Gaby could see them. Not that he cared. He jumped over her crumpled shape and was up the steps, only hesitating long enough to grab the bannocks and bolt the cellar door behind him. Then he was through the scullery and into the kitchen. Fly opened his eyes and gave a soft growl. "Easy boy," Gaby whispered. "It's only me." He bent over to ruffle the dog's ears. Fly sighed and closed his eyes again.

All he had to do now was turn the big key of the outer door, and step into the yard. Less than a minute after his pebble hit its mark Gaby was out the back gate and down the narrow lane.

He ran as fast as he could, determined to reach John Steel's farm as soon as possible. The great earl would be there. This story would be worth more, much more than a tiny coin.

# Chapter 4

The church clock struck the half hour. Marion woke with a start. Daylight was streaming through every crack in the shutters. Time she was up. Bess probably had breakfast ready by now. She smiled at John snoring quietly by her side, then slipped out of bed to dress quickly and hurry downstairs.

She opened the kitchen door to be met by swirling smoke and the smell of burning porridge. Rushing through the fug she pulled the long arm of the swee away from the heat of the fire then grabbed a cloth to flap at the smoke and drive it into the scullery beyond. The outside door was unlocked so she yanked it open, and stood there till the air cleared.

Back in the kitchen she saw how the porridge was stuck to the pot in a congealed, black lump. And yet the bowls were set out in a row, with a fresh cheese, and a pile of bannocks. She could even sniff bread warming in the little side oven.

Apart from the burnt porridge everything was ready for breakfast. Where was Bess? Maybe in the yard? Marion went out to find the small space deserted although the gate into the lane was slightly open. This bothered her.

She stepped into the lane, looked up and down, saw nothing. This had her hurrying back indoors to wake John. "Ah canna find Bess onywhaur."

He blinked at her. "Mibbe she went oot for somethin."

"No when the porridge is on the go. It's burnt black. Somethin's wrang. Ah can feel it."

John smiled. "Ye and yer feelins."

"Are often richt. Come an help me luk."

He slid from the warm bed and followed her downstairs. "See." Marion pointed to the burnt glob that should have been porridge, and the table set ready for breakfast. "Bess wis in the middle o this when somethin distracted her."

John frowned and went into the scullery to check that the cellar door was still locked. It was, and the bolt was in place. He looked at the door then opened it. Apart from a blast of cold, damp air there was no sound or sign of any movement below. He called out, "Gaby. Are ye awake?"

No reply.

"Wheesht," Marion warned. "Nae sae loud. Ye'll wake the bairns. Thur still asleep in the press bed at the far end o the kitchen. Thank God the door wis shut. Withoot that they'd hae been choked tae death wi the smoke frae yon burnin porridge."

John stepped back, locked the door again, then searched about the kitchen for a candle. Back on the top cellar step he held the lit candle at arms length. The flickering flame was useless against such dense darkness. All he could do was strain his ears and try to catch any sound. The silence was deep, and still, and not right. He stepped down one step, listened, then edged down again, waited, then took another two steps. Now the faint light showed some sort of figure huddled against the bottom step. "Richt Gaby. Let's hae ye." John jumped the remaining steps and was about to poke the figure when he realised there was too much body for such a scrap of a man. He held the candle steady and Bess's white face loomed into the guttering flame, her eyes a fixed stare, skirt up round her waist, one leg twisted under her body.

He raced up the steps and into the kitchen, and minutes later Marion helped him lift the limp, heavy body. They struggled to carry Bess's weight and could hardly avoid bumping her from step to step.

Once in the kitchen her faint gasps of breath reassured them although they were horrified at her staring eyes.

"Hoo did this happen?" Marion asked. "Whit wis she dain in there? An whaur's Gaby?"

"Long gone," John replied. "Ah think ah ken whit happened. Luk at that mark on her broo. See hoo deep an roond it is. If ah'm no mistaken that wis made wi a pebble frae the burn. Bess must hae taen peety on Gaby an went intae the cellar wi some food for him. Thur's a water jug sittin by the door, an some crumbs. Nothin surer but the ungratefu rat taen a shot at her wi his sling. The pair soul didna staund a chance. It's a wunner he didna kill her."

"It micht happen yet," Marion whispered. "We need tae git her intae a warm bed. She must be near frozen lyin in that cauld hole."

Once upstairs they wrapped Bess in a thick blanket and the big quilt she'd sewn herself. The warming touch of the wool and soft cloth seemed to tell her she was safe at last. The staring eyes flickered then slowly closed.

When Marion saw this she went to the kitchen and boiled up a pan of water, filled a big bowl, and lugged it up to the bedroom. She hurried downstairs to find a piece of soft muslin, and sprigs of lavender and chamomile leaves to steep in the warm water before bathing Bess's filthy face and hands. She began to wipe and pat the scratches, and rising bruises. There was no reaction. Bess remained unconscious.

"Shud ah wake the bairns?" John asked.

Marion nodded. "Tell them Bess had a wee accident an needs a rest. Tell them tae bide quiet while she sleeps but dinna fricht them. They've hud enough scares thae past few days.

The earl of Airlie was less than pleased when his men reported they'd seen no sign of John Steel. He would have been even more displeased if he'd known they hadn't bothered to look for the man.

Steel had escaped for the second time. Instead of catching the felon and teaching him the lesson he deserved Airlie began to realise he was facing a challenge.

Keeping this farm under his personal control would prove difficult and bring little return. Anyway, it was too far from his lands in Strathmore. A quick sale seemed the best option. This way revenge could still be sweet, albeit a compromise. He stood in the middle of the simple kitchen and barked out orders, about preparing a list of livestock, implements, house contents, even personal items, ready for a sale by the end of the week.

"Sir. This auld ragamuffin wis in the yard." A trooper came into the kitchen and pushed Gaby towards his master. "He says ye'll want tae speak tae him."

Airlie scowled at the filthy apparition. "Whit are ye aifter this time?"

"Tae assist yer lordship in yer quest." Gaby took off his cap and flapped it at Airlie. "Ah thocht ye'd want tae ken John Steel's whauraboots. Mibbe gie me a wee…"

"Reward is the word ye're aifter." Airlie studied Gaby in much the same way as he might look at a beetle about to be crushed under his boot. "I'm aw ears my man. Jist tell me whit ye ken."

He leant forward to grab Gaby's lapels and jerk him clear of the floor.

This wasn't the reaction Gaby had hoped for.

"Weel?" Airlie shook him.

"Steel's in the village. At Bess Weir's hoose. It's the second on the left, at the end o the kirk square."

"Hoo dae ye ken this?" Airlie shook him again.

"Ah wis in the hoose, saw him clear as yersel. His wife's there tae. Bess is a cousin. Likely she felt sorry for them an taen them in, in spite o yer warnin."

Airlie let go of Gaby, headed for the door, shouting an order to mount up.

"Sir, whit aboot a wee coin or twa?" Gaby scrabbled after the great earl.

Airlie whirled round. "Dain yer boundin duty is yer reward." With that he called for his horse to be brought forward. A moment later a line of troopers clattered out the courtyard.

Gaby stared after them and swore with disappointment.

Hooves rattled across the cobbles in the kirk square. The noise rang through Bess's house. John and Marion stared at each other then down at Bess's still face. Her eyes remained shut but she seemed aware of what was happening and whispered, "Troopers. Quick John. The loft."

John turned and ran along the narrow corridor. Marion followed, carrying a chair which she placed below the loft hatch. John jumped onto the chair, reached up, and pushed the wooden panel to the side. He grasped the edge of the frame and pulled himself through the space then slid the panel back in place.

Marion took the chair back to Bess's room, and was calling the two boys to join them when she heard the back door burst open and Airlie's loud voice ordering a full search of the house. "And bring Steel tae me. I want a word afore we hang him."

A few minutes later Captain McCann pushed open Bess's bedroom door. He stopped at the sight of one woman in bed, the other sitting holding her hand, and two terrified children standing by the window. A collie's nose poked out under the bed, and there was a long warning growl. Without raising his voice McCann said,

"Whaur's Maister Steel? The earl's aifter him. I hae orders tae fetch him oot."

"He's no here." Marion tried to sound calm. "He left mair than an hoor ago for Lanark."

The captain looked at her anxious face. He didn't argue and went downstairs to tell his master.

"I dinna believe a word," Airlie roared. "Search every inch, every corner. Mak sure ye miss naethin."

For half an hour the house was over-run by troopers poking here, opening cupboards, going down to the cellar with a lantern, even looking under Bess's bed where Fly managed to nip a searching hand. Eventually they reached the top landing and stood below the loft hatch. The captain turned to the two troopers following him. "Fetch a chair. I'll go up and luk."

The two troopers dragged one from the bedroom.

"Haud it steady." The captain jumped onto the chair and stretched up to reach the hatch. He slid the wooden panel to the side and they all stared at the dark square beyond. It seemed quiet enough. He looked back at the troopers. "I'd best mak sure." He pulled himself into the loft space and began to crawl along a thick beam. After a few inches the circle of light from the troopers' lantern vanished. Velvet dark wrapped around him. It seemed pointless to go any further. He stopped, stayed perfectly still while his hearing did the searching. Slowly his ears tuned into the air. Within that stillness he thought he heard something akin to the faintest wave of breath. It seemed close by. He stiffened, held his own breath, and listened harder. This time he was sure he could feel a sense of warmth mingling with the cold air. He leant his head towards this. And there it was. Another's breath, so soft, so gentle it was almost imagined.

Hand on his thick tunic belt he touched the handle of the little knife he carried, ready to swipe through the dark space. He opened his mouth to call for assistance then thought of Marion Steel, the look on her face. He stopped, blinked in the dark, and listened again. Had to be. And he should. It was his duty. Airlie would be delighted. And then...

McCann winced at the thought then turned to crawl back along the beam to the open hatch. He stared down at the two waiting faces. "Naethin."

"Ah'll tell the commander." One of the troopers hurried downstairs.

Two floors up McCann heard Airlie's angry response. What if the old earl doubted his trusted captain? But why should he? Him and his grand opinion of himself.

McCann slid back through the space, carefully closed the hatch, and returned to the kitchen where Airlie was pacing up and down. He saluted his master. "Sir. We can find nae sign o Steel in this hoose."

"Are ye sure?" Airlie sounded almost desperate.

"Nane, sir. Mibbe yon tinker wis havin ye on. I wudna put it past him. Will I order the men tae withdraw?"

Airlie didn't answer.

"Sir?"

"Whit aboot Mistress Steel?" Airlie snapped. "The troopers say she's upstairs. Aifter whit I tellt her it's pure defiance."

"Sir. There's a woman in the bed upstairs. She looks richt poorly. Mistress Steel is sittin wi her. I think she's only here tae help a sick relative."

"Are ye going saft? Hae ye forgotten we're dealing wi felons against the king? Whit aboot oor duty tae uphold the law? Fetch the mistress doon this instant."

Five minutes later McCann led Marion into the kitchen.

Airlie glared at her and clenched his fist. For a moment it looked as if he'd strike her as a substitute for the man himself. Several of the troopers stiffened and stepped back. Their reaction seemed to affect Airlie's rage. He stood straight, closed his eyes, face tightened as if fighting the temptation to lash out. When he blinked again the faces were still watching. He glared at them but instead of lunging at Marion he pointed a gloved finger. "Mistress. This is yer final warning. Leave here this instant. And dinna dare come back tae this hoose, or ony ither hoose in this village, nor seek ony help frae ony villager, or ye'll aw hang. Is that plain enough for ye?"

Marion nodded. "An ma boys?"

"Gang wi ye."

She turned, ran upstairs, and came back with her two terrified children.

Airlie pointed towards the back door. "Get on the ither side o that door afore I chainge my mind."

"Whit aboot ma cousin Bess? She hud a bad fall. She's richt nae weel."

"Did ye hear me Mistress Steel? Get oot ma sicht afore I dae something ye micht regret."

Marion and the two boys walked out the kitchen, through the scullery, across the yard, and into the lane. They didn't look back.

Captain McCann followed them a short distance and watched the three, slight figures disappear into the brightening morning. He sighed. At least they'd had the chance to walk away. He thought about it, remembered that moment in the dark loft, the sense of breathing. He sighed, nodded to himself and whispered, "So be it."

He was about to turn when Airlie roared, "McCann! This is a waste o time. Get the men ready tae move oot."

The trusted captain smiled and marched into the house to obey his master.

# Chapter 5

The sound of hooves had barely faded from the church square when Bess heard John's boots clatter down on the hard wooden floor of the back landing. The troopers hadn't found him. But what about Marion and the boys? The polite captain had taken them downstairs to that terrible, old earl. They hadn't come back. All the comings and goings, the troopers searching her house and her knowing where John was hiding had been bad enough. The earl's voice was worse. She could still hear the rage in it.

Her head pounded, her eyes hardly focused, every limb ached, and her temper rose as she thought about that tinker. "Jist wait," she hissed. "Ane o thae days."

John peered round the edge of her bedroom door. "Hoo are ye?" Before he could say any more Fly shot out from below the bed and bounded towards him.

Bess smiled. "Nae worse than ah wis. An glad tae see the troopers didna find ye. But nivver mind me, whaur's Marion an the weans?"

"Nae idea. Ah cud hear naethin up there in the loft."

"She went doonstairs wi yon captain an then the auld earl wis shoutin. Ah think he flung her oot, or the troopers hae taen her awa. Itherwise she'd be up here by noo."

"Ah best try an find her."

"No," Bess insisted. "Ye need tae bide put for a while. Ah heard yon captain say there wis nae sign o ye here. Anither thing, he came back afore the troopers left an whispered that yer farm is up for sale on Friday, the beasts alang wi the implements. Why wud he dae that?"

John said nothing. He didn't want to admit that same captain must have guessed where he was in the loft. Granted it had been pitch black but they'd only been a few feet apart. As for the sale, Airlie's determination to destroy him was no surprise. But why had the captain told Bessie about it?

The back door opened. Fly growled. John looked round the room then dived under the bed as light feet clipped upstairs towards the bedroom.

Bess smiled at the thought of John's broad shoulders squashed between the bed frame and the floor then whispered, "It's awricht. It's oor Rena. Ah ken her step."

Rena came into the room, took one look at her mother in the bed, and ran forward, "Whit's happened tae ye? Wis it thae troopers? Whaur did that dug come frae?"

"The troopers nivver touched me. Ah hud a wee accident."

"The dug belangs tae me." John poked his head out from under the bed.

Rena jumped back and then recognised the red face.

"Sorry Rena." He scrabbled out of the tight space and stood up. "Ah wis jist bein carefu."

"Ay weel. Ye didna ken it wis me." Rena still looked anxious. "So whit's up?"

"Ah'm on the run."

"Ye an a wheen ithers aifter Bothwell."

John nodded. "Things are bad. Yon grand earl flung Marion oot oor farm. She ended up here wi Bess an thocht it wis safe. It wisna. Gaby the tinker got wind. He came tae the hoose. Luckily ah wis jist ahint him an managed tae lock him in the cellar."

"Is he still there?"

"If only. The auld deil got oot when yer mither went intae the cellar wi some food for him. It wis early in the mornin. We wur still asleep. Insteid o bein gratefu he attacked pair Bess an left her for deid at the bottom o the steps. He locked the cellar door ahint him so it wis a while afore we found oot whit happened. By that time he wis awa tellin the troopers whaur tae come."

"That's why they came gallopin intae the square as if thur tails wur on fire." Rena sat down beside the bed and took her mother's hand. "Ah wis richt feart when ah heard thae men arrive. When they gaithered in mither's yard ah didna ken whit tae think."

"Hae ye seen Marion?" John asked.

"She hurried by wi baith boys a while back. Ah wis ower feart tae gie her a shout."

"Did ye see whaur she went?"

"It seemed lik the Lanark road." Rena shook with anger. "When ah git haud o yon tinker."

"Us baith," John agreed.

"Nae way." Bess joined in. "Ye'll leave him tae me."

"Luk at ye." Rena smiled at her mother. "Ye cudna bat a flea."

"No the noo," Bess admitted. "But aince ah'm better an git the chance ah'll tak great pleisure in skinnin him. An dinna try tae stop me."

"We wudna dare." John turned to Rena. "Noo ye're here ah'll leave ye tae yer mither."

"No, John! Please. Wait a wee while" Bess struggled to sit up. "Marion's a clever lass. She kens hoo tae tak care o hersel an the boys, an ither folk will keep an eye oot for them. Jist mind whae yon earl is aifter. He'll hang ye as soon as luk at ye, an then whit guid are ye tae wife an bairns?"

John shuffled back and forward and finally nodded.

That night Marion and the boys had a bed under the moon and stars. Wrapped up in her cloak they snuggled down in the middle of the old birch wood on the other side of the village. Rabbits and scuttling mice kept them company, along with the occasional swish of a bat, and their heather mattress was far from uncomfortable. The two boys were excited to lie back and watch the tiny twinkling lights come and go above the leafy branches, and not once did they mention supper.

The bed in Bess's spare room was comfortable. Not that it mattered. John tossed and turned, and worried about Marion, his boys, his farm, what to do next. That was how he was awake to hear the soft clip clop of a horse and the squeak of a cart-wheel crossing the church square.

He jumped out of bed and pulled back one of the shutters to see Sandy Gillon, his wife and daughter with a load of furniture and baskets. It looked as if they were slipping away from the village. Why else would they be on the move so late at night?

Bess had told John what had happened to the curate, how Claverhouse had saved him from hanging. John knew the commander wasn't a man to do such a thing without reason. So what was the great man up to? Did Sandy Gillon know what it was? Was that why he was sneaking off in the dead of night?

After the soldiers had gone Sandy sat in the front room for a long time staring at the wall. Meg sat beside him, her mind still seeing that thick hemp rope dangling from the beech tree, the noose waiting for his neck.

When he finally turned towards her his face was gaunt, eyes blurry with tears, hands clenched as if to stop them from trembling. He seemed to have aged. There was something else though, a glimmer of another Sandy.

He reached out and held Meg's hand. "Ah'm sorry lass. Ah wis a fool for ivver thinkin ah cud be a curate. Me and ma big heid, cairried awa wi wantin tae be somebody, forcin ye tae gang alang wi it. As for this god-forsaken place." His voice hardened. "It's bad, an bad enough but yon fancy commander made it a hunner times worse by kiddin on he wis dain me a kindness when he wisna. The fly deil wants me tae preach God's word on Sunday then spy on the village for the rest o the week. Ah've tae report back tae himsel. Naebody else. That's the reason ah escaped the rope. But ah'm no havin it. Ah'm no tellin tales. No for him. No for onythin."

"But ye'll huv tae." Meg burst into tears.

"No ah'll no. We're oot o here."

"Whaur? We canna gang back tae Lanark."

"Glesca. Intae the city. In amang hunners o faces naebody's likely tae care whae we are or whaur we came frae. That way we can stert again, wi a new name if need be. Ah've still got ma shoemakin tools. Folk aye need thur shoes fixed. Ah'll soon find work. Ah did it afore. Ah'll dae it again. Ah'm a guid tradesman. We'll dae aricht."

"An nae mair hankerin aifter religion?"

"Ah promise."

Meg hugged him. In spite of everything she almost felt happy.

They began to pack their belongings. In a few hours everything they wanted to take away was loaded into a cart. Even the horse and trap the sheriff had provided was hitched to the back rail.

"Dae ye think we shud?" Meg looked doubtful.

Sandy laughed. "Aifter whit we've been thru? We deserve it."

John signalled to Fly and tiptoed past Bess's room where her daughter Rena was sleeping in a chair beside her. He was glad she'd arrived. Bess would be well looked after. Now seemed a good time to slip away, find out if Marion and the boys were safe.

He unlocked the back door and tiptoed through the back yard. At the gate he stopped and listened but Fly gave no warning prick of his ears. Together they hurried along the narrow vennel, past the end of the village square, onto the main street. When he turned the corner by the bakehouse he saw Sandy Gillon's horse and cart up ahead. This brought his Juno to mind, now captive in her stable, about to be sold. Something would need to be done about that.

He overtook the slow moving cart and Sandy Gillon almost dropped the reins when John appeared alongside.

"It's me," John whispered. "Ah'm no here tae try an stop ye. Whit ye're up tae is nane o ma business. Ah jist wantit tae tell ye ah'll no forget whit ye did for me."

"Ah had tae," Sandy stammered. "Whit yon earl wis plannin wisna richt."

"Ay weel. Thank ye. Ah'm gratefu." John raised his hand in salute, nodded, and hurried on ahead of the cart.

"Whaur's he goin?" Meg asked.

"Maist like tae luk for his wife an bairns. He's a hard road in front o him an if yon earl gets a haud he'll no even hae that tae contend wi."

"Maybe we shud ask if he wants a lift into the toun?"

"Withoot his wife an bairns, ah dinna think so. An we're no hingin aboot here waitin till he finds them."

A few minutes later they reached the crossroads. In a moment they'd be on the Glasgow road with Lesmahagow behind them. Ahead lay uncertainty. This time Meg didn't mind. The Sandy she knew and loved was back. From now on she'd make sure he stayed that way. "We'll be fine. Ah can feel it." She leant back and squeezed his arm.

# Chapter 6

Marion sat in the little birch wood beyond the village. Terrified and exhausted she was relieved to sit among the slender trees while the boys dozed by her side. Above the wood a full moon slid in and out of wispy clouds, the glimpses of light and shadow reminding her how quickly things change. Only two days ago she'd been at home hugging John just back from Bothwell. And then Sandy Gillon had galloped into their yard. And then. She could hardly bear to think about it.

Moonlight streamed through the leaves above her head to light up every blade of grass. Maybe it was too bright. Maybe she should have gone further into the wood, into the shadows. And what about food? The boys would be hungry when they woke.

The high pitched squeal of a fox on the hunt startled her, brought a shiver as she imagined the long red body slithering through the long grass, nose pointing, searching.

A nighthawk swished through the air, dived into the long grass, then rose again. She turned to follow its flight and caught another movement. A dark figure was walking along the road from the village. She watched its progress, caught her breath when it stopped almost parallel with the little wood. It seemed to be watching or listening. Move on. Please move on. The dark shape stepped away from the hard shale to plough through the long grass towards the trees. She braced herself and slipped her hand in her dress pocket to grip the little paring knife she'd carried from the farm.

The figure had almost reached the first line of trees, close enough to see the outline of a dog, a familiar dog running alongside. She leapt up and raced forward, almost knocking John over as she hurtled into his arms.

They swayed and turned together, holding the moment before sitting down beside the sleeping boys. Fly nuzzled in between them, demanding attention.

Neither spoke.

Finally John gave her another hug and said, "Ah cud see ye clear against the moon."

"Ah wisna thinkin. An the boys wur ower tired tae go ony further. Aw ah wantit wis tae sit doon an git things straight in ma heid. But ah cudna. No aifter yon earl. The way he's aifter ye is terrifyin. Whit did ye dae tae mak him lik that?"

"Ah whacked the great man aff his horse at Bothwell Brig. Insteid o killin him ah hurt his dignity. That seems tae be mair important than spairin his life, an noo he's desperate for revenge. He's makin a guid job o it, claimin oor farm, an meanin tae sell oor beasts, oor implements. Ivvery scrap we huv is tae go on Friday. The captain whae searched Bess's hoose tellt her afore he left."

When the boys woke they couldn't wait to tell their father about the soldiers prowling all over Bess's house, how the horrible old man had shouted at Ma, ordered them to leave then threatened something terrible if they dared come back. "An we canna gang hame either." William's eyes filled with tears.

"We'll find somewhaur else. It jist happens ah ken the vera place. Even yer Ma disna ken aboot it."

Marion looked doubtful but John laughed and kissed her brow. "C'mon, ah'll show ye."

They lifted their jackets from the damp grass and set off behind him.

He went further into the birch wood then veered off to the side and came out on the edge of the moor. After a mile through the heather they began to climb a long slope towards another wooded area. Instead of going into this shelter John turned left, along the first line of trees till he reached the edge of a steep gorge. The sides were covered with yellow broom and whin bushes. John didn't hesitate and pushed his way into the bushes.

Marion and the boys followed, the branches closing round as they scrambled and slid down the steep slope, right to the edge of a fast running burn.

"Whaur noo?" Marion gasped with all the effort.

"This way." John jumped from stone to stone to the other side, then followed the burn further into the narrow valley, towards the sound of rushing water. Through the early dawn light they saw a little waterfall gushing from a rocky outcrop.

John pointed to the right of the waterfall where a sheer rock face was glinting in the first rays of the rising sun. More broom and tall ferns grew near the rock face. "Ower there. Ahint thae bushes."

The boys ran past the bushes and disappeared. Marion went after them and found a long, narrow cave with a level floor. Once inside she could stand up without bumping her head. It didn't even feel damp or cold. "That wis clever John. Wi a brush oot an a fire lit we'd dae weel enough in here. Or mibbe no." She hesitated. "The smoke micht gie us awa?"

John pointed to the long cracks above. "These run a lang way frae here. By the time ony smoke seeps oot it'll be far enough awa. Aw the same we need tae tak care an no attract attention."

"In case the troopers find us?" William sounded anxious.

"Dinna worry. We'll be fine. Noo, on ye go an gaither some twigs an leaves for kinlin. While ye're dain that ah'll gang up the burn tae a deep pool an dae a bit o guddlin. Wi a bit o luck we'll hae somethin tasty tae eat afore lang."

Within an hour John had caught and gutted three fat trout. After a struggle with his tinder box the dried leaves spluttered, and flamed, began to feed on tiny twigs, then more leaves, gradually teasing more and more till the fire was blazing away. Now he speared the fish on a long stick and stuck them into the flames to smoke and cook.

Marion and the boys sat down beside him while the fish skins sizzled and spat. For the first time in many hours the Steel family was almost content.

Once the boys were asleep, John said, "Ah need tae go doon tae Waterside for a word wi Gavin."

"Must ye?"

"It canna wait. But dinna worry. Ah'll be back afore mornin."

Marion nodded towards the sleeping boys. "Whit if they wake up?"

"Tell them ah'm awa tae see aboot mair tae eat, some blankets, an mibbe a plate, an a cup, an a knife. They'll like that."

"Ye canna cairry aw that back yersel."

"Ah dinna mean tae. Ah'll ask Gavin tae tak a horse an pannier ontae the moor as if he's collectin heather. That way he can cairry the stuff wi naebody ony the wiser. Ah'll tell him whaur tae mak the drap then aw we need dae is collect it. Much as ah trust yer brither ah dinna want him kennin whaur we are. Whit he disna ken canna be forced oot him. Richt noo ah need tae tell him that ah want Juno oot the farm afore yon sale on Friday."

"Ye canna."

"Trust me." He kissed her and hurried out of the little cave before she could say any more.

John sat in Rachael Weir's kitchen at Waterside and explained his plans.

Rachael nodded. "Ye best tak somethin back for the mornin. Ah'll gie ye a bag o meal, a loaf, an a wee cookin pot. Whit aboot bowls, an spoons?" She hurried through to the scullery and came back with a bulging fishing bag. "Come mornin Gavin can tak ither stuff up tae the broken tree, ahint the pine wood, an hide it amang the twisted roots."

John turned to Gavin. "Dinna pit yersel at risk. If Airlie kent ye wur wi me at Bothwell he'd be aifter ye as weel."

"Aifter aw the bother he's causin it's a peety ye didna run him thru when ye hud the chance."

"Weel ah didna, an it's ower late tae chainge things. Noo whit aboot Juno?"

"Juno?"

"Ah want tae steal her awa frae ma farm afore the sale."

"Hoo come?"

"By openin the stable door an bringin her across the moor tae this farm."

Rachael frowned. "Ah suppose the troopers'll jist staund by an watch?"

"Ah wis thinkin aboot a wee distraction tae tak them awa frae the farm. A few meenits is aw ah need. If Gavin lichts ane or twa firecrackers by the wee bridge that micht dae it. Mind hoo we made some last year tae amuse the weans."

Gavin nodded. "Thur's still some left in the shed. It's fine an dry. They'll still be fine."

"Hoo's aboot gien it a go the morn's nicht?"

"An fricht the wits oot thae troopers?"

"Jist mak sure thur lukin the ither way while ah spirit ma guid horse awa."

Gavin's eyes shone with excitement.

Rachael looked at them both and shook her head.

The two boys woke to see a porridge pot bubbling over the fire.

"Jist lik magic," Marion teased as they sat up to rub their eyes. "The fairies wur here. They even brocht bowls an spoons."

William screwed up his face.

John laughed. "It wis me brocht the stuff frae Granny Weir. She even sent some bread. Ye'll no go hungry this mornin."

Most of the morning was spent gathering a supply of wood and leaves, and stacking it inside the cave. John guddled for fish again. This time Marion wrapped them in a parcel of thick dock leaves and left them to bake in the embers of the fire.

Later on they climbed up to the moor and made their way to the broken tree. The promised supplies were there, even the extra treat of a full cheese, a pan of milk, and some ale. Back at the cave Marion soon had it all safely stacked on a rocky shelf, well above floor level.

"Whit aboot Juno?" she asked as she folded blankets and laid them in the farthest corner.

"She'll soon be safe in yer brither's stable."

"Hoo come?"

"Nivver mind." John tapped his nose. "Ah'll tell ye aifter ah've done it."

The earl of Airlie had spent the night at Logan Waterhead farm. He'd even slept in John Steel's bed. It was big, well made, and comfortable, with thick blankets and a soft quilt. The earl had enjoyed none of it. The thought of the man he was desperate to capture was disturbing enough but the sense of that man's presence in the room was a further torment.

Before daylight he was up to rouse the sleeping men, and demand his breakfast. Even half-awake they could see his temper. The bellows blew into the dying flames in the kitchen range, fresh logs fed the rising flame, and a decent meal with the freshest of eggs was ready in record time.

Once fed Airlie's mood seemed to improve. He took a walk outside to look at the stock and the implements. Everything was in good order. The cattle and sheep were well fed and healthy. They should fetch a good price in the sale.

When he came back into the kitchen he asked Captain McCann about preparations for Friday.

"Nae worries sir, the notices are up in the village and the sale lists are complete. I checked them masel. The men did a guid job."

"In that case there's naethin tae keep me here. I'll awa tae Lanark and see if Clavers is still wi the sheriff. I'd like a word aboot the way he means tae patrol this district and keep a luk oot for Maister Steel. I'll tak the sergeant and twa men wi me. We'll be back early on Friday." Airlie didn't add that he couldn't bear to spend another night in this farmhouse.

As soon as the earl was gone the captain set the remaining men to do yet another check on all the sale items. He wanted nothing to go wrong on Friday. With a bit of luck a good sale might appease the old man and encourage him to think about returning north to his duties at Strathmore. Back on home ground, attending to his estate might help his master forget about the dent to his pride that had become a ridiculous obsession.

John Steel lay in the heather and watched the comings and goings around his farm. After years of hard work he was about to lose everything. No doubt the old earl had also claimed the two tenanted farms and taken the rent for himself. John wondered what his tenants made of all this. Not that he could do anything about it. But Juno was different. This thought cheered him up and he crawled back over the lip of the hill to spend the rest of his day setting rabbit snares. One way or another his family needed to be fed.

It was after midnight. The summer night had only just gone hazily dark. The young trooper on guard at the farmhouse door was struggling to stay awake. Captain McCann had ordered a night guard. The young man thought there was no need and resented being ordered to stand in one spot for hours on end.

Sleep crept a little closer. The young trooper's eyelids drooped, his head slumped forward. He closed his eyes. A loud bang shattered the still air. "What the...?!" He jerked upright. A bright flash soared above the farm track. "Jeesus!" He turned and hammered on the farmhouse door. "Sir! Sir! Wur unner attack!" A second bang convinced him. Another bright flash lit up the trees beside the farm track, the dancing shadows like figures creeping forward.

The farmhouse door opened. The captain appeared as a third, even louder bang, shook the ground. Again there was a bright flash.

"Oot here!" the captain roared. "At the double! Muskets ready."

Several men stumbled out to position themselves against the nearest outhouse.

"Doon there." The young trooper pointed down the narrow track. "It seems tae be comin frae the wee bridge. Ah'm shair ah saw folk creepin aboot amang the trees."

Another bang made them jump.

No one thought to look behind, to the back of the yard, where the stable door had just opened and a beautiful, black horse was about to step out after being cooped up for two days.

John led Juno round the corner, jumped on her back and was gone.

Gavin had the troopers full attention. Clutching a tar torch he ran along the line of firecrackers he'd laid by the bridge. The fuses lit easily and a cracker exploded every few seconds. The effect was even better than he'd hoped. Another five crackers banged and flashed and it was all over. Time to slip into the night, leaving the troopers to make sense of the past few minutes.

The noise stopped. The troopers waited, expecting more to come. Apart from the cackles of disturbed birds all was quiet. The captain signalled his men forward. Wary of possible ambush, each musket ready to blast anything they might meet, they edged down the track. They reached the turn in the track and met no one. The bridge seemed deserted except for drifting trails of smoke and the smell of spent gunpowder.

The captain sniffed the air. "Fire crackers. Fire crackers tae git oor attention and bring us doon here. It must be the hoose they're aifter. Quick. At the double."

The men ran back up the track. Once in the courtyard McCann ordered a full search of the house. "Check every room, every corner then tak a look roond the byre and the sheds."

Within minutes he heard, "The black horse is missin."

"So that's it." Dominic McCann had to laugh. "And nae prize guessin whae's taen it. Aw thae bangs and flashes wis a perfect distraction tae lure us doon tae the bridge while the rebel we're aifter got on wi stealin his ain horse frae his ain hoose." He laughed again.

"Ye'll no be laughin when his lordship hears aboot it," a trooper warned.

The captain nodded. "Worth it when ye think aboot the cheek o the man."

Friday was a difficult day. Airlie arrived, buoyed up with the prospect of a successful farm roup. News of John Steel's latest escapade soon tore a hole in his good humour. As expected he flew into a temper at the thought of being made to look a fool yet again.

"It cudna be helped, sir." A red-faced McCann tried to explain about the surprise element, how the noise and the flashes had added to the confusion. "It wis weel planned sir, and weel done."

"And we've lost the price o a guid horse. Buffoons. That's whit ye are. A bunch o useless eedjits."

"We thocht it wis an attack, sir." Lieutenant Ross dared to speak up.

"Thocht!" Airlie roared. "Ye dinna ken the meanin o the word. Yer stupidity is beyond belief. I've a guid mind tae stop a day's pay." He stomped into the house and sat down at the kitchen table to study the sale list.

An hour later there was no sign of anyone arriving for the sale. The men began to fidget as they waited for another outburst from their master. Strangely enough Airlie continued to sit at the kitchen table, staring at the long list of sale items, saying nothing. He seemed to sense that his grand intentions for revenge were not working out as he intended.

After another hour still no one had arrived. Airlie stood up. "Nae takers."

"So it seems, sir." Captain McCann agreed. "And it's no as if folk dinna ken. We put up notices roond the village, jist lik ye said."

Airlie stared at the ceiling and the captain watched his master's lips move while his eyes flicked back and forth. He seemed to be in the midst of some private argument.

The captain had the sense not to interrupt.

After a few nods then shakes of his head the great man turned towards McCann. "If I canna dae this ane way I'll dae it anither. Tell the men tae round up the beasts and drive them tae Lanark market. They'll fetch a guid price there."

"Whit aboot the implements, and the ither stuff?"

"Load up whit ye can on the carts aboot the place. It aw goes tae market. Aifter that I'll get a tenant tae run the place. That should sort oot Maister Steel."

"Ay sir. I'll see tae it richt awa." McCann signalled to the men and walked out to the courtyard to give them instructions.

"Folk aboot here must think weel o this Steel," the sergeant remarked as he led the first cow from the byre.

"Luks like it," the captain agreed. "This is the first time ah've seen a farm sale wi nae buyers."

"Dae ye think the auld man's bitten aff mair than he can chew this time?"

The captain didn't answer but inside he was smiling.


That afternoon Lesmahagow main street had a surprise. A cart loaded with farm implements and baskets of squawking hens lumbered in front of another piled high with furniture. Behind this came a line of cows and a flock of agitated sheep with a disgruntled platoon doing their best to keep the reluctant beasts in order. This kind of work was not to their liking. Nor was it proving an easy task, and they still had ten miles to cover before they reached Lanark market.

Bess's daughter Rena watched this performance from her mother's bedroom window and counted the animals as they passed. "Ah think John's aboot tae lose everythin." She shook her head. "Whit's the world comin tae when the likes o this can happen?"

High on a ridge above his farm John Steel had watched his cows and sheep walk down the rough track, over the little hump-backed bridge, and away along the road to the village. They were closely shepherded by Airlie's troopers. It was easy to guess where they were going for behind them lumbered two big carts heaped with implements, hand tools, milk churns, even hens in baskets perched among Marion's best pieces of furniture. It felt as if his life was walking away from him, and he thought about that day not many months ago, the day his family had set out for Loudon Hill, to hear that preacher and enjoy a day in the sun. Somehow it had all gone wrong. He'd lost his farms, his beasts, his livelihood, and become a man on the run with a vengeful nobleman on his tail. That sunny morning in June when his horse and trap clattered down the track he'd been smiling, with no idea what a difference the rest of that day would make to his life.

Airlie watched John Steel's cattle being led into the sale ring at Lanark Market. After a ten-mile hike from the farm they'd been dusty and tired, but an overnight rest in a holding pen, some hay and water, a good wash, and they looked like the fine beasts they were.

There seemed keen interest in them. The price rose quickly when the bidding began. The town butcher took all the hens and was keen enough to agree a price outwith the sale. He was even happy to add a little extra for the willow baskets. The farm implements fetched a decent price too, as did the milk pans and churns. So they should. They were the best of stuff. Marion's prize pieces of furniture fell short and went for next to nothing. Everything else made up for it and Airlie was content with the result. He'd managed to deprive John Steel of home, livelihood and fill a bag with silver merks for himself. It would do till he laid hands on the scoundrel.

Captain McCann stood beside his master. "A guid sale, sir. Ye must be pleased."

Airlie nodded. "Jist the man himsel tae catch and I'll be content."

"But surely sir," the captain's voice grew persuasive, "yer obligations at Strathmore must be pressin on yer mind. The estate must be missin yer attention. Wud that no be better than fashin yersel ower ane rebel? Aifter aw, ye've hud him named as a felon wi a price on his heid. It's only a maitter o time afore somebody whispers tae the law and he's caught. Richt noo he's on the run wi naewhaur tae go. Ye've deprived him o awthin."

"Except his life," Airlie growled. "But ye're richt. We've been awa a while and need tae be heading up country."

"Will I tell the men?" McCann sounded relieved.

"Nae sae fast." Airlie stopped him. "A tenant needs tae be gotten for that farm. I dinna want tae gie Steel the chance o creeping back the meenit ma back's turned."

"I unnerstaund whit ye're sayin, sir. But think aboot it." McCann grabbed his chance. "The locals didna come tae the farm sale. Whit chance hae ye o findin ane willin tae tak on the farm?"

"If that's the case I'll jist luk further afield. There's a tenant up at Strathmore I'm meaning tae move oot. Insteid o evicting him I'll offer him the Steel tenancy."

# Chapter 7

Airlie's platoon had barely galloped away to Bess Weir's house in the village when strong hands grabbed hold of Gaby. Clear off the ground he swung back and forward like a rat as the two remaining soldiers hustled him across the cobbled yard, out through the close, to hurl him onto the track beyond.

He'd been thrown out of many a place and knew how to twist his body, play the injured victim, when he'd only suffered a few scratches or a dent to his pride. Maybe he looked a scrap of an old man but Gaby was neither helpless nor old. The life he led had weathered him more than most, and the pack he carried everywhere had bent his shoulders, making him stoop like a man beyond his years. It suited him to be seen as a poor, old soul. His clear, sharp eyes were the only give away, but few bothered to take a proper look at such a ragamuffin.

Both soldiers laughed and wandered back inside the farmhouse. Gaby watched them go then spat in the dust and scrabbled after his pack lying a few yards away on the grass.

Returning to the village would be unwise; maybe time to put some distance between himself and Lesmahagow. He thought about Lanark, but the sheriff there seemed to take orders from Airlie, and that great man had just proved what kind of man he was.

Strathaven was in the opposite direction. That might be better. Not far away yet far enough. Tomorrow would be market day, plenty of people about with money in their pockets. Gaby had plenty of trinkets and ribbons to tempt the unwary. And of course there would be one or two customers after his secret potions in the bottom of his deerskin pack. The desperate and unhappy always seemed to hear whispers of his special tinctures and what they could do. Those customers never argued about price, all they wanted was relief from their torment.

With a final curse against Airlie and his men Gaby wiped the dirt from his pack and scuttled away. At the end of the farm track he turned away from the village and cut across the fields towards the Strathaven road.

When he reached the crossroads he stopped and sat down. There was no hurry. He could easily reach Strathaven before dark and find somewhere to bed down. Right now he was more concerned with his rumbling stomach. "Penniless an starvin. Whit a mixture." That's when he thought of Davie Shaw at Bellscroft farm. Davie was old, probably very old, lived alone, and was well known as an eccentric skinflint with an ill temper and a sharp tongue. Through years of calling at the farm Gaby had learnt to pander to the old man's moods, to wheedle a bite of supper, and sleep in the drafty barn. Davie enjoyed a moan and a rant against everything and anything, and it was no trouble for Gaby to nod, or shake his head and seem interested in whatever was said. A small price to pay for a good slice of ham and cheese.

Davie had given up keeping any cows, too much bother milking, and all that money spent on extra hay for winter-feed. Hens had taken over, wandering and scratching everywhere. Once a month he'd take baskets of eggs to Strathaven market where he always managed to sell them a little cheaper than anyone else. He was known for it, and usually returned with empty baskets and a full purse.

If Gaby managed to gain a night in the barn and then helped the old man load his cart he could probably beg a free ride to the market.

Mind made up he retraced half a mile of road then tramped across a broad meadow before he saw the long, low, straggle of unkempt buildings that formed Bellscroft. Nothing was ever tidy here; implements lay where Davie dropped them, the barn had a gaping hole in the roof and none of the house walls had seen paint in years, for Davie Shaw had no inclination to bother with any appearance, even his own. Money was meant to make money with as little outlay as possible, and the little it did make was secreted away. Davie's only weakness was his stomach so Gaby was almost sure of a decent meal. And Davie knew how to brew a good ale, strong and warming. An evening in the company of this difficult old man, having his ears nipped with all kinds of nonsense, would be well worth it.

There was no smoke spiralling above the chimney. This was unusual, for summer and winter Davie's fire was ever on the go.

Gaby knocked at the yard door and waited. No answer, not

even the old man's rasping, "Whae's there?"

He knocked again then lifted the latch and stuck his head into the gloom. "Davie. It's me."

Silence.

Baskets of eggs were stacked on the flagstones ready for morning but no sign of the old farmer.

Gaby hurried through the outer scullery and into the kitchen. There was Davie Shaw slumped in his big chair.

Gaby laid his pack on the floor and tiptoed towards the sleeping figure. He was about to lean forward, to touch the rounded shoulder when the old man's eyes met his. They were wide open, unblinking.

"My Gawd." Gaby jumped back and studied the frail, raggedy figure. "Deid as a doornail." He shook his head. "On his ane tae." This thought almost brought a wave of pity as he stared at the lined face, the mouth still sagging from its last gasp, and the broken stumps of teeth sticking out like some leering animal. In death Davie Shaw was less of a pretty sight than in life. Gaby was glad to look away and turn his attention to every corner of the cluttered room, to see if there was anything worth slipping in his bag.

Even by Gaby's standards there was little, but on the table was a new cheese and a full loaf. He tore off a hunk of bread then used his horn handle knife to cut a big chunk of cheese. "Waste not want not," he whispered to his silent observer and stuffed the rest inside his pack.

Behind him the big grandfather clock chimed the hour. The sound broke the silence like a warning. What if someone else appeared, a neighbour, a relative, anyone? What would they make of a tinker with an ill reputation standing in the kitchen of a very dead old man? What would Gaby say? Would he be believed, or would it turn into something altogether different? Where Gaby was concerned this was usually the way of it.

"Best git oot. An nivver let on ah wis onywhaur near the place." He turned to lift his pack when he had another idea. He stopped. "Mibbe no tak lang, an it's a peety tae miss the chance."

He began to search the kitchen, poking into every corner but finding no sign of what he was after. He hurried through to what Davie referred to as his guid room and searched again. Still nothing. He scampered upstairs to the only bedroom, looked under the ramshackle bed, lifted the stained mattress to find a trail of mouse droppings. Next came the big wardrobe. It was empty. He pulled out the bottom drawer. This time he found an old, mouldy top hat.

Undeterred he tore up the lid of a blanket kist at the foot of the bed. Here he discovered clothes, layer after layer of jackets, waistcoats, breeches, fine linen shirts, each carefully folded between protective sheets of cotton, and still in good condition. At the bottom sat several pairs of buckled shoes, rarely worn by the look of them, from a long forgotten time when Davie Shaw must have cared about his appearance.

Next he tackled the chest of drawers against the wall. Again nothing. He was about to give up when he looked down and saw two long lines scrieved into the wooden floor. This chest had been pulled out then pushed in again; and more than once or twice to make such deep marks.

He grabbed the top corners and tried to pull the chest towards him. It barely moved. He waited a moment, took another breath, then tried again. A mixture of excitement, determination, and as much brute force as he could muster seemed to do the trick. Slowly the little ball feet of the chest scraped across the worn lines on the floor. Behind the chest was a hole in the wall, a neat space where plaster had been carefully chipped away then several bricks removed. "Ah kent it." He thrust his hand into the hole and touched a rough hemp bundle. He poked it and heard a tiny clink. His fingers ran across what seemed like a good-sized bag.

He eased Davie's stash from its hiding place and laid it on the floor, before untying the string round the top. Inside was a rare mix of silver and gold coins. He lifted one out. It gleamed in the light, a glint of a better future.

"Guid o ye tae mind me in yer will, Davie." He tied the bag shut again and laid it aside while he struggled to reposition the chest of drawers exactly as it had been before.

He lifted the bag and checked its weight. It was heavy but he'd gladly carry this one.

At the bedroom door he stopped. "Why no?" He went back to the blanket kist and chose a full outfit for himself. "Micht be a wee bit big, but nae maitter." He hurried down to the kitchen, stuffed everything into his pack, gave a wave to the silent figure in the chair, and was out and away across the yard.

His plans had changed. No need now to bother about the market. No need for selling or begging. Everything would be different. To do this he'd need to go farther afield, far enough to disappear and re-invent himself.

Like Meg and Sandy Gillon, who'd crept away from their manse in Lesmahagow, Gaby headed for the city, for Glasgow.

At dusk he left the main road and pushed his way into a dense clump of yellow broom. The thick, pliable fronds easily bent then closed behind him. Soon he was out of sight in the middle of the bushes. Here he opened his pack and removed everything except the tiny phials of special tinctures. There might yet be a use for them. The rest could go.

He cut a patch out of the grass, pulled back the square sod, then used his old horn spoon to dig into the soft earth. The only hindrance was the tangle of roots but he was patient and worked round them till there was a deep enough hole for his trinkets and ribbons. He dropped them in. It was a good feeling to let them go, pile in the soft soil then pat the grass sod back in place. Now he had plenty space in the deerskin bag for his new-found wealth, and his new suit of clothes.

Job complete he lay back and stared up at the green curtain above his head. Whatever he did next there must be no mistake. This was too important a chance to allow it to vanish as easily as it had arrived. He began to work out a story about himself, who he was, and where he was going. Being naturally devious helped. Once he started it was easy to convince himself. Feeling pleased he ate some more of Davie's bread and cheese then closed his eyes.

Sleep was broken with a mix of dreams. First he was a grand gentleman, everyone bowing and scraping, doing his bidding, then it changed and he was climbing the gibbet, with a crowd baying at him for stealing an old man's life savings. Several times he sat up with a start to check the hemp bag was still in his pack before he was content to lie down again.

Eventually he gave up and spent the rest of the night rehearsing his new story. Invention had saved him on many an occasion.

Sometimes he did it just for fun. This time his whole future depended on it. He had to get it right, starting with a new name. It had to match his new character, help him wear it like a second skin, and allow his imaginings to roll off his tongue like the truth. He tried a few but none seemed convincing. And then it struck him. "Davie Shaw wis guid at gaitherin money an hingin on tae it it. Wi a name lik that ah micht jist dae the same." And so Gaby, or Sam Galbraith as was, became Davie Shaw as is.

He ate more bread and cheese then crept out from the protective circle of broom. Once on the road again he walked into the brightening dawn with a spring in his step.

When he reached Hamilton he headed for an inn in the centre of the town. It was a tidy looking place, well painted and maintained, a respectable house, with no space for riff raff, the sort of place he'd never dared approach till today.

A stout woman was washing down the outside tables. When she saw the new Davie she flapped her wet cloth at him. "Nae tinks allooed."

Davie bowed and took off his hat. "Quite richt maam. But appearances are no aye whit they seem. Ah'm a pair man ah'll grant ye, but nae tinker."

"So ye say."

"Indeed maam. Fallen on hard times a while back but noo on ma way tae claim ma inheritance."

"Inheritance." The woman laughed. "Ah dinna think so."

"Whither ye believe me or no it's the truth. Ma faither wis a weel kent Glesca merchant, sellt the best o cloth tae the gentry. He even kitted oot the guid duke hereby. The duchess bocht bolts o cloth for hersel as weel. She even hud ma faither mak them up, special like."

"So whit are ye dain wanderin the country lik some ragamuffin?"

Davie pulled a face and bowed his head. "Ma faither an masel hud a bit o a fallin oot."

"Ah think ye mean he flung ye oot."

"Ay. An ah deserved it. Ah wis stupid enough tae think ah cud mak ma ain way. It didna work oot. Ah've been livin haund tae mooth these past years, an ower ashamed tae gang back an say sorry."

"So whit's chainged noo?"

"Ah hud word frae a lawyer. God kens hoo he found me but he did, an sent a letter tellin me ma faither wis deid. The auld man hudna forgotten me. He still thocht o me as his son. Ah'm in his will, his sole inheritor. Ah've been tellt tae present masel at this lawyer's office in Glesca afore the end o the month an everythin ma faither hud will be mine. The man musta kent ah wis on hard times for he sent me a wheen merks tae git me there on time." He held up a silver merk. "Wud this gie me a room fur the nicht, a bite tae eat, an a gless o brandy tae toast ma auld faither fur mindin his renegade son?"

The woman stared at the coin and smiled. "Ah think ye'll need plenty hot watter tae wash awa yer past afore ye sit doon in ma dinin room fur ony dinner."

"Jist whit ah'm thinkin," Davie nodded. "David Shaw at yer service. Davie tae ma freends." He patted his deerskin pack. "Ah hae a decent set o claes in here. Aff wi ma rags, a bit wash, an ah'll be a new man."

"Ah'm Mistress Scobie. This is ma place since ma guid man passed awa. In ye come. But mind we want nae nonsense."

"Ye'll hae nane."

He was led upstairs to a room overlooking the busy street. It was clean, sweet smelling, with a large comfortable looking bed in the middle of the floor.

"Pit yer things doon an we'll git sterted." Mistress Scobie hurried away and after a few shouts from below two men lumbered into the room with a big, metal bath. They laid it beside the new guest, treated him to a suspicious look, and retreated without a word. Servant girls came in with jug after jug of hot water till the bath was half full, then their mistress bustled in. "Ye'll need these Maister Shaw if ye're ivver gonna shift that dirt." She handed him a pile of towels, a large bar of soap, and a stiff brush.

After the door closed he stood a moment to stare at the steaming water. This would be a new experience.

An hour later he emerged from his bath like a butterfly from a chrysalis. He was spotless, if a little red with all the scrubbing, and smelling sweeter than he had in years. He wrapped himself in the luxury of soft towels then pranced round the room like a delighted child. The clothes came next. He spread them on the bed and studied them. "They say claes can maketh the man." He pulled the linen shirt over his head and ran his fingers across the fine weave. It felt good. Even after years in the old kist it still looked fresh enough. Next he tried the breeches, the embroidered waistcoat and the heavy, worsted jacket. They proved a reasonable fit and the quality of the cloth would certainly give credence to his story.

Stockings and shoes on, he practiced walking up and down the room for a shoe with a heel felt awkward compared to his ground down old boots. Finally satisfied, he was ready to make his first appearance as a new man.

Mistress Scobie nodded approvingly when she saw him come downstairs. "No bad. No bad. But whit aboot yer hair, an yer beard? Thur's a barber's shop twa doors doon. It wud be worth yer while."

"Hoo much wud that be?" Davie played his role of the poor inheritor. "Ah huvna claimed ma inheritance yet."

"Three bawbees shud dae it."

"In that case – " He made his way to the barber's shop.

The barber tutted and shook his head. "Sir, if ye dinna mind me sayin, yer hair's awfy needin attention. As fur yer beard..."

"That's whit ah'm here for. Dae yer best an ah'll add anither bawbee tae yer price."

When he left the barber's shop the change was complete. He looked different. He felt different. He was different.

Feeling quite the gentleman Maister Shaw took a walk through the town, pleased how some people even smiled and nodded in his direction. He kept walking until he reached the banks of the river where he had a good view of the Duke of Hamilton's fine palace and manicured grounds. It all seemed like a good omen.

Wandering back to the inn he asked about the nearest stable, visited it, and bought himself a fine, brown gelding, a good, second hand saddle and a harness. After arranging to collect the animal in the morning he went back to the inn to sample Mistress Scobie's cooking.

She did him proud. He enjoyed every bite. Finally she brought over a glass of brandy and sat down opposite him. "Ye're uncanny interestin, Maister Shaw. We dinna see mony lik ye comin in here."

"Ah hope no mistress. Ah wis oot in the cauld fur years. Nae life at aw. But noo ah huv ma chance tae gang furrit an be somebody again." He winked at her and raised his glass. "Aw thanks tae ma faither. Ah'll no let it slip awa this time."

Mistres Scobie smiled. "Guid luck tae ye then. A man that kens his faults an hus learnt his lesson is a rare bird indeed."

Davie smiled back and accepted the compliment.

Davie's first night in a proper bed was a delight. He slept as if floating on a cloud. But he was still up early, down for breakfast and eager to start the next stage of his journey.

He paid his dues and added a bit extra which pleased Mistress Scobie.

"Aw the best," she called after him as David Shaw, in his new role as a sober, upright gentleman, clothed in best worsted cloth and buckled shoes, sat astride his fine horse, his precious pack secure in his saddle bag while he trotted out of town and along the Glasgow road.

It so happened that Meg and Sandy Gillon arrived in the city at the same time as a certain gentleman who'd journeyed from Hamilton. He approached their loaded cart, dared to give them a nod, and a good day as he drew alongside.

"Whae's that?" Meg stared after the stranger trotting into the crowd ahead. "Dae ye ken him?"

"Jist somebody bein freendly," Sandy replied. "Nivver seen him afore."

# Chapter 8

Meg watched carts, traps, horses, and a mass of people filling the street ahead. Back in Lanark there was always a familiar face or voice. Here everyone was a stranger. And then she remembered why they were here. Suddenly she was scanning the crowd for a different reason.

Sandy saw her anxious expression and tried to reassure her. "Dinna worry. Ah've learnt a sair lesson an mean tae pit things richt frae noo on."

"Ay." It was barely a whisper but enough to encourage him as they trotted further into the maze that was Glasgow.

Further on they found themselves in a cobbled square bounded by elegant, sandstone houses, each with a marble pillar either side of an ornately carved front door. Rows of tall windows gleamed in the sun. People with money must live here. The crowd around them seemed unimpressed and hurried on.

Instead of following them Sandy turned to the right and trotted into a narrower, quieter space which seemed to lead round the back of the impressive frontage on the square. Another right turn took them into another cobbled square, not such elegant houses this time, but well enough built and in good repair. Just beyond this they could see a row of shops with people busy shopping. Between the tall buildings they glimpsed the sparkle of the river. This excited Meg and she squeezed Sandy's arm as he drove the cart across the square.

He smiled. "Different tae auld Lanark, eh? We'll gang on an explore a bit mair afore we luk for an inn. If we find a guid ane we'll bide a nicht or twa then think aboot somethin mair permanent."

"Can we afford tae?" Meg asked.

"Nae fear." Sandy patted his jacket pocket. "We stuck oot Lesmahagow lang enough fur the sheriff's clerk tae send oot ma second quarter's money. Ah huv it here. It'll see us thru till ah'm up an runnin wi ma new shop. Thank God ah kept ma tools an bits o leather. Fowk here need shoes fixed same as onywhaur. Ah'll be earnin afore oor money runs oot."

"Whit if the sheriff comes aifter us?"

"He disna ken whaur we went. Onyway, he'll be lukin fur the Gillons an thur lang gone. We'll hae a new name as weel as a new story aboot oorsels. By the end o the week ah'll hae a beard tae hide ahint as weel. Meet Jamie Gray frae Ayrshire. Ma grandfaither's first name wis Jamie an ma mither wis a Gray."

"Whit aboot oor wee hoose an yer shop in Lanark? Ye rented them tae Henry Seaton while ye wur a curate. Will he jist tak them ower?"

"Naw, naw. Ah'll git a lawyer tae send Henry a message that ah'm oot the country fur the time bein an need the rent paid tae ma appointed representative. Ah trained Henry masel. He wis reliable as a journeyman. He'll no let us doon. An it'll dae nae harm if he lets oot that we're far awa."

For the first time in many weeks Meg began to feel hopeful that maybe her own Sandy was back in his skin.

Within days the new Jamie found a vacant shop two streets up from the river. Within weeks he was earning a return on his advance rental with several customers already recommending his work to others. Things were looking up for this shoemaker who said he'd come up from Ayrshire to try his luck in the big city.

Meg was much happier. They'd managed to rent a tiny, two-roomed cottage in a long row behind an inn on the edge of the docks. Meg had brought her pots and pans and knives. Already she was supplying a pot of soup every day to the inn, and earning a few extra groats. They had no furniture but there was good money in repairing old boots and shoes. Another month should provide a decent bed, table and chairs. A few weeks hardship was easy to bear.

City life seemed to suit her, she felt safe, well able to play her new part as Mrs. Gray. She even enjoyed spinning the stories of her imagined past.

Wee Isabel had so much happening around her it was easy to forget about Lesmahagow. And she liked the novelty of becoming an Elizabeth.

While Sandy Gillon was vanishing into crowded Glasgow Hugh Bawtie, from the Vale of Strathmore, was about to reach his destination in rural Lanarkshire. He was not a happy man and the closer he came to Lesmahagow the worse he felt. The Earl of Airlie had ordered him south to take over the tenancy of John Steel's farm and Hugh Bawtie had no option but to obey.

His angry wife and three resentful children sat beside him on the slow moving cart. The journey hadn't been easy, over rutted roads, rough tracks – sometimes no track at all. That's when they'd been scared, crossing the loneliest stretches of the countryside, having to sleep in the open.

Their livestock was left behind in Strathmore and Helen Bawtie couldn't forgive the old earl, even though he'd paid them compensation for the beasts. Helen had built up a good milking herd and now her work meant nothing. Hugh had tried to tell her they'd find good replacement stock at Lanark market but she refused to believe him.

As they approached the village they heard a loud shout and a military troop galloped towards them.

Helen looked scared.

"Dinna fash yersel. We huvna done onythin." Hugh stopped the cart and waited for the soldiers.

To his surprise the leading horseman barked out, "Are ye the Earl o Airlie's tenant farmer frae Strathmore?"

Hugh nodded.

"We're here tae escort ye tae yer new farm, an see ye settled. Airlie sent word tae expect ye, an see ye're luked aifter."

"Nae need sir. We're weel able tae luk oot fur oorsels."

"Oor order is tae provide escort, an that's whit ye'll tak. As weel as that I'm tae leave three troopers on the farm tae mak sure ye bide safe."

"Safe?" Helen looked even more scared. "Is this no a respectable place?"

The soldier laughed. "We're mair concerned wi yer new farm. It belanged tae a rebel whae's still on the loose an micht be aifter causin ye some trouble."

Helen turned to Hugh and whispered, "We've trailed aw this way tae land oorsels wi a problem? Ye shud hae stood up tae auld Airlie an tellt him naw."

"An git landed wi a bigger problem?" Hugh turned to the trooper. "Thank ye sir, lead on."

The procession through the village drew plenty attention. Everyone guessed where it was going. No one was pleased to see the new arrivals.

For six weeks the Bawtie family tried to settle into Logan Waterhead farm. No one called, and when they went into the village no one spoke. As for finding someone to work on the farm, Hugh had more sense than to ask.

Worse of all was putting up with three soldiers who were supposed to be protecting the farm. They did nothing, ate too much, spent each evening at the village inn then came back demanding supper and more ale.

Many a night Hugh and Helen cursed their old master who'd turned their comfortable life upside down and forced them to become unwelcome strangers in a strange place.

From a hidden vantage point on the moor it was easy for John Steel to watch the new tenants' problems at Logan Waterhead. He did nothing to disturb them or make life any more difficult than it was.

When Hugh Bawtie went to Lanark market he discovered the truth of Airlie's compensation. His money only stretched to four milkers and ten sheep. Disappointed at this further set-back he trailed back with his new beasts. By the time he reached the road to the farm he was in the depth of depression. Nothing was going right and his money was almost spent. If only he'd been able to stay in Balkeerie. If only, he wished. If only he could be somewhere else.

Just before the turn-off to the farm track he met a young man coming towards him with a loaded cart. The young man pulled into the side, then waved Hugh forward.

As he drew level Hugh nodded his thanks.

To his surprise the young man spoke. "Been tae market?"

"Ay. It's been a lang and wearisome day. Ah only managed tae buy four milkers an ten sheep. Whit guid's that tae a man used tae a fu herd an a proper flock?"

"That bad?"

Hugh shook his head. "Worse. Ah'm forced here as a tenant

fur ma maister Jamie Ogilvie an no allooed tae farm ma richtfu place back at Strathmore. Ah nivver wantit tae come here. An noo ah'm here everythin's wrang. The land's different tae up by an ah'm nae acquaint wi hoo things are done aboot here. An am left wi haurly ony beasts, nae hens, money near run oot. Ivvery day it gits harder wi three troopers tae feed an watter beside oorsels. Thur supposed tae be protectin us but aw they dae is eat an drink, an laze aboot."

"Can ye no send word tae yer maister, tell him things are nae workin oot?"

"Ye wudna say that if ye kent Airlie."

"Soonds lik ye huvna yer sorrows tae seek." The young man nodded again and clicked his horse on.

Little did Hugh know that he'd been talking to John Steel's brother-in-law. Later that night Gavin met John on the moor and repeated Hugh Bawtie's tale of woe.

John smiled. "Mibbe ah shud gang an hear his story fur masel."

"Whit aboot the troopers?"

"Come nicht thur awa at the inn fur hoors on end. An it jist so happens ah hud a wee bit news that micht appeal tae Maister Bawtie."

Gavin frowned. "Whitever it is, be carefu."

Next evening John watched the troopers set out on their usual visit to the village inn before walking down to the farm and crossing the courtyard like any visitor. At his own door he knocked and waited.

Hugh Bawtie opened the door and peered at his unexpected visitor.

"Evenin." John smiled and took off his bonnet. "We twa need tae hae a word."

"Whit aboot? Ah dinna ken ye."

"Ye will sir. If ye jist hear me oot it cud be worth yer while."

"In that case, ye best cam ben."

John stepped into the familiar kitchen, which wasn't familiar any more. Marion's big dresser with her collection of plates and bowls was gone. No settle by the fire, where he'd sat of an evening. A woman on a high-backed chair, darning a stocking, occupied the space. Only the blazing fire with its flames dancing across the white walls seemed the same. Somehow the strange table in the middle of the floor summed it up.

Hugh Bawtie stared at John as if trying to work out why this stranger had suddenly appeared, and why he seemed almost friendly. "So whit are ye aifter? We dinna git visitors here. Are ye seekin work?"

"Ah heard aboot yer difficulties," John said. "An thocht ah cud suggest a way oot."

"Hoo wud ye dae that? Assumin of coorse ah hae ony difficulty. Tae be blunt sir, ye ken nuthin aboot me."

"Ye spoke tae a young lad the ither day. Ye met him on yer way back frae Lanark market an seemed keen enough tae unburden yersel."

Hugh nodded. "A lot o guid that did me. The price o decent beasts ran awa wi ma money. Thanks tae yon auld skinflint o an earl ah'm reduced tae four milkers an ten sheep. In ma ither farm ah hud a fu flock, twelve guid milkers, an a wheen hens. This lot can haurly keep us goin never mind feed thae troopers ah'm forced tae keep. Thur awa tae the inn. When they cam back they'll be wantin fed, an shoutin fur mair ale. Ma pair wife's dementit tryin tae streetch oor rations tae feed the beggars." He stopped as if realising he'd said too much. "No that it's ony o yer business, sir. Whae are ye onyway?"

"John Steel."

Hugh Bawtie jumped back. "Him that's – "

"On the run frae yer auld earl. Him as wis the richtfu owner o this farm."

Hugh stepped further back. "Noo, luk here. Yer problems hae nocht tae dae wi me. Ah'm the legal tenant here, sent against ma will by Jamie Ogilvie. When yon auld deil says jump ye dae it. He jist mairched intae ma kitchen in Balkeerie an tellt me tae pack up. The estate factor hud a lang ee fur ma farm, an wantit it fur his son. Nae doubt he suggestit me fur the tenancy doon here tae git rid o me. Him an the maister are richt thick. It wis nae use arguin. No that ah'm needin tae tell ye aw this but mibbe it'll help ye unnerstaund ye're no alane in bein ill-used. Ma farm at Balkeerie is a grand place. It runs lik clockwork. The Vale o Strathmore hus guid land, an disna back ontae a wild moor lik here. The grass grows lush, an sweet. The beasts fatten up weel, an gie plenty milk. Enough tae sell aboot the doors as weel as mak fine cheese. Here ah hae naethin, an nae chance o haein onythin. Ah'm stuck an canna gang back, an ah canna see masel survivin here muckle langer. In ma ain way ah'm as bad aff as yersel."

"Haurly." John shook his head. "Ah huv tae live on that wild moor an watch ma back at ivvery turn. Ma pair wife an bairns git the same ill-treatment."

Hugh Bawtie's attitude softened. "Ay weel, ah'm sorry aboot that. Bit jist the same, whit are ye aifter? Ah canna gie ye back yer farm. It's nae mine tae gie."

"Ah wis mair thinkin aboot offerin ye anither yin."

"Hoo come? Ye're haurly in ony poseetion."

"Jist listen. Ma mither's cousin heard hoo things are an offered me the rent o a farm in a wee place doon Ayrshire way. Ah huvna seen the place but he says it gies a decent livin. He suggestit ah chainge ma name fur a fresh stert withoot yon earl on ma tail ony mair."

"Ah'd grab it if ah wis ye."

John frowned. "This is ma farm, alang wi twa ithers. It belanged tae ma faither afore me, an his faither afore that. Ah've ivvery intention o bidin here till ah git the chance tae claim back whit's mine."

"Ye micht hae a lang wait."

"Ah'll tak that chance."

Helen Bawtie laid down her darning and joined in the conversation. "Maister Steel, are ye sayin whit ah think ye are?"

John nodded.

"It soonds ower guid tae be true. Ye dinna ken us. We dinna ken ye. Why wud ye be aifter helpin us?"

"If ye leave this farm Airlie will nivver persuade onybody aboot here tae tak on the tenancy. Think aboot the bother an expense o sendin anither o his ane men aw the way frae Strathmore when he's beginnin tae think aboot ither things, mair pressin things fur his ain estate. Aince this place is empty ma wife an bairns can come in oot the cauld afore the winter sets in."

"Will the law no jist pit them oot again?"

"Airlie wis the prime mover in aw this. Noo he's awa up north ah doubt if the law will chase aifter a wummin bringin her family intae the shelter o whit wis thur ain hame."

"Ah see." Hugh looked down at the floor, shuffled his feet. "An ye think this wud work?"

"Why no?"

"Ay weel. We've been ill-used aready. Mibbe yer suggestion wud hae us jumpin oot the fryin pan intae the fire. An whit if we git caught? Airlie's no a man tae cross."

"Ye'll no be caught. Trust me. Think aboot hoo things are richt noo."

"Cudna be worse," Helen cut in.

Hugh looked up, gave John a hard stare then turned towards his wife.

She nodded.

"Richt. That's it then. Ye twa seem agreed." He held out his hand. "Whitivver ye did tae git on the wrang side o Airlie has ma approval. As for trustin ye. We'll see. It'll aw depend if this farm ye talk aboot is as guid as ye say, an far enough awa frae yon auld deil tae let me lead ma life the way ah want. Bit whit aboot oor beasts? Ah canna run a farm withoot them an money's ower ticht tae buy ony mair."

"Ye tak them wi ye."

"Whit aboot the troopers? They'll no staund by while we walk awa."

"Ye wait till thur awa at the inn then ah'll lead ye across the moor withoot leavin ony trace. Ah'll tak ye tae a freend o mine on the ither side o the moor. Ye can rest there a wee while then ah'll see ye on the rest o yer journey, show ye the farm, an yer new landlord."

"Ah'm sorry tae soond sae suspicious. It's jist – " Hugh's apology was interrupted by the sound of hooves rattling up the farm track.

"Aince things are sortit ah'll be back." John turned, was down the little hall, out in the yard, and round the back of the byre before the three troopers reached the courtyard.

A few minutes later he was walking across the heathery moor, whistling to himself, and smiling at the stars.

# Chapter 9

A month passed before John Steel came back with the news about the promised farm. Hugh Bawtie had almost given up. Now he could hardly wait.

"Jist git ready," John grinned, "an we're aff across the moor lik ah said."

"Whit aboot oor stuff?" Helen Bawtie wailed. "We've nae money tae buy new."

"Ah've got ma brither-in-law Gavin sortit on that score. If ye load yer cairt he'll tak it tae his farm an hide everythin till the fuss dies doon. Aifter that he'll drive roond by the road an meet up wi ye at yer new place."

"Aw that way?" Helen looked surprised. "He disna even ken us."

"He spoke wi yer man on the way back frae Lanark market. It wis Gavin tellt me aboot yer problem wi Airlie. By helpin ye he's tryin tae gie his sister the chance o gettin intae her hame, an aff the moor afore the winter sterts. We'll mak a start aifter the troopers huv left fur the village inn."

"Can ye wait three days?" Helen asked. "That way ah can pit stuff awa discreet like withoot the troopers smellin a rat, an on the nicht we can load up quick."

"Friday then?"

"We'll be ready."

On Friday evening the troopers set off for their usual session at the village inn. They'd hardly reached the beech avenue at the top of the road when the Bawties were loading the cart. Minutes later John and Gavin joined them and began to organise the beasts. An hour later the farmhouse door was locked, John had the key in his pocket, and the little group started up the rough track towards the moor.

Gavin drove the loaded cart to his own farm without meeting anyone.

John's collie nipped at the cows' heels while Hugh's dog kept the sheep in order. They made a good team and the beasts gave little trouble. At the end of the track they stepped onto the rough grass and heather. Minutes later a line of dark shapes disappeared into the deepening dusk and began a long night trek across the open moor.

The troopers had a great time at the inn, winning enough at cards to buy a few extra rounds of ale. They lingered long past their usual time, singing and boasting, and tormenting the serving maid.

Eventually the innkeeper's patience gave out. He managed to cajole them from their seats and steer them across the floor towards the door. Even as they were wondering what this was about he opened the door and pushed them out. The door banged shut. The big lock clicked. The bar dropped into place. Now on the wrong side of the door their fun was over. Fists hammered on the hard wood. Angry voices demanded entry in the name of the king. The door remained shut. Gradually the swearing and shouting tailed off. With a last threat the troopers loosened their horses from the hitching rail and made several attempts to climb into their saddles.

Each man slumped forward against his horse's strong neck and hung on. This was nothing new. The beasts knew what to do and ambled forward to carry their riders back to the farm.

Once there the three revellers slid off their horses and managed to pull the stable door open. But that was enough effort and the beasts were left where they stood.

"Noo fur supper tae roond aff a guid nicht." Fergus, the oldest trooper stumbled across the yard and fell against the farmhouse door. He expected it to swing open. It didn't budge. He pushed harder. It shuddered. "Chris sake." He clicked the sneck. Still nothing. His mood changed. "Open up! Wur back."

His friend Gilbert joined him. "Thur's nae lichts flickerin. They must be in bed."

"The door's ticht shut."

"Alloo me." Gilbert heaved his shoulder against the door. It shuddered again. He rattled the sneck then hammered on the door. "C'mon. Oot yer bed Bawtie. Open this door. We're needin fed."

The door remained shut. There was no sound from inside. The two troopers stared at each other in the pale moonlight then sat down on the doorstep to wait for the third trooper who'd gone behind the byre for a pee. As they sat the cold air began to clear their dull wits. Something wasn't right. Bawtie and his wife were reluctant hosts but they never made any criticism, and always had supper ready when their lodgers came back from the village inn.

Lieutenant Ross, the youngest trooper, staggered towards them. "Whit are ye sittin there fur? It's supper time." He stepped over the two bodies sprawled on the step, clicked the sneck then looked down at the two upturned faces. "The door's locked."

"Ay." The other two tried to stand up. "An we want in."

All three began to hammer on the door but no farmer appeared. Ross soon gave up. "Tae hell wi this. Ah need tae lie doon afore ah fa doon."

The other two followed him back to the stable and seconds later they were sprawled in the hay, snoring loudly.

Come morning the troopers woke with pounding headaches. They stared up at the cobwebs strung across the stable rafters and tried to remember how they'd got there. Eventually Fergus sat up. "It must hae been a guid nicht. Ma heid's dirlin." He lurched forward and staggered off the hay. "C'mon, a bowl o porridge'll pit us richt. The auld wife will hae it ready by noo."

Out in the yard he noticed how quiet the place was, and the byre door still shut. He thought about it then walked round the courtyard. Not an animal to be seen or heard. "Here," he called back, "ye best cam oot. Somethin's wrang."

The other two appeared, rubbing their eyes as they stared at the empty yard. They opened the byre and found no cows. They walked to the far end, opened that door, and looked out at the sheep pen. Yesterday it was full of sheep, now there was only champed mud and a swinging gate.

They went back to the stable. Their horses were standing where they'd left them, still wearing their harness and saddle, but the big farm cart that usually took up the far corner, was gone.

"Ah dinna like this." Fergus ran across the yard towards the farmhouse. He rattled the door. Nothing. He tried the sneck. Still nothing. He peered through the kitchen window. The fire was unlit. The table and chairs were gone. He ran round to the front of the house and looked in at the bedrooms. Empty. He ran back to the courtyard. "Bawtie's done a runner. An it's oor job tae keep an eye on him."

"Chris." Ross groaned. "The captain'll hae us on a charge. It micht even mean a whippin."

"No if we hae a guid story," Fergus suggested.

"Lik whit?"

"We wur duped. Bawtie an his family kidded on they wur ill. We went intae the village fur a doctor. They disappeared while we wur awa."

"Naw, naw." Gilbert shook his head. "We wudna aw go."

"Whit then?"

"We aye go tae the inn so we cud say twa o us went there fur a nicht at the cairds. Ane wis left tae guard the place. We need tae say that. Crichton wud expect it."

"An then whit?"

"Bawtie said he wis needin mair logs fur the fire. Oor freend wis happy tae help an went tae the oothoose. While he wis bent ower fillin the basket Bawtie sneaked up ahint him, cracked the pair soul on the heid, tied him up, an shut him in the oothoose. When we cam back the door wis locked an it took a while tae brak it doon. Aifter that we found oor freend trussed up lik a turkey amang the logs. Thur wis nae sign o Bawtie or his family, an we've nae idea whaur they went."

Ross nodded. "That soonds mair like it. But we need tae mak it soond richt afore staundin in front o Crichton. Noo he's a captain thur's nae haudin him, aye wantin tae prove he's the great *I am*. We dinna want tae be caught oot. Ye ken whit that means."

This had them practicing the story, checking every detail till they felt confident of backing each other up.

"Richt," Ross grinned, "ane mair thing we need tae mak sure oor story hauds watter."

"Whit dae ye mean?" Gilbert frowned.

"Crack on the heid. Crichton needs tae see the evidence." Ross smiled at Gilbert.

"Naw naw." Gilbert stepped back as Ross nodded to Fergus who obliged and gave his friend a whack.

Gilbert groaned and dropped to the floor.

"Gie him anither tae mak sure," Ross ordered. "On ye go man. He'll no feel it this time. The captain'll find it hard tae argue wi a guid lump on the back o the heid."

"An then whit?" Fergus grinned.

"We wait till oor pair comrade comes roond then heid for Lanark wi a convincin tale."

On the Cumnock side of the moor the Bawtie family were recovering after their adventure. It had been an eventful journey, shuffling through long, rough grass, tripping over heather roots, and all the time walking into a depth of darkness they'd never experienced before. Not that this seemed to bother John Steel. He plodded on as if he knew where he was going while the two dogs kept the cows and sheep in a steady line.

And he did know the way. Before dawn began to light this world of undulating hillocks and valleys he'd delivered them to his friend John Brown's farm and settled the tired animals in the byre. Mrs Brown welcomed the family, made a fuss of the sleepy bairns, and sat them down to a proper breakfast as if entertaining total strangers was the most normal thing to be doing so early in the morning.

While the Bawties were eating they learnt how the next part of their journey would be easier. John Brown was a carter. He travelled all over Ayrshire delivering parcels, packs, furniture, even animals, his carts being extra big, broad, and high sided. Space enough for four milking cows and ten sheep.

"We're travellin in style." Helen sat back to enjoy the changing scenery as they left the moorland and headed along the road towards the coast. "Luk Hugh. Up aheid, rollin fields an guid land."

He smiled back and felt happier than he had for weeks. Every mile was taking them farther away from the earl of Airlie. Soon they could begin to forget how unfair he'd been, how he'd nearly ruined them.

Two loaded carts trundled up a long hill that led to what was known as the Maidens. Reaching this part of South Ayrshire had been a long, wearisome trail. Now daylight was fading and it was beginning to rain. Helen Bawtie was too tired to care. She'd fallen asleep, her head nodding with every jolt of the cart, her arms still round her three children who were also sound asleep.

Exhausted as he was Hugh Bawtie tried to stay alert to check out this new land with its varying shades of green and gold suggesting good growing soil.

Round the next corner came a wider view of his future. There was a half-moon bay with a small, stone harbour at its tip and a long line of low houses straggling back along the shore-line. Fishing nets strung out in front of the houses covered every inch of ground right down to a wide stretch of smooth sand. Behind this a patchwork of fields led up to a densely wooded hill.

The evening held a stillness, as if waiting, while tiny raindrops pattered on the sea surface as the soft grey merged with the leaden sky.

Just before the village the carts left the road and followed a narrow track towards a small fort-like building with a wide, arched gate at the front.

A tall, thin man in a long overcoat stood beside the gate. As the carts drew near he stepped forward with a smile. "Guid tae see ye again, John. Are ma new tenants wi ye?"

John smiled back. "Ready and willin."

Helen woke with a start and looked at the strange face staring up from the side of the cart.

"Doon ye come, maam." The stranger held out his hand to help her down from the high cart. "Welcome tae Maidenheid. Ah'm yer new landlord. Name's Archibald Kennedy, Archie tae ma freends."

"Why, thank ye." Helen stumbled down to stand beside Kennedy while Hugh lifted down the children who immediately hid behind their mother.

"Guid tae meet ye, Maister Kennedy." Hugh held out his hand. "Gled tae be here."

As they shook hands Kennedy nodded towards John. "This man recommended ye insteid o himsel. He seems set on bidin whaur he is. Ah dinna unnerstaund why an tried tae chainge his mind. But he's set on dain things his ain way so his loss is yer gain. Ah'm shair we'll dae fine. Come awa thru an see whit ye think o the place."

He led them into an enclosed courtyard. "Up aheid that white washed bit is the hoose. Weel laid oot wi twa bedrooms facin the sea. Yer bairns shud like that. Thur's a big kitchen. The range works weel an lichts nae bother. The kitchen windae faces oot here. Guid fur keepin an eye on things. Thur's a wee scullery alangside the ootside door an a pantry. Ye'll find bits o furniture tae. Ma last tenant deid sudden like. He'd nae family. Naebody tae lay claims so ah thocht it best tae jist leave the stuff be. If ye dinna want onythin jist say."

"Indeed no." Helen shook her head. "We hae some furniture comin but no much so whitivver's here will dae jist fine."

"Ye're welcome." Kennedy nodded and pointed to the brightly painted green door of the house. "Did that masel an the wife scrubbed the doorstep tae freshen the place up. Richt noo she's inside getting a meal ready."

"We didna expect – " Hugh began.

"It's naethin." Kennedy stopped him. " We'll stert as we mean tae gang on. Noo let me tell ye aboot the rest. On yer left's the byre, clean an waitin for yer beasts. The milkhoose is at the far end. The milk pans an pails are still ther. Three arched doors on the ither side tak ye intae the stable and a guid hay shed. Ahint ye, alangside the gate are twa henhooses an a pen fur calves or sheep. In the centre is a guid drawin well." He stopped as he ran out of breath.

"It's mair than we hoped fur." Hugh Bawtie could see himself working here, making it a real home. "Wur mair than happy tae tak up yer offer sir. Ye'll no regret takin us on. An wur grateful tae John here. Withoot him – "

"That'll dae." John Steel looked embarrassed. "Ye'll dae fine here but think aboot chaingin yer name. Bawtie's no vera common aboot here an ower easy minded. Ye dinna want word gettin back tae Airlie."

"Ah've tellt folk ma new tenant is Hugh Graham." Kennedy turned to Hugh. "Ah didna mention whaur ye wur comin frae. Ah thocht ye cud deal wi that yersel."

"Nae problem, sir."

John nodded. "Noo let's git thae carts emptied an yer beasts sortit."

"Ay." Archie Kennedy hurried over to help John Brown who'd started to open the back of his cart.

Once the beasts were settled everyone followed the inviting

smell of food into the farmhouse kitchen where Kennedy's wife was waiting with soup, bannocks, fresh baked bread, and platters of fried fish, fresh caught from the bay.

Archie Kennedy took John Steel and John Brown by the arm. "Ah ken ye're baith keen tae be awa hame. But no the nicht. Tak time tae sit doon, enjoy a meal wi us then bed doon aside the fire till mornin. Ye can be aff by daylicht an feelin better for it."

The two Johns readily agreed and joined the others at the table. The mood was quietly happy, the Bawtie family glowing with pleasure. John thought how Marion and the boys might have fitted in here, enjoying life without fear of harassment. And here he was, giving that opportunity to someone else.

Later, when John bedded down on the rag rug by the kitchen range, warm and comfortable he was uneasy enough with himself to remain awake while everyone else fell asleep.

After a while he rose and tiptoed past John Brown, snoring gently on the settle.

Fly joined his master as he lifted the outer latch and together they slipped into the courtyard to take a little path through the wood towards the sea.

Once past the trees he stood a moment, pleased how the moonlight could show him a great horseshoe of a bay with a stone harbour at one side and the faint shape of Arran on the other. Behind the harbour loomed the huge pudding shaped rock known as Ailsa Craig.

The sea was calm, only a few waves breaking nearest the shore where a mixture of rocks and gravel and sand offered a resting place for long strands of dark seaweed.

Between John and the sea stretched a dense patch of gorse with the narrowest opening leading into it. Once inside the path twisted left and right, scuffing past jaggy gorse and soft broom tall enough to form a green tunnel. Underfoot was soft and sandy and so narrow his shoulders kept catching on the gorse thorns. Among all this climbed purple vetch, pink willow herb, and the tiniest, sweetest-smelling pink and white wild roses, all adding to a sense of something new as he listened to the sound of the waves beckoning him on. And then he was out on the edge of the beach itself.

The rain had stopped; the air was fresh, clean, almost tingling.

The moon grew brighter, sailing in and out of wispy cloud trails and turning the smooth sand almost silver.

Once across the sand John stopped with his toecaps almost touching the water's edge. Fly stood behind him while John stared out beyond the bay, past the odd shaped island, on towards endless stillness. Even with bright moonlight there seemed no way of seeing where sky touched the sea.

"Jist lik masel," he whispered. "Naethin ivver clear." Closing his eyes he listened to the lap, lap of waves, gentle but relentless, ever moving, changing. Tomorrow they might roar and crash, full of fury, determined, even dangerous.

He opened his eyes, looked down at the soft foam gliding over tiny pebbles, hiding them for a moment then pulling back only to do it again. Jist lik ma ain mistakes. Heart rulin the heid, ower an ower. Whitivver possessed me tae think that Hugh Bawtie comin here wud somehoo mak life better for Marion an the boys, let alane masel? "Eedjit again." His voice sounded harsh. "Will ah nivver learn? Think man. Think."

Fly gave a soft growl and snuggled against John's hand.

"Ay weel," he ruffled the soft ears, "us twa thegither."

Fly wagged his tail and they went back to the farm together, slipped into the kitchen to lie down on the rug again, and this time fall asleep.

The two Johns were up, ready to leave as daylight crept across the sea and onto the fields around Maidenhead farm.

As John reached his cart Hugh Bawtie ran over to him and grasped his hand. "If ah can ivver dae ye a guid turn."

"Ah'll be in touch." John squeezed the outstretched hand. "Aw the best, an tak care."

Hugh and Helen Bawtie stood in the courtyard of their new farm. Their new landlord stood beside them and shook his head as John Steel and John Brown drove the two carts back along the farm track towards the coast road.

Sheriff Meiklejon looked up from his steaming plate of stew and glared as captain Crichton appeared on the other side of his dinner table. From here Meiklejon issued orders, bossed his overworked clerk, and received visitors, but only by invitation. This particular one had barged in unannounced. "This is maist inconvenient, sir." His tone betrayed his dislike of the captain.

Crichton clicked his heels and stood to attention. "Ah bring disturbin news."

"Indeed?"

"The tenant in John Steel's farm at Lesmahagow has disappeared. Naebody kens whaur."

"Naethin tae dae wi me. Claverhoose is yer maister. Tell him. He's weel in wi yon earl that's taen ower the farm."

"So ah will, sir. So ah will. But."

"But whit captain? Ah'm at ma dinner. It's gettin cauld."

"Ma platoon wis ower by Lesmahagow tae check oot the farm aifter the three men billeted there brocht news aboot Airlie's tenant disappearin. We went intae the village an discovered the kirk wis shut up, ticht as a drum."

"Whit?" Meiklejon leaned forward.

"The villagers said yer curate's awa. Horse an cart wis loaded wi baskets then the family taen aff durin the nicht, alang wi his fancy new horse an trap."

"When wis this?"

"A few weeks ago."

"An naebody let on?"

"So it seems."

"That village has much tae answer for. An Gillon's jist been paid anither quarter. At the start I clothed him, his wife, an his bairn, gied him a horse an trap." Meiklejon pushed his plate away. "Thrum! Up here this instant."

Feet clattered up the stair in response to the roar and a small, fat, harassed looking man stuck his head round the door.

"Come in an hear this." The sheriff signalled to the captain. "If ye'll jist obleege me sir by repeatin yer story."

Thrum groaned. This meant more work, more hassle. Wisely he said nothing.

"I'll hae Gillon, so ah will!" Meiklejon thumped the tabletop. "This time he'll hang, an commander Claverhoose canna stop me." He glared at Thrum. "Ye heard whit the man said. Dinna staund ther, ah need the richt men tae search oot this runaway. Ye ken whae I mean."

"Ye need tae stert lukin fur anither curate," Thrum dared to suggest.

"That kirk bides shut." Meiklejon thumped the table again. "Thae villagers will be tellt tae attend the ane in the next village. The walk will dae them guid. Ah hope it rains ivvery Sunday. They deserve a guid drookin aifter the way they've let me doon. Ye can draft a letter tae the meenister at Blackwood informin him aboot the extra bodies he can expect in his kirk frae noo on."

"Ah cud mention yer missin curate tae ma commander," the captain cut in. "He hus mony a contact tae help in yer search for the man."

"Mmm." Meiklejon considered this. "Ye cud be richt. It'll dae nae harm tae hae extra een on the luk oot. Noo whit aboot the farm?"

"Whit Airlie disna ken will no hurt him. He'll jist mak an awfy fuss an solve naethin. Ah intend suggestin tae Claverhoose that the farm is left empty fur a while. It micht tempt Mistress Steel tae try sneakin in again. When she does her man will no be far ahint. That way we micht bring the maitter o Maister Steel tae a satisfactory conclusion. Airlie gits haud o Steel, an so will ah. Ah'm as keen tae catch that rebel as the auld man."

Meiklejon smiled. "Of course, there's a wee grudge atween ye and Maister Steel."

Crichton flushed and hoped the sheriff would make no further mention of the fiasco where John Steel had not only bested the captain but made him look a total fool.

"Richt." Meiklejon waved the captain away. "Report tae Claverhoose. See hoo he taks yer suggestion. Meanwhile ah'll deal wi thae Lesmahagow villagers."

"Sir." Crichton saluted again and marched out looking rather pleased with himself.

# Chapter 10

On his way back from Maidenhead John Steele had plenty of time to think how his life had changed. He'd begun the year worrying about draining the bottom field in time to sow the spring barley, then there was lambing, and calving, and making sure he'd enough eggs for the market. If only he could go back to that.

Lucas Brotherstone had started it all, him and his precious conscience, persuading the fool to use his pulpit to speak out against king and government. As for what followed, John wished he'd hardened his heart instead of allowing himself to be sucked into this nightmare.

Marion was his main concern. That last night before he'd marched away with the village platoon, the night before he became an official rebel, he'd only wanted to forget the responsibility he'd taken on, wanted nothing but the warmth and security of her love. She'd been every bit as keen, encouraged him, over and over till they were both exhausted. Caution played no part in their need for each other. What followed was almost inevitable – and she'd said nothing till it showed. All because she didn't want to worry him. Now she was struggling to climb up the steep sides of the little gorge they'd grown to think of as home. The cave itself did well, more or less wind free, and once a fire was lit it seemed almost cosy. It might be safe from the troopers but no place for a new baby, especially with winter coming. And yet here he was driving a cart along, following John Brown, and whistling to himself.

Helping Hugh Bawtie escape from Airlie's clutches had been a mad idea, imagining his own family could go back to Logan Waterhead and somehow be allowed to stay there. Hoo on earth did ah manage tae dream up sic a notion? Faither wud hae said it wis madness. Tellt me brae plain. He pictured his father shaking his head as he often did at some of his son's ideas. Many's a time an argument would follow with John going his own way only for his father to be proved right. It was just the way of things. They both knew this.

Suddenly his father's sense and reason were beside him. He could hear that familiar voice whispering, "My farm."

That made him stop the cart and think about it. Westermains had lain empty since the old man had set out for Bothwell the day before the battle. He hadn't been seen since. Nor had he been officially declared dead.

A rebel on the run had no right to anything let alone setting set foot in that farm. Marion and the boys were different. They could even live there. Neither Robert Steel nor Marion had broken any law.

When the two carts returned to Priesthill John helped John Brown unharness the horses and rub them down after their long journey. As they worked he took the chance to say, "Ye did weel an ah'm grateful fur yer help."

John Brown smiled. "Whit's a freend for? But if ye dinna mind me sayin, yer effort for Bawtie wis nae use tae yersel. Ah near said but ye seemed set on dain it. Ye must hae kent or wis it the thocht o rattlin the grand earl again?"

"Ay an naw. God kens why ah thocht Marion cud go back hame tae oor ain farm. Ah wisna thinkin richt. But ah've come tae ma senses an ken whit ah shud hae done. Ma faither's farm's empty an it's no under ony law regardin the rebellion."

"That maks sense," John Brown agreed. "Yer auld man's no likely tae come back but he's no officially deid an the law canna claim ye've inherited it an tak it aff ye. No yet onyway. Marion an the boys shud be safe there."

John was hurrying down the track from Priesthill when he saw a cart crawling up the long, winding track towards him. This cart was driven by John Brown's partner, Gus McPhail. One delivered to the city, the other travelled all over Ayrshire.

As soon as they met Gus asked, "Hoo did ye git on? Did ye git yon farmer delivered safe an soond?"

"Nae problem. It wis a great help hain twa big carts."

"Ye did that man a real kindness. An him a stranger."

John shook his head. "Ah wis thinkin mair aboot masel. If ah got him awa frae the farm ah thocht it wud alloo ma ain family back in. Ah wis wrang. But it disna maitter. Ah've ither plans noo.

86

Ah'm thinkin aboot Westermains."

"Yer faither wud approve. Shame aboot him disappearin lik that."

"We dinna ken whit happened, nivver heard hunt nor hair but we can guess."

Neither spoke for several minutes then Gus said, "Him an me wur guid freends, got intae mony a scrape as boys. An we bid close. Ah wis a witness at his weddin tae yer mither. We aye trusted ane anither, kept in touch thru the years. Mibbe that's why he tellt me somethin special a year ago. He cam ower ane day an went oot on the cart wi me. Drivin alang on oor ain, we cud talk private like. That's when he tellt me aboot yer inheritance."

"Whit?"

"Yer inheritance. No sae much whit it wis but whaur it wis. If onythin happened tae him ah wis tae tell ye it's in an auld, black tin, at the back o the milk hoose, in the far corner, on a wee shelf ahint the pails."

"Wis he no jist windin ye up?"

"Mibbe." Gus smiled. "An mibbe no. Aw the same ah'd tak a luk. Yer faither wis a fine man. He did me the honour o trustin me an ah've said nuthin so far. Noo it's time ye kent."

John went to Waterside to tell Gavin about the journey to Maidenhead.

Gavin grinned. "Yer wee trick caused a richt fuss. The troopers must hae gotten a rollickin frae thur captain. Ah wis on the knowe above yer farm watchin when a hale platoon came tae check oot the place. Aifter that they made for the village tae badger folk. No that they got ony answers except findin oot the curate wis awa. Aifter that ah think they high tailed for Lanark."

"Nae doubt they'll be back. But richt noo ah need tae see Marion an the boys safe afore the winter sets in. Ah'm takin them tae Westermains. Ma faither's no there, nor likely tae be. Thur's nae reason why ma family canna bide in the farm. An ah'll no mind some comfort masel. If the troopers come gallopin up the track it's lang enough for me tae jook oot an disappear afore they arrive."

"Peety ye hadna thocht o that frae the stert insteid o bidin oot on the moor. As for movin Hugh Bawtie, whit guid did ye think that wud dae?"

"Whit way did ye no pit me richt aboot ma daft notion?"

"Keep yer hair on. Ah'm jist sayin."

"Ah ken whit ye're sayin." John shrugged. "An yer richt. Ah need tae think things oot insteid o divin in."

Gavin laughed. "Ah wudna ken ye if ye did."

"If ye say so." John had the grace to admit the truth before he left Gavin and began his walk across the moor, back to the secret gorge, to be met by two excited boys and a white faced Marion.

She seemed very tired. The strain of the past few months was having its effect. When he told her his plan she simply said, "When?" and burst into tears.

Late that evening four shadowy figures and a dog crept off the misty moor, crossed the first field above Westermains farm and headed for the farmhouse. Shut up for months it smelt cold and fusty inside but once the big range was lit warmth and light flooded the kitchen to bring one corner of the house back to life.

Everything was exactly as Robert Steel had left it. John stared round the familiar kitchen with the big dresser, the settle by the fire, the scrubbed table and high back chairs his mother had been so proud of, the lustre jugs, the little copper pots on the shelves, even the rag rug he'd played on as a child. Now that the candles were lit it looked like the real home it was.

John scooped up his two boys. "Noo ye're snug as a bug. This time the law canna shift ye. Ah'm the rebel, no ye, nor yer ma, nor yer auld grandpa." He gave them both a hug. "Lets see aboot puttin ye twa intae a proper bed for a chainge."

For the first time in months John lay in comfort, his toes warmed by a hot brick from the stove, a linen sheet, and a thick, woollen blanket covering him. Best of all Marion was curled in his arms, sound asleep. Next door his two boys were content and safe. He smiled and fell asleep, and only woke when grey dawn crept in at the window.

For a moment he wondered where he was, then felt the warm, soft body by his side. He relaxed, and almost drifted off again when he thought of Gus's message.

John lay there staring at nothing, thinking about that word 'inheritance'. Finally he gave in and slipped out of bed. His feet touched the cold, stone floor. He shivered, then went on, tiptoeing through the house to the door which led to the milk house. The sneck clicked and he opened the door to meet a cold blast from this space with its thick walls to keep the fresh milk as cool as possible. Three steps down, past the metal milk-skimming bowls, all neatly stacked, and there in the far corner, like Gus said, were three milk pails. He lifted the first and looked behind it, then the second, then the third. He stretched his hand further, reached into the deepest corner, found the shelf, and felt the smooth metal of a tin, an almost flat tin, about twelve inches long, maybe three deep. He lifted it. Turned it over. Peered at it. But the dim light in the milk house made it difficult to see. He hurried back to the kitchen. The room was still half dark so he lit the table lamp for a proper look.

There was no seal, no special fastener. Just any old tin. The lid came off easily. Too easily for anything important to be inside. So it seemed for all he found was a single piece of folded paper, tied with a short length of string, the same as his father had used for many a job about the farm. The paper was smooth, good quality, in contrast to the rough string. He loosened the string then lifted the paper from the tin. As he unfolded the paper a gold ring dropped out and rattled on the kitchen table. He lifted the narrow, gold band with finely champhered edges and balanced it on the tip of his fourth finger. Now he could see a row of strange symbols cut into the gleaming metal. He turned it and saw a tiny, dark blue and gold flecked stone set in the middle of the symbols. He pushed the ring further down his finger. It was large enough to slide over his joint. This ring was meant for a man, yet he'd never seen his father wear it.

He turned the golden circle a few times. It was beautifully made, smooth and unscratched as if it had never been worn. This made sense, for when would a hard working farmer ever have the chance to wear such a fine thing? He couldn't remember his father ever mentioning jewellery. His mother, yes. She'd always treasured the little locket her husband had given her on their wedding day.

Even more curious he opened the stiff folds of the paper and read –

*I James McAvoy, incorporated goldsmith of*

*Glasgow, do hereby guarantee the safe keeping of*
*gold on behalf of Robert Steel of Westermains*
*Farm, in the parish of Lesmahagow, in the county*
*of Lanark, till such times as the aforementioned,*
*or a nominated third party, may require to retrieve*
*it or draw down a portion.*
*Hereby truly stated and promised this day Friday*
*6th August 1649, in the presence of the same*
*Robert Steel.*

The signature James McAvoy was made with a great flourish. Below it John saw his father's spidery scrawl beside a fancy, red seal with an intertwined J & A.

He read the whole thing again. Whatever it was, it was a secret his father had seen fit to keep for thirty years.

He read the address along the bottom line, folded the paper again, and this time put it and the gold ring in his inside jacket pocket. The black tin had served its purpose. This piece of paper best stay close till he confronted James McAvoy.

The rest of the day was given over to organising the house, helping Marion arrange things as she wanted. It was only after supper, once the boys were in bed and safely out of earshot that he mentioned the paper in the tin and showed her the ring.

"My it's bonny. Did yer faither nivver mention it?"

"No a word. But ah mean tae find oot." John held out the piece of paper. "See for yersel."

She read the strange words several times. "Whae's this McAvoy? It says he's a goldsmith. Whit did the auld man want wi the likes o him?"

"Nae idea. An sittin here will bring nae answers. Ah'll need tae gang intae the city an find oot."

Marion nodded. "It seems important. Bit ye'll need tae tak care. No be recognised."

"Ah want tae ken so ah'll tak that chance."

Rather than travel by horseback John walked over to Priesthill and begged a lift into the city with Gus McPhail. Gus's cart was in and out the city nearly every day. No one would give the carrier's cart a second glance. If need be John could slide below the top cover and stay out of sight.

John felt obliged to tell Gus the reason for this visit and held out the piece of paper. "See that address at the bottom. Dae ye ken whaur it is?"

"Ay. Ah can drap ye aff at the very door, or as near as ye like."

It was a cold journey. They were both chilled by the time they reached the city. "My that's a cauld wind." Gus McPhail pulled the collar of his overcoat further over his ears. "Feels lik snaw. Mind ye, it's no puttin them aff." He nodded at the street heaving with carts, horses, men, women, children, many carrying baskets or pushing loaded handcarts. "They're heidin for the market alang by the Gallowgate." He glanced at John hunched beside him and guessed it was more than the freezing temperature. He took off his wide brimmed hat. "Here. Pit this on. Pu it ower yer een an hide yer face if it'll mak ye feel ony happier. Noo fair exchange, gie me yer blue bunnet for the day."

John felt safer with his face in shadow, not that anyone seemed to glance his way.

"Ye're fine." Gus gave him a nudge. "Naebody here kens ye've a price on yer heid. Onyway, nuthin beats bein pairt o a crowd. Best way tae disappear."

John nodded and hoped Sam was right but he still wished the cart could move more quickly through the crowd.

When they passed the massive Tron steeple Gus gave it a nod. "Fine sicht. Five storeys high and built wi the best o stuff. Thae merchants ken hoo tae flaunt thur wealth an let us pair fowk see hoo important they are." He pointed to the right. "Three doors alang that street is the hoose ye're aifter. Ane o the finest in the city. Maister McAvoy is a weel respected man wi the best lined pooch for miles. But dinna be pit aff. They say he's an honest man. Nae side aboot him, an perfectly at hame amang the likes o us."

"Ah hope so." John made to jump down from the cart.

"Haud on." Gus grabbed his arm. "It's only a few mair yards tae ma first stop at the vintner's. Ye can help me lift aff the barrels an then slip awa. That way it luks as if ye're workin wi me. Aifter that ah'll gang on an meet ye again at the tap o the High Street aboot four o'clock. An ah hope ye'll hae some guid news by then."

John watched Gus's cart merge into the crowd then walked back through the crowd to the Tron. Hat pulled down in case of any stares he stopped on the opposite side of the street then slid into the shadows of a narrow close to study the frontage of the McAvoy building. It was a grand looking house; at least three storeys of golden sandstone with tall, graceful windows glinting out at the street. Two sets of marble columns on either side of the entrance set the main door back a few feet and protected it from the continuous trail of carts, horses, and people. This was an important residence with a long, brass bell pull alongside the shiny black door. On the wall was a well polished, brass plate inscribed with the name James McAvoy, Goldsmith.

The black door opened. A well-dressed gentleman came out. The door closed again. Several minutes passed. Another well-dressed gentleman ducked out of the crowd, approached the door, pulled the bell pull. The door opened. The man stepped inside. John stayed where he was watching the great and the good come and go as if on some regular business.

After an hour it was time to make a move. He pushed his way across the busy street, and stood by one of the pillars to wait his chance. As the door opened he was round the pillar to duck past an elderly gentleman about to step onto the broad, white step.

Before the man realised what had happened John was across the black and white tiled floor standing before a long, carved table piled with papers.

Behind him the elderly man muttered, "Manners sir," and slammed the door shut.

A young man sitting at the table, jumped up. "Something wrang, sir?" He blinked at John. "Hae ye an appointment?"

John held out the folded paper. "This'll explain why ah'm here."

The young man took the paper, spread it flat on the table before putting on a pair of half-moon reading glasses. He skimmed through the words, then looked up at John. "A meenit sir." He shot out from behind the table, ran across the hall, and raced up the marble staircase at the far end.

He was back in no time, all respect, ushering John upstairs. "This way sir. Ma grandfaither is keen tae meet ye."

At the top of the stairs he pushed open a pair of double doors and waved John into a beautifully proportioned room, painted in softest grey, with three elegant windows overlooking the busy street. An intricately patterned carpet, the biggest John had ever seen, covered much of the floor. Outside and inside this house spoke of wealth, and comfort, and elegance.

Opposite the windows was an ornately carved fireplace of white marble. A gleaming candelabra sat at either end of the broad mantelpiece. Even in the daylight twelve candles twinkled along with the gentle flames from a log fire, adding warmth and life to the quiet room. Close by the fire, in a carved, padded chair, sat an old man wrapped in a red tapestry cloak trimmed with fur. In his hand was John's piece of paper. He looked up and smiled. "In ye come, sir."

John nodded to the lined face. It seemed friendly enough but the steady gaze from a pair of astute eyes were another matter. "Guid day sir. Ah'm John Steel, son o Robert Steel frae Wester Mains Farm near Lesmahagow." He walked across the fine carpet and held out his hand.

The old man grasped his hand. "I can see the likeness."

John ploughed on. "Ah'm hopin ye'll be able tae explain the meanin o the bit paper ah brocht. Ah've only come because ah hae reason tae believe ma faither is deid."

"I'm sorry tae hear that." The old man sighed. "I can explain it aw. But first, wud ye happen tae hae the ring wi ye?"

John nodded and dug it out.

James McAvoy took the beautiful little ring and laid it in the palm of his hand. He smiled at the perfect, golden circle. "It's been a lang time since I saw this. I made it masel for Robert Steel. It wis oor extra precaution. Ring and receipt belang the gither. Whae ever cam wi ane had tae hae the ither. Yer faither wis a cautious man."

John nodded. "Ye made a braw job o the ring. It's a fine piece. But richt noo ah'm aifter some answers. Whit dae the symbols mean? An that wee stane, set in the middle, is awfy unusual."

James McAvoy laughed. "Jist me indulgin masel. I wanted tae mak somethin that spoke for ma client. The stane is Lapis, said tae bring oot the enduring qualities o honesty and compassion in whaever owns it."

"Ye got that richt then." John's eyes smarted. "Bit whit aboot the symbols?"

"The runes. They spell oot 'tae yer ane sel be true.' No that yer faither needed remindin. But here, sit doon We need tae talk. It's a lang story."

John sat down on the padded chair opposite and stared at the dancing flames of the fire while he waited for the old man to begin.

"It aw sterted wi the mine."

"Mine?" John stared at James McAvoy. "Whit kinda mine? Ye must be mistakin."

"It wis afore yer time. Likely yer faither nivver saw fit tae mention it. He'd nae interest in coal. In fact that's why he asked me tae deal wi the maitter."

This sounded unbelievable, or impossible, or both.

"Yer faither had an auld uncle wi a coal mine by Cambusnethan. It wis a guid, deep seam, and did weel. At least it did till the man wis killed in an accident. Yer faither wis surprised tae find himself inheriting sic a thing. He kent naethin aboot working a mine nor whit tae dae wi it. That's hoo I got involved."

"But ye're a goldsmith?"

"Whae dabbles in this and that and whiles the ither. I suggested yer faither micht alloo me tae find him a suitable buyer for the mine."

"But hoo did ma faither ken aboot ye in the first place? He nivver mixed wi goldsmiths or the like. In fact he wis rarely in the toun."

"We met by accident. Near yer ain village as it happened. My carriage wheel cam aff on the main road and I wis stranded on a richt miserable day. The rain wis dinging doon. I'd nae idea whit tae dae, and wis feeling sorry for masel when yer faither cam alang and taen peety on a weary traveller. Believe me I wis richt gled tae see him. He saw tae the sortin o the wheel then taen me tae his farm for the nicht. I wis his guest for three days afore the damage wis fixed. When I left yer faither refused ony payment, so the least I cud dae wis suggest I'd be available tae help him if he ivver needed ma services. Twa years later he inherited the mine and minded aboot me. That's hoo this connection began."

"So whit happened wi the mine?"

"I found a buyer, willing tae pay the richt price and tak it ower wi nae fuss. I did the paper work and wis able tae bring in 50,000 merks for yer faither. He seemed weel enough pleased wi ma effort."

John almost choked.

"Aifter that he asked me tae invest the money. Said I'd ken best whit tae dae. He left everything in ma haunds and went back tae his farm. Year on year I'd get in touch. Year on year word cam back telling me tae keep going. So I did. The interest tae date is still bringing a healthy return. Mibbe yer faither made nae use o his windfall but he has provided weel for yersel. Ye're a wealthy man Maister Steel."

John looked as shocked as he felt. "Somethin lik this taks a bit o gettin used tae. Richt noo aw ah hae is a thoosand merks on ma heid as a declared rebel agin the government. Ye see ah wis at the Battle o Bothwell Brig. On the wrang side as it turned oot. Ma faither disappeared somewhaur aboot ther. Ah believe he wis killed."

James McAvoy blinked. "Ay weel. Terrible times we're living in. Believe me I'm sorry for yer loss." He fell silent for several minutes then said, "Rebel ye micht be. But whitever ye've done, or nae done, I suspect ye've been wranged. And I'm sorry for that tae."

John looked relieved. "Ah hope ye'll conseeder keepin up yer guid work an luk aifter me as weel as ye did for ma faither." He leant forward and touched the old man's arm.

"Pleasure sir. And thank ye for yer trust. Noo whit aboot some money on account? Tae keep ye going? Hoo aboot a thoosand merks in a bag tae tak awa?"

"A thoosand merks on ma heid an noo a thoosand in ma pooch."

They both laughed then James McAvoy rang a little bell he had balanced on the arm of his chair.

The young man appeared. "Some paperwork tae be done, grandfaither?"

"Ay. And dig oot a thoosand merks for Maister Steel. It needs tae be in a strong bag. He's a lang journey hame." James McAvoy turned to John. "If ye're willing, William here will draw up a new contract atween oorsels, and then we'll baith sign."

John stood up. "Will ah come back later for that?"

"Nae need sir. If ye're happy tae gang intae the dining room doonstairs we can offer ye a bite tae eat while the legalities are sorted oot. Or mibbe ye'd raither tak a luk aboot the toun?"

John shook his head. "Bidin oot o sicht suits me fine, an a bite tae eat wud be richt welcome."

They shook hands again and John followed the young man downstairs.

The dining room was every bit as impressive as the room upstairs. John stared at the massive, polished table broken only by the march of six silver candlesticks along its top. He turned to William McAvoy. "Hoo aboot a bite in the kitchen? It wud be less bother."

"Not at aw, Maister Steele. Ye're a valued client and must be treated accordingly. Grandfaither wudna want it ony ither way."

John sighed and sat down. "Bread an cheese will be fine."

A serving girl, in a spotless dress and apron, laid a silver tray in front of John. She bobbed a curtsey and left him staring at a selection of best cheeses, three different kinds of cooked meat, bread, bannocks and a bowl of steaming soup. He sniffed. It was chicken. His favourite.

He ate every scrap then moved to a seat by the window to watch what was happening in the street. In the hall he could hear William occasionally talking to someone, the scrape of a pen on paper, well-shod heels clacking across the tiled floor as customers came and went. It was an orderly, reassuring sound. For the first time in months he began to feel safe and calm. If only, he thought. If only it could aye be like this.

The outside bell jangled. A faster, lighter pair of feet pattered over the tiles. John moved to a chair by the slightly open door and listened.

"Has yer maister thocht ony mair aboot ma wee proposeetion?"

John stiffened. That voice. No. Couldn't be. Not in a place like this?

William's voice sharpened. "Jist wait a meenit, sir. I'll go up and ask if grandfaither wants a word wi ye." William's feet climbed the stair, while the hall and the visitor waited in silence.

John crept forward and peered round the edge of the door. In front of the hall table he saw a respectable looking figure in a long, black, woollen overcoat with a fur collar to match. He seemed at ease here, and his clothes had cost a bonny penny. John's guess had to be wrong.

And then the visitor turned and began to pace back and forward. Something about the man's build, his movement, the slight stoop, the almost secretive footfall was reminding John. He'd seen this man before, in different clothes, in different places, but he'd seen him. More than that, he knew him.

He waited till the figure turned then pulled the door open and stepped out. "Sam Galbraith."

The man stopped in his tracks, looked stunned but quickly recovered. "Naw sir. Ye're mistaken."

John stared at the face, now clean shaven, powdered and dusted, looking quite the gentleman, glaring out below a fine green felt hat with a grouse feather stuck in it. The half smirk was the same. Those wary eyes hadn't changed. "Gaby. Ah ken it's ye. Stop pretendin."

The man backed away. John reached out to grab hold of the overcoat. The man ducked to the side. John followed. "Ye're no gettin awa this time." He managed to grab the left sleeve. "Come here ye auld deil." He pulled the coat towards him and made himself an easy target as a little knife slipped out from the right sleeve to thrust forward.

He barely felt the stab of the blade though something made him gasp and let go of the thick, woollen sleeve.

Half way down the stairs William called out, "Maister Shaw. Whitever are ye daing?"

Maister Shaw didn't reply. He was almost at the door, hand stretched out to turn the handle. The door opened, banged shut, and the figure vanished into the street.

John turned to William. "Ah think ah've jist made a mistake an allooed that auld deil tae git the better o me."

William gaped at the sticky red ring spreading across the front of John's shirt. He grabbed a hand-bell on the table and swung it above his head.

"Whit the...?" James McAvoy leant over the bannister. "For God's sake William move yersel. Maister Steel needs help. Get twa men frae the kitchen tae help the pair soul upstairs then send for Agnew."

"Will I get somebody tae come frae the garrison?"

"Naw. We'll deal wi this oorsels. We'll see tae the victim first, then we'll see aboot Maister Shaw."

Gaby slipped through the crowd, desperate to get away before anyone in the McAvoy household could raise the alarm.

With luck his knife had hit the right spot and put an end to John Steel telling that stuck up old goldsmith who he really was. As for being Davie Shaw, that had to stop. That's the name they'd come looking for. And come they would. These kinds of people always did.

As he ran he felt more and more resentful. If only John Steel hadn't appeared at that very moment. Seeing him had been a shock, a man on the run in a posh house like that.

He went straight to his lodgings in Black Friars Wynd. He'd chosen carefully, had enjoyed living there, playing at being a gentleman well able to afford the high rent for such a respectable address. Those snooty nosed merchants expected no less from anyone they'd consider doing business with.

He stopped at the front door, took a deep breath, then sauntered in as if nothing was amiss. The old manservant he'd hired came out of the kitchen. "Ye're early back sir. Ah wisna expectin ye. Are ye aifter somethin tae eat?"

"Here Jamie." Gaby held out a few bawbees. "Ma mornin's business has gied me a richt drooth. Tak a jug doon tae the ale shop. While ye're at it gang tae the baker for a fresh baked loaf, an then see if ye can find a nice bit o cheese. Ye ken the kind ah like."

"The shops are aye steery at this time o day. Ah micht be a while afore ah'm back." The old manservant shuffled into the kitchen to look for a jug then, still complaining, was out the back door and away.

Gaby wasted no time. He was up the stair, into his bedroom, to pull his deerskin satchel out of the big wardrobe. As his faithful companion for years its many pouches still held many of his special potions. They'd be coming with him. His precious bag of money took up most of the space and added to the weight. Finally in went receipts from a collection of merchants, innkeepers, and the like, for Gaby's way of making money had turned out to be much the same as diddling the public at the fairs he visited when still a tinker.

Minutes later he was out the back door, hurrying away from his grand house, heading for the stable to collect his chestnut horse. He even took time to press a coin into the stable lad's hand and whisper, "If onybody asks ye nivver saw me."

The boy nodded and helped the fine gentleman saddle up.

With a final warning Gaby trotted off along the Gallowgate like any self-respecting citizen going about his normal business.

Once clear of the city Gaby urged the horse to gallop, to put time and distance behind him. He was well into open countryside before slowing to a trot. Now he felt safe with his nose pointing towards another city and another hiding place where he could disappear, start again with yet another name, another story. So far so good. Tomorrow he'd be someone else. This wasn't a problem. Stories were his stock in trade, and he'd plenty money to make things easier. Since arriving in Glasgow he'd almost doubled what he'd stolen from David Shaw at Bellscroft Farm.

"Ay." He nodded to himself. "They say that a chainge is as guid as a rest."

John had no option but allow himself to be carried upstairs, undressed, and gently laid on a huge, four-poster bed. It all felt surreal, as if none of it was happening. And when Doctor Agnew appeared to bathe and clean and bind, then force a little sedative down his throat, it was a relief to fade into sleep. But as he did he could still see a certain face, grinning in triumph, at besting him yet again.

Outside the promise of snow arrived. A myriad of flakes swirled and whirled as Glasgow settled under a white blanket.

John woke and tried to sit up. His side throbbed. He ran his fingers over the tight bandages round his middle and realised it wasn't a dream after all.

"Ye were lucky." James McAvoy was sitting beside him. "And dinna think aboot moving. Agnew says ye're tae bide still for a few mair hoors. And dinna worry aboot yer lift hame. The man wis at the door spiering aboot ye. I had William tell him ye'd been delayed and needed tae bide ower a day or twa tae sort oot some mair business. He said he'll ca back for ye."

"Thank ye." John flapped his hands and closed his eyes again.

Much later, after a bowl of soup and another dose of ill-tasting herbs, John was able to tell James McAvoy about Gaby.

"A richt rascal," the old man said. "He introduced himself as Davie Shaw, said he'd got rid o his farm doon Dumfries way and come tae live in the toun for a chainge o life. Something aboot the story didna add up. I've heard mony a fanciful story in ma time, gotten used tae weeding oot lies so I didna bother arguing or even questioning him. I bid polite but daing business wi him wis oot the question. I think Maister Shaw cam back thinking he micht chainge ma mind."

"Shaw?" John shook his head "It jist so happens that an auld farmer, aboot twa miles frae masel, wis found in his kitchen, deid as a door nail. They said he'd slept awa in his chair. His name wis Davie Shaw. Ah'm sure it wis aboot the time Gaby escaped frae the cellar in ma cousin's hoose. He near killed the pair wummin wi a stane frae his sling. That's why ah wis sae angry when ah seen him, large as life paradin aboot yer grand hall."

James McAvoy shook his head. "It micht be a coincidence but mibbe oor freend helped yon auld farmer tae sleep afore making aff wi his siller? Jist a thocht. Lik I said, I wisna much taen wi Maister Shaw and his story. Aifter whit ye've said it micht be wise tae search oot this rascal and stop him afore he does ony mair harm."

John nodded. "Tak care. He's as slippery as an eel, an that's jist the stert."

"Dinna worry." James McAvoy smiled. "I hae guid men at ma disposal, every bit as devious and clever as Maister Shaw. Trust me, he'll get his comeuppance. Noo rest easy. Ye'll be a new man in the morning."

While John Steel slept the snow transformed everything it touched. Come morning the whole of Glasgow was dressed in white and more or less at a standstill. Cart wheels spun, went nowhere, or slid out of control; even walking was difficult. John accepted the inevitable and agreed to stay where he was till Gus would be able to return and collect him.

The McAvoys gave him every attention with his wound bathed and salved every few hours. Tasty meals appeared at regular intervals, never the same thing twice. The doctor suggested proper rest, which was enforced by the old man's will. John had never been so spoilt. He was grateful but most of the time his thoughts were racing ahead, trying to guess what Marion would say when she heard his news.

Four days passed before the weather changed from freezing ice and snow to driving rain. The streets ran with water but at least the city traffic was on the move again.

When Gus came to the door John was ready in minutes, saying his thanks to the McAvoys, accepting the promised bag of money.

James McAvoy came out to see his guest away. "Carefu hoo ye go," he warned. "Bide safe and leave oor freend tae masel."

"Help findin him wud be appreciated but ah still want tae deal wi him masel."

James McAvoy smiled and pulled his cloak hood over his ears. "Ay weel. We'll see. Meanwhile awa and gie yer family the news aboot yer chainge o fortune."

John and the old man shook hands. John climbed up on the cart. His eventful visit was over.

The old man watched the cart trundle off then made his way back to his favourite chair by the fire. He sat a little while to warm himself, then reached for his faithful bell to summon his grandson. "Richt William. We've been a bit remiss allooing this Davie Shaw tae slip awa sae easily. Nae doubt he thinks he's safe so it's time tae send the twa Jamiesons aifter him."

William nodded and hurried away to the dingiest, darkest howf at the bottom of the Gallowgate where two of the cleverest, most devious brothers in Glasgow were sure to be found, arguing over an everlasting game of chess, while sharing a large jug of Spanish claret.

Six hours later two men in black cloaks stood in James McAvoy's beautiful sitting room. "We turned ower Maister Shaw's hoose an hud a word wi his auld servant. The eedjit wis still hingin aboot expectin his maister tae come back. He kent nocht ither than tellin us whaur his maister kept his horse. The lad at the stable said he wis lang gone. Nae surprise sir so whit noo?"

James McAvoy nodded. "Jist spread the word whae we're aifter, hae a wee luk in as mony corners as ye can, and we'll reel the beggar in afore long. I'm a great believer in patience being rewarded." He handed them a small bag of two gold coins and a few merks. "Ye ken whit tae dae. Come back aince ye git haud o Maister Shaw, or mibbe ye'll be bringing me news o the deil's untimely death."

Both men nodded, and left the old goldsmith to sit back and toast his feet beside the fire.

Gus and John's journey out of Glasgow was far from pleasant on an open cart. The rain battered down and a sharp wind added extra bite. Head down and huddled into his thick coat Gus sat beside John with never a word. Miserable as he might be with his eyes full of water and his cheeks stinging, to say nothing was unheard of. Eventually John lost patience. "Ye've lost yer tongue an yer face is lik soor milk. Whit's wrang?"

Gus sighed. "Ah wis jist tryin tae work oot the best way o tellin ye."

"Tell me whit?"

"Ye'll no like it." Gus began to talk and John listened.

# Chapter 11

November was a dark, wild month with constant rain lashing Glasgow's filthy cobbles. It washed away some of the usual stink and muck, and reminded the residents that their leaking boots and shoes were needing attention before the real winter set in. One after another they found Sandy Gillon's tiny workshop, at the end of Bernard's Wynd. Every day the pile of repairs grew. Every day, Sandy earned more money.

This morning was no different. Sandy was bent over his anvil, mouth full of sprigs, tapping away with his little hammer, fixing yet another worn out sole. He'd lost count of how many he'd done so far and was thinking about a rest and a bite to eat when the shop door swung open. "Jist a meenit." He tapped in a few more sprigs then left his bench to greet the new customer.

The door was still open. Sandy hurried to close it against the blast of cold air then stopped short when he heard, "Wud ye be Sandy Gillon by ony chance?"

Sandy turned towards the speaker then pointed to the door. "If ye tak the trouble tae read ma sign it says J. Gray shoemaker."

"Wis that aye yer name?"

"Born and bred." Sandy tried to hide his alarm by sounding annoyed. "Whit has ma name got tae dae wi onythin? Are ye aifter a repair, or jist in oot the rain tae torment a busy man an keep him aff his work?"

"Ah meant nae offence." The stranger sounded apologetic. "Ye jist minded me o somebody ah kent in anither toun. He wis red heided as weel."

Below the dripping rim of a hat Sandy saw a thin, pock-marked face with a long, blue-veined nose, sharp like a cockerel's beak. At any other time he might have found this amusing except for the two intelligent grey eyes looking at him, as wary and sharp as any fox.

The stranger grinned and his trap like mouth opened to show dark spaces in an irregular row of teeth. "Hoo lang tae sort these?" He held out a pair of very old, scuffed, riding boots.

"No afore the end o the week," Sandy said. "Ah'm awfy busy."

"That'll dae fine." The stranger leant across the counter and seemed to be studying Sandy while he examined the boots.

Sandy's neck reddened but he kept his voice steady. "Twa soles, new heels, an the leather needs waxin. Ye micht be better aff wi a new pair."

"Ah'd raither hae them fixed." The stranger pulled his hat over his eyes and turned to go. "Friday then. Guid day, Maister Gray."

Sandy watched the stranger battle into the rain and disappear up the narrow wynd. *Guid day Maister Gray* rang in his head. The way it had been said meant exactly the opposite. It wasn't a good day. It was the worst of days. Frozen with fear he stayed put for several minutes before survival clicked in. He ran to the door, turned the key, pulled the bar over then retreated to the farthest corner of his workshop and quickly packed up his tools. In a few months he'd established himself as a good tradesman with much better to come. Not now, if he wanted to keep his head on his shoulders. The promise of a new life, a good life in this city was over. But first he had to find Meg, tell her what had happened.

He found her in the kitchen of the Black Bull Inn. She'd just delivered her daily pot of soup and was enjoying a gossip with the landlady, Elsie Souter.

One look at Sandy's white face worried Meg until she saw he was carrying his bag of tools. Now she was scared.

"No a word," he whispered. "No till we're back in the hoose wi the door ticht shut."

Meg turned to where her daughter was playing with a kitten. "Pit doon that wee beastie. We need tae gang hame." She frowned at Elsie and shrugged.

Elsie saw the look on Sandy's face and simply nodded as all three hurried out the back door of her inn.

Meg and the child could hardly keep up with Sandy as he almost ran along the little lane to their tiny cottage then hustled them both inside and banged the door shut. "Richt. Whit's up? Ye luk as if ye've seen a ghost."

"As guid as."

Meg gaped as he told her about his unexpected visitor at the shop. "Are ye sure?" Her voice trembled. "Did the man really say Sandy Gillon?"

"Clear as day. Ah near choked when ah heard it. The sheriff

must hae sent yon stranger aifter me. Richt noo his spy will be awa tae the law seekin help tae arrest me. Aifter that it's back tae Lanark. An ye ken whit that means."

"No unless they catch ye." Meg began to throw clothes into a basket. "We need tae pack up an git oot o here richt awa. We'll go tae the inn. Elsie'll hide oor stuff. Mair tae the point somethin she tellt me micht be whit we need. C'mon. Git on wi it."

Sandy was too desperate to waste time asking what she meant and within an hour the Gillon family were sneaking in the back door of the Black Bull. Meg quickly found Elsie and they had a whispered conversation.

"God sakes." Elsie grabbed one of their heavy baskets and led them down to the cellar. "Put thae baskets ahint the barrels, oot o sicht. An noo back up the stairs." This time she climbed all the way to the furthest away attic bedroom. "Safest room in the hoose. Ower mony stairs." She patted Meg's arm. "Bide here till ye're settled then come doon tae the kitchen an gie me a hand till the freend ah spoke aboot arrives." She glanced at Sandy and Isabel. "Yer man an the bairn best bide here." With that she clattered downstairs again.

The Gillons stared at each other then Sandy whispered, "Whae's this freend?"

"Come an luk oot." Meg crossed to the tiny window and pointed to a large, brick built building beyond the back yard of the inn. "It belangs tae a Maister Middleton. He's a weel respected merchant aroond here, an a member o the toun council. He's a guid freend o Elsie's an sups in here maist dinner times. She's tellt me aw aboot the grand things he's done."

"Whit's that tae dae wi us?"

"Everythin. Ah intend askin fur his help. He's no jist a wealthy man he's richt God fearin. Since yon battle at Bothwell Brig mony a Presbyterian is on the run. Elsie says he's helped a wheen tae escape."

"But ah wisna a Presbyterian ah wis a curate. He'll no like that."

"Ah'll jist huv tae tell him the truth then."

"Ye cannae dae that."

"Aifter the mess ye got us intae a dose o the truth micht be jist whit's needed."

Sandy groaned but didn't argue.

"Noo ye need tae bide here wi wee Isabel. Ah'll awa doon an help Elsie in the kitchen till Maister Middleton comes in. Ah've asked Elsie tae sit him in a quiet corner an introduce me."

Sandy watched the door shut and listened to Meg's heels rattling down the bare, wooden stairs. He could hardly believe what she'd suggested. He shook his head and climbed onto the bed. Isabel jumped up beside him and snuggled into his arms. They lay there together, one content and half asleep, the other staring at the wooden ceiling, trying not to feel so desperate.

Isabel was sound asleep when there was a light tap at the door. A well dressed, elderly, white-haired man opened the door and introduced himself as William Middleton. His voice was soft and polite.

Sandy jumped off the bed and gave the old man a decent handshake. "Please, sit doon."

"Nae need. Whit I have tae say will only tak a few meenits." William Middleton made sure the door was firmly closed then turned back to Sandy, "I understaund ye've fallen victim tae yer ain stupidity."

Sandy blushed and looked uncomfortable.

"Weel micht ye luk ashamed. Yer wife has tellt me yer sorry tale o greed and pride. If ye dinna mind me saying, they mak an ill mix that's hard tae resist."

Sandy looked even more uncomfortable.

"Yer wife believes the sheriff at Lanark played on yer weakness and duped ye intae thinking ye could deal wi men's spiritual souls instead o the soles they walk on." The old man smiled at his own joke.

"It wis far frae amusin, sir. Ah landed in a richt pickle."

"Indeed ye did." William Middleton's voice hardened. "As for trying tae be a curate – hoo cud ye dae sic a thing, daring tae tak ower a parish aifter the richt meenister was forced oot for speaking the truth agin the government's wrang ways? Toadying tae the great and the guid is bad enough but pretending tae be something ye've nae richt tae canna be justified. Whit ye did wis wrang. But I suspect ye ken that yersel. Ye certainly deserved yer comeuppance. Ay, and ye ken that tae. Yer wife has asked for ma help. Much as I disapprove o yer antics I dae feel sympathy for yer predicament. At least I dae for yer lang suffering wife and bairn. We've had a wee talk and I've explained hoo ye micht escape frae whit's coming next."

Sandy gaped at the old man.

"I hae a briggait anchored at the tail o the bank, waiting for high tide the nicht. If ye're willing ye can be on it, alang wi yer guid wife and wee bairn."

"Whaur tae sir?"

"Across the watter tae Holland. Much o ma business is ower there. Ye'll find it a God fearing place whaur honest endeavor is expected and weel rewarded. Ye'll no be on yer ain. There's anither passenger, a young man on his way tae Utrecht, tae study at the Presbyterian college there."

Sandy was speechless.

"Yer wife spoke aboot Claverhoose. She seems tae think he has a special interest in ye. If that's true ye'd best put a wheen miles atween yersel an yon man. He's richt powerful, and mighty dangerous wi a reputation tae match."

"Whit aboot the cost o oor passage?"

The old man smiled. "Dinna fash yersel. A few extra passengers mak little difference. Whitivver money ye hae ye'll need tae set yersel up and luk aifter yer family. Aince ye're established ye can think aboot it and send ower whit ye conseeder worthwhile. I'll leave it tae yersel."

Sandy flushed bright red and listened to instructions about being collected then rowed down river to join the briggait *Marianne* before she sailed.

"And mind," William Middleton warned, "ye canna be late, for the boat moves on the cusp o the tide."

"We'll no miss a chance lik this, sir. We'll aye be grateful. An rest assured payment for oor passage will come as soon as ah'm able."

"Jist mak sure ye tak better care o yer wife and wee bairn."

"Ah mean tae dae richt frae noo on."

William Middleton nodded and gave Sandy a firm handshake. "Be ready tae leave by eight." With that he left the room and made his way back downstairs where he called for his dinner then sat there smoking his pipe, as calm and content as on any other day.

Up in the attic Sandy wept with a mixture of shame and relief while his little daughter slept on as if nothing was amiss.

When the stranger left Sandy's shop he hurried to the nearest garrison. It was a good way off, at the top of the High Street. At the entrance he spoke to the sentry on duty and showed him his letter with Sheriff Meiklejon's seal. "Ah need tae speak wi yer captain on a maitter o some urgency."

The sentry studied the official seal then stared at the unkempt figure. "Ah tak it ye're in disguise. Ye dinna luk lik a man the captain wud want tae speak wi."

The stranger nodded. "In this kinda work it's the only way tae git results."

This seemed to satisfy the sentry. "In thru the arch, richt across the cobbled yard. The captain's quarters are at the far end. Tell the man at the door whit ye're aifter. He'll see ye up the stairs tae himsel. But dinna expect a guid reception. It's dinner time an the captain isna keen on bein interrupted when he's eatin."

The stranger thanked the sentry and hurried into the garrison. Moments later the next soldier on duty was accompanying him up twisted stone stairs to the captain's quarters to gently knock at the door.

"Whit is it?"

"Special visitor tae see ye, sir."

The door yanked open and a well-turned out officer glared at them both.

The stranger spoke up. "Sir, ah'm sorry for ma intrusion but time is o the essence." He offered the letter. "This will explain it aw."

The captain frowned, took the letter and walked back into the room without inviting the stranger to follow him. After a few minutes he reappeared and waved the letter. "Ye best come in."

The stranger bowed and stepped into the captain's quarters. It was a spartan place with an almost miserly fire in the hearth, no carpet, only a well swept stone floor, clean bare walls and a small sparkling window, very different to Meiklejon's hot, stuffy, smelly place of business with its heavy tapestries and thick, filthy rugs. In the middle of the room was a large table with papers arranged in order, ink and quill to hand. By the flickering fire was a well-polished settle. At one end sat a half eaten meal on a pewter plate along with a mug of ale. The captain sat down and read the letter again. Finally he looked up. "And ye are?"

The stranger took off his hat and bowed again. "Hugh McBride, sir. Ah hae a rovin commission frae the sheriff at Lanark."

"As ane o his spies?"

"No exactly sir. Ah tak on aw kinds o work."

"I'll bet ye dae." The captain laid the letter beside his dinner plate. "This letter asks for assistance as necessary. So whit kinda help dae ye hae in mind?"

"Ah need tae mak an arrest, sir. Ye'll see frae the letter that ma maister's maist anxious tae catch a runaway suspected o a serious offence."

"Whit has this felon done?"

"Nae offence sir but ah'm no at liberty tae say. It's raither a delicate maitter."

The captain frowned. "I see mention here o commander Claverhoose. Why did he no pen this letter?"

"Claverhoose is a busy man, aw ower the south o Scotland aifter rebels on the run. He asked the sheriff tae tak on this responsibility while he gits on wi enforcin His Majesty's orders in the south west."

"I see." The captain stared at his visitor. "In that case whit can this garrison dae for ye?"

"Ah need twa strong men tae come wi me tae Bernard's Wynd an help me arrest the felon ah'm aifter. Ah ken exactly whaur he is an want tae catch the deil afore he disappears. Aifter that, if ye'll be guid enough tae keep the man locked up ah'll see aboot transport back tae Lanark. Baith the commander an the sheriff will be gratefu fur yer assistance."

"Very weel." The captain went to the top of the stairs and shouted, "Carson. Find me twa aff duty men and bring them up here."

Five minutes later Carson appeared with two broad shouldered men. They all saluted, and stood to attention.

The captain nodded towards McBride. "This man comes at the behest o the sheriff at Lanark tae arrest a fugitive on a maist serious maitter. He needs help tae mak the arrest at Bernard's Wynd an bring the man here. Aince he's in the main cell ahint the stable ye're tae guard him nicht an day till he's taen back tae Lanark."

"As ye wish, sir." McBride bowed again to the captain and

signalled for the two men to follow him.

McBride hurried down the High Street. All he had to do was close in. The job was as good as done. Sheriff Meiklejon would have his revenge on Sandy Gillon while McBride would enjoy counting the promised bonus.

Most of the way from the High Street was down hill. He kept up such a pace that his two companions were almost running behind. His desperate hurry made no difference. Sandy's shop was locked up with no sign of the man himself.

The two soldiers watched McBride bang at the door then rattle the handle. "Luks lik yer fugitive's been tipped aff."

"Mibbe." McBride gave the handle another rattle. "We'll ask aroond here. This is a narrow wynd, somebody must hae seen or heard somethin. Somebody must ken whaur he bides. Ask in the shops alang this side. Ah'll tak the ither side."

It paid off. Soon they were crossing the little footbridge over the Clyde, heading for the row of cottages where Jamie Gray was said to live.

McBride hammered on the door then peered in the window. There was no sign of anyone. "Damn an blast." He kicked the door several times. A young woman poked her head out of the house next door. "If it's Maister Gray ye're aifter he left a while back, wife an bairn wi him, an a load o baskets. By the luk o them thur nae set on comin back."

McBride stood and fumed. Why had he been so stupid? Mouthing the name was as good as a warning. No wonder Gillon had grabbed his chance. "Richt," he snapped at the two soldiers, "we'll try the inn at the end o this lane. It's by the river an the merchants' sheds are nearby. A place lik that hus plenty fowk in an oot aw day. Thur's aye gossip."

Meg was coming out of the kitchen with a tray of food for Sandy and Isabel when she saw three big men come barging in the front door. Two were in uniform and the third, a strange looking man wrapped in a cape, made her look again. She'd seen him before. She drew back into the shadows and hoped they wouldn't notice her. That face with the beak-like nose wasn't one to forget. Worse than that, it belonged to Lanark. She didn't know the man's name, or anything about him other than she'd seen him near the garrison. That was enough. She waited till the three men turned into the main drinking room then ran upstairs, imagining they'd seen her and were following behind.

When she reached the attic bedroom she burst into the room. "Quick, lock the door. Thur's a man wi twa soldiers doonstairs. The man's frae Lanark. Ah've seen him afore. Ah'll bet he's the yin that wis in yer shop this mornin."

Sandy leapt off the bed. "Long thin face, nose lik a beak?"

Meg nodded and burst into tears. "Thur here fur ye. Whit'll we dae?"

Sandy turned the key and leant against the door. "They huvna found me yet, an mind Elsie said this is the safest room in the hoose. Thur's nae reason why yon man or the soldiers wud climb aw the way up here. No unless somebody directs them. Elsie's nae likely tae dae that."

Meg said nothing and leant against the door listening for the slightest sound. None came. Gradually she began to relax but nothing would persuade her to unlock the door, or creep downstairs to find out what was happening.

An hour later Elsie tiptoed up to the attic. The door was still locked. "It's me," she whispered through the keyhole. "It's aw by wi. Ye're safe."

Meg unlocked the door and peeped out. "Ah'm sorry Elsie but ah saw twa soldiers an a queer lukin man come in. Ah'd seen him afore an panicked. When ah tellt Sandy he said it wis the same man as wis in the shop this mornin. Ah jist kent he wis aifter Sandy. Ah hudna time tae tell ye."

"Ye wur richt tae disappear. The man in the cape wis fu o questions, askin ma customers aboot a Sandy Gillon, sayin he wis red heided, an a shoemaker new cam tae the toun. Ane or twa must hae jaloosed whae it really wis but God luv them they didna let on. Somethin aboot him seemed tae pit them aff. Ah offered the soldiers an the man a pint an promised ah'd keep an eye oot. The soldiers didna seem bothered but the man wis richt put oot. He said he'd be back the morn tae see if ah'd heard onythin. Thank guidness ye'll be awa by then. Whit time did Maister Middleton say ye'd tae be ready?"

"Eight," Sandy replied. "It shud be dark by then."

Elsie nodded. "Aifter whit's happened ye best bide here an jist come doonstairs near the time. Ah'll hae yer baskets placed ahint the cellar door ready tae collect. Meantime ah need tae git on as if naethin's amiss." She gave Meg a quick hug. "Stop worryin. It'll be fine. Maister Middleton's nae a man tae let ye doon." With that she left the Gillons to sit out the hours till eight o'clock.

Just before eight a handcart rumbled along the dark lane behind the Black Bull Inn. The back gate was pushed open by a tall, square-shouldered man and the cart rattled across the cobbled yard. It stopped by the kitchen door. Elsie Souter peeped out behind a guttering candle, and the man jumped onto the doorstep to whisper something. A moment later three shadowy figures slipped past her to join the man. They were carrying heavy baskets.

"Maister Middleton sent me," the man explained. "Ah'm Henry. Ah've a wee skiff tied up ahint ma maister's yard. Anither hoor an ye'll be doon river an boardin the boat that's waitin fur ye. Noo gie me yer baskets." He loaded the cart and began pushing it towards the open gate.

"Wait a meenit." Sandy turned back to the watching Elsie. "Oor horse an trap is kept in the stable at the end o Benjamin's Row." He held out a piece of folded paper. "Tak this. It's yer receipt."

"Whit for?" Elsie sounded confused.

"It maks oot ye've bocht the horse an trap. The trap's in guid order an the horse is a fine fella. He works weel. Ah made oot the receipt while we wur waitin upstairs. Ye mair than deserve it fur yer generous help." Sandy squeezed Elsie's hand and turned back to the waiting cart.

"That wis a kind thocht," Meg whispered.

"We owe her far mair than that," Sandy replied. "Withoot her we'd be locked up by noo, an ah'd be facin a hangin."

"Best git on," Henry reminded them. "Jist in case."

They didn't need a second telling and followed him as he pushed the loaded cart down the lane towards the river.

Once on the path along the river bank there was a faint glimmer of light from a row of houses close by. "Is this way safe?" Sandy asked.

"Ay. Nae bother," Henry replied. "Ma wee jetty's jist alang here.

Ah'm a regular ferryman, takin merchants back an furrit across the river every day. Onybody seein us will think naethin o it."

When they reached the jetty Henry pointed at the tiny rowing boat tied to one of the posts on the bank. "That's it. Climb in."

Meg stared at the black, watery space between her and the boat. She didn't move.

Henry grasped her arm. "If yer man steps in first he can guide ye ower. Ah'll keep a haud as weel, an then lift ower yer bairn. C'mon maam, time's gettin on."

Sandy nodded and stepped into the little boat. It rocked twice. He almost fell over but quickly recovered his balance and stretched out his hands to catch Meg as she jumped the space with her eyes tight shut. When she landed the boat rocked even more and some water splashed inside. "Chris sake." Henry sounded annoyed. "Sit doon. Baith o ye. Ah'll fetch the bairn ower masel. Aifter that bide still while ah load the baskets."

Isabel was soon in her mother's arms and Henry quickly dealt with the heavy baskets. This done he loosened the rope, pushed the little boat away from the jetty with an oar, then jumped in as it swung clear. The boat rocked even more and water splashed again. Meg swallowed a squeal, held Isabel even tighter, and tried not to look at the dark water swirling so close to the edge of the boat.

"Richt." The big man climbed past his passengers to reach the centre seat. He sat down, holding the oars upright while he allowed the boat to pick up speed with the current. Satisfied at last he dipped the oars in, and began the rise and fall of a steady rhythm, pulling the skiff through the water as if it was the easiest thing in the world. "Wur in luck the nicht. Nae moon an nae stars means naebody can see or guess whaur we're goin. An nae worries. Ah've done this mony a time."

"This is worse than ah thocht," Meg whispered and prayed that Henry did know where he was going.

The journey down river seemed never ending. It wasn't helped when the river widened and the shadowy banks disappeared leaving nothing but foul smelling water on all sides. The further they went the colder and damper the air became, wispy trails rising from the water's surface to settle round them like a blanket. They sat there shivering, feeling miserable, not knowing where they were, or where they were going. The only reassurance was Henry's solid shape rowing steadily and smoothly, whistling softly to himself.

They'd almost given up believing they'd ever arrive anywhere when Henry suddenly stopped rowing and turned to point ahead. "Wur nearly there." Looming out of the dark they could just about make out a faint but enormous shape.

"Is that oor boat?" Sandy asked. "It's some size."

"Ay. Ane o the best in the maister's fleet. Ye cudna dae better." Henry steered towards the dark shadow. "An ye're lucky the nicht wi the watter sae calm. Ye'll hae nae problem climbin aboard?"

"Climbin? Whit dae ye mean?" Meg gasped.

"Only way. Unless ye want tae swim tae Holland." Henry pulled the skiff even closer and slid along the side of the boat. Somebody seemed to be watching for him. High above a lantern light swung out then a gruff voice called out, "Henry?"

"Ay," Henry laughed. "Whae else?"

They all watched a thick rope ladder snake down through the damp tendrils of air which now had a tang of salt.

"Is this the sea?" Meg whispered. "Ah've never seen the sea. Noo ah'm no jist on it but expected tae climb up above it."

"Ye'll be fine," Henry said. "The end o the ladder's near enough tae grab. Naethin tae fear."

"Naw," Meg said. "Ah canna. An whit aboot ma bairn, she's ower wee? An ma baskets?"

"Dinna worry aboot yer baskets. Jist hing on tae the ladder an stert climbin up. Ah'll cairry the bairn. Tell ye whit, me an the bairn will go first an show ye hoo easy it is." He turned and held out his arms to Isabel who didn't seem in the least afraid of this stranger. "Richt lass." Henry lifted the little girl and stood ready to start the climb. "Haud ticht roond ma neck. Twa meenits an ye'll be safe on the deck up there."

Isabel clung to Henry. Up they went then slid over the ship rail to land on the solid wood deck. Isabel was delighted and leant over the side to wave while Henry more or less slid back down the rope ladder and into the little skiff.

Meg gaped at him then up at the tiny, white face. It was a long way to climb to reach that face. Unlike her daughter, she was expected to climb.

"Will ah come ahint ye? Mak sure ye dinna slip?" Henry sounded confident.

She nodded then closed her eyes, and kept them shut as she grabbed the rough rope to begin a long, slow haul, feeling for each rung, pulling herself a few more inches, steadying herself, taking a deep breath, sucking in the strong smell of painted wood close by her nose, forcing herself to try again. It seemed to last forever but she did reach the top where Henry gave her an extra push, into a pair of willing hands waiting to pull her safely over the rail and onto the deck.

"It wis easy!" Isabel ran forward and hugged her mother.

Meg nodded and tried to stop her legs shaking.

A stout man in a tight fitting uniform appeared. He was holding a bright lantern. "Ye did weel, mistress. No the easiest way tae come aboard. There's a pile o rope ahint ye. Sit doon. Get yer breath back till yer man arrives."

Minutes later Sandy's legs slid over the rail and the uniformed man stepped forward to wave him into the pool of light. "Ower here sir. Yer wife is needin a wee sit doon aifter her climb. Let me welcome ye aboard. I'm Peter Jones, captain o this ship, the *Marianne*."

Sandy shook hands with the captain. "Thank ye sir. It's guid tae be here."

"Nae worries. We'll tak guid care o ye and yer family, and see ye safe in Holland. Ma maister is maist parteeclar aboot that."

"He's a fine man," Sandy admitted. "Thur's anither doon below in the wee boat. Excuse me a meenit. Ah need tae thank him." He hurried to the side of the boat and leant over the rail to call his thanks to Henry.

The ferryman was busy linking each basket to the hoisting rope so Sandy waited till this was complete then roared his thanks. Henry looked up, gave a cheery wave, then pushed the skiff clear of the big boat, and disappeared into the darkness.

Sandy turned to the captain. "Ah hope wur dain the richt thing."

"Rest assured." Captain Jones swung the light of his lantern towards a low arched door further along the deck. "This way folks. Yer cabin's ready and waitin. Dinna worry aboot yer baskets. Ma men will see tae them."

# Chapter 12

The skyline of Rotterdam slowly began to appear from the sea mist. As it came closer it brought sharp-pointed roofs and soaring spires, which then became tall, narrow buildings, painted in colours the Gillons had never seen before, very different to the squat, grey huddle of Glasgow.

Captain Jones stood beside them and smiled at their expressions. "New place, new ways, new folk, an a new life. In a few months it'll seem lik hame. Holland welcomes the likes o us. Ye'll dae fine."

Sandy said nothing and hoped this was true. He glanced at their travelling companion who stood on the other side of the captain. Lawrence Scott was on his way to study at the Presbyterian College in Utrecht. He'd already arranged to take lodgings with one of the tutors and had suggested the Gillons should tag along and see what help might be available. Lawrie had been a lively and entertaining companion who'd helped make the days at sea more bearable. He seemed to enjoy playing games with Isabel, and they'd raced back and forward across the deck for hours on end. Not at all the person Sandy imagined as a future Kirk minister.

Just after the *Marianne* docked a horse and carriage came through the harbour gate and drew up close to the water's edge. Two men dressed in black with matching wide-brimmed hats, jumped out and stood staring at the upper deck of the ship. Suddenly one took off his hat and began waving it in the air.

Sandy watched the antics. "Somebody doon there's seems anxious tae attract yer attention,"

"Whaur?" Lawrie leant over the rail.

Sandy pointed. "Yon fair haired man in the black coat, wavin his hat as if demented."

"Oh my," Lawrie gasped. "It's Cameron. Richard Cameron."

"Whae?" Sandy looked blank.

"He's only the cleverest student ivver tae cam oot Saint Andrews, an the best speaker on ony topic. I'm tellin ye his words can move the heart an the brain in a way ye'd haurly believe. Ane meenit he's bringin tears tae a gless ee, next meenit he's urgin action wi nae haudin back. He wis ordained ower here but they say he's set on returnin tae Scotland. An no jist as a meenister. He's determined tae tak on the king himsel an point oot the error o his ill thinkin ways. It luks like he's meanin tae go back on this ship."

Sandy shook his head. "Ah wis a sorta meenister fur a wee while. The law kept pokin its nose intae ma work, aye tellin me tae dae this an dae that. When ah didna dae as ah wis tellt ah got intae an awfy pickle. Ah ended up runnin awa. An that wisna the end. The great an the guid sent the law aifter me till ah wis forced tae flee the country or face a hangin. Ma pair wife an bairn had nae choice but come wi me."

Lawrie's eyebrows rose. He gave Sandy a long, hard look.

This made Sandy wish he'd kept his mouth shut. He coughed, looked embarrassed, and turned away to speak to the captain.

Lawrie stared after him then shook his head at this revelation. Five minutes later he seemed to dismiss it and was down the gangway, running over to the fair haired stranger, shaking his hand, introducing himself, bowing and scraping as if meeting royalty.

Meg watched the performance. "That lad's gettin cairried awa wi himsel. An ye ken whit that means." She looked at Sandy. "Ye got cairried awa an luk whit happened."

Sandy blushed and turned away to busy himself with the unloading of their baskets and then make a proper goodbye to the captain and his crew.

The Gillons were hardly off the gangway when Lawrie grabbed Sandy's arm and pulled him forward to meet this special person.

"Sir." Sandy held out his hand. "Lawrie tells me ye're Richard Cameron. A raither special meenister."

The fair-haired stranger laughed. "Meenister ay. Hardly special though. Aw I dae is follow the Lord, keep ma conscience clear an try tae mak ithers see the truth o the Word an bide clear o the deil. Frae whit I hear his lang shadow is noo spread across Scotland an it needs stoppin. That's why I'm on my way hame, tae speak the truth on this maitter and rally whit support is needed tae put oor pair country back on the richt path." His tone was calm and measured but something about the words sent a shiver through Sandy.

To Sandy's relief Meg stepped forward to introduce herself and ask Richard Cameron about life in Holland. He answered her politely then waved to his black clad companion who was still standing by the open door of the coach. "Lucas. Thae folk are new here and fu o questions aboot the place. I need tae go on board the ship and speak wi the captain. Mibbe ye cud see tae them?"

"I'll dae ma best." A thin, worried looking man stepped forward. "I'm Lucas Brotherstone, ane o the tutors at the Presbyterian College in Utrecht." He smiled at Lawrie. "I tak it ye're ma new student."

Sandy stiffened at the sound of the name. This was the very man he'd replaced, the man who'd lost his wife the day he'd been flung out of his parish. A man like himself, who'd run away, but for very different reasons, yet he daren't tell him, not unless he wanted to jeopardise this new future before it had even begun.

He gave Meg a warning glance and saw her jaw tighten, and then the briefest nod. He offered Lucas his hand. "Ah'm Sandy Gillon. This is ma wife Meg an ma wee lass Isabel. We hud help frae a Maister Middleton tae come ower here, an noo wur lukin tae mak a new life fur oorsels."

"I hae reason to be grateful tae that same man," Lucas Brotherstone said. "If Maister Middleton wis involved ye had a problem wi the law, or the government?"

"Ay." Meg jumped in first. "Sandy wis on the wanted list fur staundin oot agin them."

This seemed to convince Lucas that Sandy was of the same mind as himself. He smiled broadly. "Welcome then. I'm sure ye'll dae fine."

"Ah hope so." Sandy grabbed his chance. "Ah'm a shoemaker an ah expect folk here need thur shoes fixed same as onywhaur."

"Indeed."

"Ah'm hopin fur work cookin an cleanin," Meg said.

"Cookin? Cleanin?" Lucas Brotherstone's face lit up. "Guid Scottish fare?"

"It's aw ah ken," Meg replied. "Ah'm no bad at it."

"In that case maam, ye're doubly welcome. If I cud persuade

118

ye tae consider workin in the college kitchen a guid few tutors an students wud be smilin for we miss oor ain style o food."

"Happy tae gie it a try." Meg looked relieved. "But first we need a place tae bide, an then Sandy needs a wee workshop. Utrecht ye say. Whit kinda place is it?"

"A busy toun, an a God fearin place wi opportunities for the richt minded. Tell ye whit. If ye've naewhaur parteeclar in mind come alang wi Lawrie an masel an see whit Utrecht has tae offer. I cud show ye the college an introduce ye tae the principal. He's aye on aboot missin guid Scots fare.

"In that case," Lawrie turned to the pile of baskets. "We'll load up an set aff for Utrecht." He winked at Sandy. "Ye never ken whit micht happen next."

Richard Cameron had slipped away. Now the little group saw him on the *Marianne's* deck, in earnest conversation with Captain Jones.

He didn't notice them load their baskets on the carriage roof, then wave, and shout goodbye. He seemed to be almost ahead of himself, back in his homeland, already facing the demons he seemed determined to confront.

This was Meg's first journey in a proper carriage. She leant against the padded cushion of the velvet seat and imagined herself as a grand lady. The jolts from the cobbled street quickly brought her back to reality and she opened her eyes to see the amused expressions of the three men. "Ah wis feelin tired," she lied and turned to look out the side window. "My, this is a busy toun."

"It is," Lucas replied, "but we'll soon be oot in the countryside, on the road for Utrecht. It's a fair journey. Ye'll need tae be patient."

"Ah dinna mind. It gies me time tae git used tae the idea o bein here." She sighed. "Ah hope ah dinna git hamesick."

"Where is hame?" Lucas asked.

Meg hesitated then said, "Lanark. It's a fine toun perched above the Clyde Valley wi its orchards an farms."

Lucas nodded. "Ay. It's a bonny place. My ane hame isna far awa. Lesmahagow. Hae ye heard o it?"

Meg nodded but didn't dare answer.

Lawrie turned to Sandy. "So Maister Gillon, whaur wis yer

charge in Lanark?"

"At Greyfriars," Sandy stuttered. "Lik ah said, ah wisna a richt meenister, mair a lay helper. Ah wisna ordained nor even licensed. The meenister there wis auld an a bit wannered. Ah did the leg work fur him, an hoose visits."

Lawrie looked puzzled. "Whit wis his name?"

Meg interrupted before Sandy could answer. "Luk. Wur leavin the toun an drivin by tidy fields, jist lik a patchwork quilt. An everywhaur's sae flat."

"It is that," Lucas agreed. "No a hill tae be seen."

The conversation tailed off. No more was said till they approached Utrecht when Lucas seemed to come back to life. "This is a fine place," he announced. "Hard working folk, guid clean living, nae problem adhering tae the truth. Ay. A fine place. I've been fortunate in my time here. Freends offering help and support, the kind o work I find worthwhile. At least I did – " He hesitated then shook himself. "Lawrie, I'm taking ye tae my lodgings in Patrimonium Stratt. Mevr Vrooman is a guid landlady. She's expecting ye, awthing's prepared, awthing taken care o." He shook himself again. "Ye see, I'm planning on leaving my post at the college."

"I thocht ye were tae be ma tutor?" Lawrie seemed surprised. "Is there a chainge o plan for ma tuition?"

"In a manner o speaking. Ye'll hae anither tutor, weel experienced an free thinking. Much as I've enjoyed being here I must mind the call o duty and follow Maister Cameron back tae Scotland. Indeed I hae nae option aifter the terrible news aboot Bothwell Brig."

"I see." Lawrie sounded impressed while Meg and Sandy looked uncomfortable.

There was an awkward silence then Lucas leant forward to tap Sandy's knee.

"Ye'll be aifter a place tae bide yersel? When we arrive I'll introduce ye tae Mevr Vrooman an ask for her help."

Meg interrupted with, "Luk at that."

Lucas smiled. "That's the Domtoren. It's a magnificent tower. A few years ago it was part of a cathedral. A great storm blew the main building down."

Meg frowned. "Soonds lik we've landed in a wild kinda place."

"Not at all." Lucas laughed. "It was back in seventy-four. I wudna worry. An mind we hae bad storms at hame as weel."

"Ay." Meg didn't look convinced and glanced at Sandy. "We'll be fine?"

"Ay." He squeezed her hand.

A week later Meg felt different. She'd been introduced to the chief tutor at the Scots College and invited to cook for the masters and students on a daily basis. Now her soup pot was ever on the go, her stew and fish pie much in demand.

Wee Isabel helped her mother in the college kitchen and the college principal, Reverend McWard, had promised her some proper tuition.

Mevr Vrooman had found them two rooms in a row of houses only a few streets away from the college and Sandy had put down a deposit on a small workshop behind the Anastraat. He'd chosen well. It was close to the Dom square and easily found. Already word had got out and customers began arriving with shoes and boots.

Life was changing again for the Gillons. This time it felt right. They could begin to put the past months behind them.

Ten days after the Gillons arrived in Utrecht Lucas Brotherstone began his journey back to Scotland. Reverend McWard came to see him off. They shook hands and the old minister said, "God speed my son. Be brave, for Ritchie Cameron needs aw the help he can get in raising the banner o the true word again for aw the world tae see."

Sandy and Meg heard this. Sandy cringed but said nothing while Meg shook her head and whispered, "Aw that pain an sufferin an he's learnt nuthin frae it."

"Whit dae ye mean?" Sandy whispered.

"Luk at him. The pair man's fair cairried awa wi himsel. Mark ma words he'll rue the day."

"Shh. They'll hear ye." Sandy warned.

Meg tutted and shook her head again.

Lucas Brotherstone had been seasick on his way to Holland. This time it was worse. He was still chalk white and shaking when the

*Marianne* dropped anchor at the tail of the bank. Scotland was waiting.

Henry McCraw, the ferryman, was surprised to see Lucas Brotherstone again. Discreet as ever, he made no mention as he rowed him up the Clyde. However, the white face seemed so helpless that Henry felt obliged to hand the traveller onto the quay at the Low Green, carry his bag to the nearest stable, negotiate a good rate to hire a horse, wait while the beast was saddled up, then lead Lucas up a narrow lane to the bottom of the Saltmarket where he gave directions to reach the Edinburgh Road.

"Thank ye, Henry." Lucas offered his hand. "Ye didna need tae dae aw that."

"Ah ken. Ye jist luked sic a poor soul." Henry gripped Lucas's hand. "Go weel, sir. Tak care. Hereaboots isna a safe place these days."

"I'm on ma way tae – " Lucas began.

Henry stopped him. "Ah ken fine whaur ye're goin, an whae ye've tae meet. Whitivver ye're intention ye're aboot tae keep dangerous company."

Lucas looked down at Henry's solemn face. "I need tae Henry. The truth must out."

"Ay weel." Henry loosened his grip. "Lik ah said, tak care."

Lucas's horse seemed to know its way through the busy streets. Nothing bothered the beast as it clip clopped on along the Gallowgate which eventually led him onto the Edinburgh Road, taking him on the last few miles of his return journey.

Lucas decided to stop and look for an inn before approaching the capital. As he turned off the road a rider hunched over a fast moving roan passed him. Little did he know he'd had a brief glimpse of Gaby high tailing it for Edinburgh and the Water of Leith, hoping to find passage on a boat south.

Once in the village of Harthill Lucas soon found a tiny but well run inn, a place to freshen up, eat a decent meal, and enjoy some quiet time to prepare for what would come next.

A few weeks ago he'd been present at Richard Cameron's ordination. It had been a remarkable event, particularly when the chief preacher laid his hands on his student's head and said, "This is the head of a faithful minister and servant of Jesus Christ, who shall lose the same for his master's interest, and it shall be set up before sun and moon, in the public view of the world."

Everyone had heard. Everyone had gasped at what it might mean. Lucas still remembered these words. How they challenged him to fight for the word, the true word. With Richard he'd have the chance to change that and do something for the cause, something that mattered.

In the morning his resolve was stronger. He carried on, determined to do the right thing this time.

Edinburgh was every bit as busy, and much more confusing than the city he'd left. It did seem a grand place, the way it stretched along a high ridge from the brooding castle to the Palace of Holyrood and beyond.

This time the horse needed directing and it took him a long time, with many askings, much turning round, then doubling back as he passed bakers' shops, skinners' workshops and wine importers, all with their different sights and smells. He wasn't interested in any of this, and kept pulling out a scrap of paper from his pocket, reading the spidery scrawl over and over as if this would direct him.

Eventually a carter put him right. "It's further doon the High Street. Nae sure whit side."

Half an hour later he spied what he was after. "At last," he muttered and dismounted to lead his horse through the narrow entrance to Trunk's Close. Beyond this dark, little tunnel was an enclosed yard of high gabled houses.

He tied his patient horse to the railing at the bottom of a twisted staircase and turned to climb the long flight of steps. He was half way up when a door above opened and a familiar figure appeared. "Guid tae see ye ma freend. I've been expectin ye. Had a guid journey?" Richard Cameron smiled a welcome as if nothing was amiss.

# Chapter 13

Sheriff Meiklejon chewed long and hard on a juicy mutton chop. Not that he needed to. It was the best of meat, and cooked to perfection by his garrison cook. It was more a delaying tactic, putting off the moment he'd have to start talking to his important guest. He peered over his well-filled plate. "Eat up, sir." He tried to sound jovial. "Simple fare but the best we can offer."

"Rest easy man." His visitor's voice was silky smooth. "Yer fare is aye guid. Nane better."

The sheriff stabbed at an ashet piled with roast potatoes. "Guid tae hear Clavers. Ye ken we aye luk furrit tae yer visits."

"As do I, Sheriff. As do I."

Meiklejon never knew how to handle commander Claverhouse. He hadn't quite worked out if he actually disliked the man. He did know he was scared of him, forever playing with words, confusing others for his own end, and now Meiklejon was once again on the receiving end. Looking a fool was bad enough, he also had to be careful for Claverhouse was seen as the king's favourite and any slip up would cost dear. After all the years of struggle and conniving to get where he was Meiklejon was loath to see any of it disappear.

The two men ate in silence till Claverhouse lifted his linen napkin, starched and waiting by his plate. He slowly unfolded the pure white cloth and wiped his lips as delicately as any woman. This always disconcerted the sheriff and tonight was no exception. He tried to cover his embarrassment by saying, "Ony mair, sir? A bit cheese mibbe?"

"I've had an elegant sufficiency." Claverhouse laid down his napkin and leant back in his chair. "Noo pour me anither glass o yer excellent claret while I hear yer report for this month. Mak it unofficial and feel free tae speak yer mind."

Meiklejon took a deep breath. "Ye mind yon curate I had installed in Lesmahagow?"

Claverhouse nodded. "He's certainly turned oot tae be a headache. Ma captain tells me Alexander Gillon has abandoned his charge."

Meiklejon reddened. "I'm still ragin at the man. And no jist because curates are a bit thin on the ground these days. The deil made aff wi the next quarter's pay alang wi a fine horse and trap. Tae think I kitted oot his wife and bairn wi the best o stuff, as weel as buyin him aw he needed tae luk the pairt."

"Quite the rascal then. Ye must be wishing I'd let ye hang him yon day at Lesmahagow. So whit's tae be done? Hae ye tracked him doon?"

"In a manner o speakin." Meiklejon's face grew even redder.

"Whit does that mean? Arrest the man. Deal wi him. He deserves tae be made an example o for flaunting the law, as weel as making a fool o yer guid sel."

Meiklejon ploughed on. "I sent three o ma best men on the hunt. Ane in parteeclar has done weel afore. He has a nose for trackin doon runaways. He nearly got haud o Gillon in Glesca, in a wee workshop. The rascal wis back at the shoemakin."

"Nearly?"

"Ay. That's when ma man slipped up. Insteid o dealin wi the maitter there and then he went tae the garrison for help tae mak a proper arrest. When he cam back wi twa troopers the shop wis shut and the bird flown."

"I see."

"Ma man found oot whaur Gillon wis stayin. He checked it oot. But the place wis empty. Wife and bairn awa tae."

"Soonds like ye've lost him."

"Naw, naw. We're still searchin." Meiklejon tried to ignore the commander's amused smile. "And that brings me tae the maitter o the empty kirk he's left ahint. Noo I ken hoo keen ye are aboot kirk attendance. But thur's the sma problem o money tae pay a curate, or a meenister, or whitever, and a guid portion o ma budget has disappeared wi Gillon. But fear not sir, I've tellt the meenister at Blackwood tae expect a bigger congregation frae noo on."

"Indeed."

"Ay. The walk frae Lesmahagow will dae thae villagers guid aifter nivver lettin on aboot the curate bein awa. It took yer guid captain tae find that oot. So, I'm wonderin." Meiklejon hesitated. "Mibbe yer captain cud keep a check on the villagers' kirk attendance for a wee while?"

"Three months then we tak anither look at the situation."

Clavers tone hardened. "His Majesty is keen on things settling doon aifter the upset at Bothwell Brig. But he wants it tae happen in the richt way, if ye tak ma meaning."

Meiklejon groaned "Ay weel. I ken it doesna luk guid but rest assured I'll no gie up till I catch Sandy Gillon and separate his heid frae his shoulders." He tried to move on. "Ye mind John Steel?"

Claverhouse laughed. "The way he tweaked Airlie's tail wis something tae behold. I've never seen the great earl sae angry."

"Mibbe ye ken that Airlie's tenant on John Steele's farm has done the same as Gillon. Family, beasts, furniture, awthin are gone. I had a wee whisper that John Steel wis at the back o it."

The commander's eyes sparkled. "Hoo did he manage that?"

"It must hae been across the moor for naebody saw them go. But I'll wager it's a plan tae get the farm empty again in the hope his ain family can come creepin back. Noo that Airlie's up north an mibbe taen up wi his ain affairs again he'll no be sae keen tae chase aifter Steel."

"Whit aboot me, sheriff? Am I no tasked wi rounding up every rebel on behalf o the crown?"

"Indeed sir. I'm jist sayin."

"I think ye're a tad oot o date." Claverhouse flapped a ringed hand. "I had a wee whisper that Mistress Steel and her twa bairns are bidin at Westermains farm."

"Whaur?" Meiklejon looked blank.

"It's twa miles alang frae John Steel's ane yin. It belangs tae his faither. Apparently the auld man set oot for Bothwell afore the battle. He hasna been seen since. Naebody kens whaur he went or whit happened altho it's a fair guess the man's deid. There's nae proof he wis a rebel, even though his son has a price on his heid, so the law canna claim the farm and lands. At least no till he's recorded as officially deid. As a named rebel his son canna claim ony inheritance so we need tae wait." Claverhouse lowered his voice. "I ken Mistress Steel wis put oot her ain farm by Airlie in the heat o the moment but I canna see it wud be richt tae put her oot o this farm. Like the auld man ther's nae proof she's been a rebel, ither than by association. Onyway, the woman seems tae be cairryin a bairn. Weel gone by her shape, or so I'm tellt. Wud it no be a Christian act tae alloo her some shelter frae the moor?

Noo that winter's coming on."

Meiklejon grinned. "And mibbe her guid man will come in aff the moor as weel." He raised a glass to the commander. "I must say that's weel thocht."

The two glasses clinked together and the two men sat back, one relieved, the other amused by the discomfort he'd caused with so little effort.

Marion looked round Westermains kitchen and smiled. Here was warmth and comfort. A place where a baby might be born in safety. At least she hoped so. It was good to be in a proper house again. What a difference it made. John said she'd every right to be here. She did believe him but she also knew it wasn't that simple. And if the troopers did arrive would she have the courage to face them?

Her smile froze. Tears appeared. It was all so unfair. Her two boys didn't deserve this. They hadn't broken any law or done anything wrong. Right now they were in the yard, playing with the dog. They sounded happy. She smiled again.

When the boys were in bed, Marion sat by the fire. She enjoyed doing this, just sitting staring at the dancing flames. Tonight her worries kept interrupting, bringing pictures of the past few months after that grand, old earl had rounded on her, and all because John had bested him. But Airlie was away now. The sheriff at Lanark was enforcing the law. In his eyes it was John he was after so why would he come chasing after her? She hadn't been declared a rebel. Surely that was as good as innocent? Maybe it was time to try and pick up some threads of how things used to be, to stop hiding and do something that any woman might do, like visiting her mother. That would be start. She thought about this. Tomorrow she'd take her sons to see their grandmother. There would be no harm in that.

When Marion woke next morning the snow that covered Glasgow had skiffed across Clydesdale and only left a light dusting. The field and hills looked bright against the dark sky, but no deep snow, no drifts to struggle through, nothing to stop her walking across to Waterside Farm. But now she was less sure if this was a good idea. She'd told the boys though, and she could see they were keen. So wrapped in their thickest coats they set out against the winter wind.

Half way down the farm track Marion realised how difficult walking had become. Her back ached so much she was forced to stop several times and pretend she was looking at the winter scene. The two boys didn't mind. They ran back and forward, sliding on little threads of ice along the rutted track while their mother held her belly with both hands and arched her back to relieve the baby's forward push. It felt so heavy now, and seemed to be slipping a little lower. This worried her. It was too soon. In the past week a pain like an ever tightening girdle had come and gone several times. Yesterday she'd been forced to sit down and take little, short breaths till it eased. She'd have to be careful now, very careful, or this restless baby might drop even further, and there was still another month to go.

Captain Crichton was not a happy man. Earlier that morning his commander had warned him that the Steel family's arrival at Wester Mains meant keeping a close watch, no more. "Ye bide back. Keep a guid luk oot. Mak a report and leave ony decision tae me."

Crichton hadn't dared argue but now he was out and about and thinking like his own man. Somehow the captain contrived to take his platoon close by that very farm. After that it was easy to swing up the track to take a look.

When the platoon halted in the yard it was obvious the place was deserted. In spite of his orders Crichton forced the house door open and ordered a thorough search of every room.

"Sir." Lieutenant McCann's tone said it all but his captain chose to ignore him.

They found no sign of John, nothing they could use against Mistress Steel. Reluctantly Crichton ordered his men to mount up and continue their patrol.

As they walked past the track leading to Logan Waterhead Marion stopped and looked across at the little cluster of buildings. No smoke rose from the chimney.

No sign of life. This persuaded her. Instead of walking on, she turned onto the familiar track, and followed it down to the little, hump-backed bridge. Here the pain in her back forced her to stop and lean against the stone parapet. The boys slid down the bank to skim stones across the frozen pools and crack thin ice at the water's edge.

As she stood there Marion thought about her old home. And then she was pulled back to her senses with the drumming of hooves on the road above. On the beech avenue she saw a glint of red and the flash of metal. Troopers, and she was standing on forbidden land. "Run boys! Hide. Quick! Oot o sicht."

As Crichton's platoon reached the end of the beech avenue he caught sight of a loan figure on the little bridge below. He reined up. The platoon juddered to a halt behind him.

"Doon there." The captain's gloved hand jabbed forward. "That woman. She luks lik mistress Steel."

Lieutenant McCann edged his horse closer. "Whit difference does that mak? The commander's orders were clear enough, sir."

"Only aboot Westermains farm. This land belangs tae the Earl o Airlie noo and he wudna be wantin ony Steel trespassin on his land." Crichton dug his spurs in. His horse lurched forward. The platoon followed in close formation.

The sound of hooves grew louder. Marion gripped the edge of the bridge parapet. The troopers weren't passing on the road, they'd turned onto the farm track. Seconds later the horses rounded the corner. The sight of their brown bodies filling the narrow space, and their hooves thundering on the ground with scattered stones flying behind, was terrifying. It was like six months ago when Airlie's platoon galloped into her farmyard looking for John.

She dived over the parapet and slid down the steep slope to the edge of the burn. She managed to stop herself before landing in the water then turned to run as best she could, stumbling over roots and stones, pulling herself along by gripping any low hanging branches.

Behind her she could hear the horses champing and snorting on the bridge. Nothing more for a minute then one rider left the others and began working his way along the top of the bank towards her. She peered up through the thick branches and saw the dark shadow.

"Show yersel Mistress Steel. Ah ken ye're ther." The harsh voice belonged to the awful Captain Crichton.

Crouched down she half-ran, half-crawled, and still she could hear the heavy hooves following her progress. Here the top of the bank was higher, the undergrowth thicker. Maybe Crichton was only guessing where she was. Anyway, she was out of breath. Had to stop. She leant against the steep side of the grassy bank and wondered what to do. That's when she felt a sudden wetness soak her legs, warming her ankles, her feet. Now she'd no choice but to find a safe corner, somewhere out of sight from the military, and away from the biting wind before she could give in to this force within her. "No yet," she whispered. "No yet." But already the girdle of pain was tightening, the spasms warning her it was time to lie down.

A few yards along she saw a small rock fall. It had torn some soil from the bank, created a little recess, enough to give some shelter. It would have to do. She crawled in and pressed against the soft soil. Terrified of being found she closed her eyes, tried to prepare herself, and tried not to call out as the pain took over.

Above her the soldier seemed to have given up. All she could hear was the sound of her own gasping, and in the background a blackbird singing away to itself as if nothing was amiss.

This baby would be her third. The first birth had been long and difficult, the second less so. This baby seemed to be in a hurry. She could feel it almost pushing by itself. Following her instinct she drew up her legs, spread them wide and began to push. One push then some short breaths. Yes. That was it. She did it again, and again, and again till she was exhausted. She lay back and stared up at the fronds of frosty grass and soil almost touching her nose. It was now or never. She had to do it. One more breath, hold it then push, really push.

Slowly, gently, almost pleasantly she felt her body let go and allow something to slide forward. She stretched her hands down between her legs and felt warm, wet hair, a round head, a tiny neck, and a pair of hunched shoulders. All she had to do now was allow the rest of the body to ease out then lean over and take a look at a round, red, screwed up face, and open mouth which brought the only sound she wanted to hear. A little whimper, another, then a clear cry. "Shush, shush." She pulled her shawl from her shoulders and wrapped up the precious bundle. She'd managed. She'd done it. But what now? If ever there was a time for prayer this was it. "Dear God," she whispered. "Ah need help."

Upstream an old shepherd was trying his luck, guddling for trout. Jo Peat wasn't having much luck and his dog was fed up sitting on the cold grass just waiting. "Anither go," he muttered and thrust his numb hands into the water again. This time it worked. He grasped a fat, brown trout. "At last!" He flung it on the bank, banged its head then checked the size. It would do. He put it in his string bag and signalled to his patient dog.

They were walking away from the bank when the dog stopped and whimpered, looking downstream as if something were wrong. Jo had heard the soldiers on the beech avenue; later he'd seen them gallop up to the empty farm and then gallop back down, and away. Now there was no one else about, and yet his dog seemed to know better. His mind made up, he followed the dog; a few minutes later the dog stopped by the rock fall and pointed its nose towards a dark recess. Jo clambered down and peered inside.

"It's me, Marion Steel. Is that ye, Maister Peat?" A woman's frightened face stared out at him.

"Ay." Jo gaped at the woman, her clothes pulled up, saw the blood, and on her stomach a little bundle. "Ah see ye've managed."

Marion nodded.

He pointed at the mess alongside. "Is that the after birth? Will ah shift it? Whit aboot the cord?"

"Ah'm ower shaky."

"Ay, weel. Alloo me." Jo took out his little knife, and the reel of cotton any self-respecting shepherd always had in his pocket. "It'll only tak a meenit." With no sense of embarrassment he cut and tied the cord then removed the after birth and buried it under a pile of stones. Job done, he took off his big coat and draped it over Marion. "Jist bide still Mistress Steel. Ah'll awa tae Waterside Farm an git help. Dinna worry. Ye'll be hame an safe, afore ye ken it."

Jo had almost reached the little hump-backed bridge when he saw Gavin and the two boys coming towards him. "Come quick!" He waved for them to follow and turned back along the bank.

They ran after him till he stopped and pointed down at a rocky overhang. "The mistress is shelterin in a wee hole ablo thae rocks. Ye'll need tae bring a cairt tae cairry her an the new bairn. She's nae bad, but she's had an awfy shock."

Gavin gaped at the old shepherd then turned to the two boys. "Richt ye twa. Ma needs help. Back we go an git the horse an cairt. Ye can run aheid an tell grandma tae git a bed ready. Quick noo!"

An hour later Marion was in bed in Waterside Farm, washed, fresh nightdress on, and her new daughter at her breast.

Jo Peat put his head round the bedroom door. "Ah'll awa then. Ye're in guid haunds noo."

Marion nodded. "Thank ye Maister Peat. Ye wur an answer tae a prayer."

Jo's face glowed with pleasure. "Ah jist happened tae be ther. An gled o it for yersel an wee Bella."

"Bella?"

"Ay. Ma wife's name wis Isabella but ah aye cawed her Bella. She wis richt bonny. Yer bairn brocht back the memory." His cheeks reddened further. "Och nivver mind me an ma nonsense."

Marion smiled. "Perfect, Maister Peat. Bella it is."

Gus McPhail dropped John off by the Waterside Farm track and watched as he raced away with barely a thanks. He shook his head and thought, *If it's nae ane thing it's anither. An nane o it deserved.*

John hurried into the bedroom and hugged Marion over and over. "Ah'm sorry lass. If ah'd been here – "

"Hoo cud ye? We baith wantit ye awa in Glesca. It wis important. Ah wud hae been aricht if yon Crichton hudna come aifter me. Ah did gie him the slip but the effort wis ower much." Her eyes filled with tears. "Ah wis richt feart for the bairn. She wudna hae survived if Maister Peat hudna cam by."

"But he did." John smiled down at the dark curly hair of his new daughter. "Ah'll aye be gratefu. An ah'm sorry for whit ye suffered."

"Dinna stert doon that road," Marion touched his arm. "We brocht it on oorsels. Baith tryin tae be rebels."

Marion's brother Gavin poked his head round the bedroom

door. "If ye can spare yer man a wee while ah cud dae wi his help in the byre."

John knew there was another reason for his summons. He handed Bella over to her mother, gave them both a kiss, and joined his brother-in-law. Once outside he said, "Ah think yon Crichton an masel hae some unfeenished business. Gus McPhail said ye'd been askin aboot the man's aff duty habits aboot the toun. That wis guid thinkin. Ye must hae kent ah'd no let this lie."

Gavin nodded. "Ma cousin in Lanark tells me the guid captain favours Maggie's Howf of an evenin, maist often on a Friday. He's there for hoors dievin the locals wi his stories."

"And?"

"Maist nichts he has his ain company back tae the garrison."

"Perfect." John nodded. "Are ye still willin tae gie me a hand?"

"Wudna miss it. Wull Gemmel an big Wull Cleland are keen tae come as weel."

"Ye tellt them?"

"Crichton's a strong man. The mair there tae haud him the better."

And so it was decided that pay back time for the captain would be on Friday night.

Crichton came out of the warm fug in Maggie's Howf and stood a moment adjusting to the dark November night. Few lights flickered in this part of Lanark but this didn't bother him, not with a belly full of strong ale and all the stories he'd been boasting about.

Maggie's Howf was a tiny inn behind the High Street. The only way through was by Bell's Close, a narrow tunnel carved between the houses. The space was so tight Crichton's shoulders brushed the lime-washed walls as he lurched along.

He'd almost reached the opening onto the High Street when a dark shape filled the gap. "Gie way," he called out.

"Jist anither meenit and I'll be thru."

The figure stood still, blocking the exit.

"I said, gie way!" Crichton barged forward, the heels of his boots rattling on the rough paving as he bounced off a solid body. Suddenly aware of another body behind he half turned. This figure was close, too close. Something hard whacked his brow. He gasped. His legs gave way. He didn't even manage to cry out.

Strong hands caught him, held him upright then carried what looked like a helpless drunk into the street and up the hill towards the Mercat Cross. There he lost his clothes, all of them, and his sword; even his new leather boots were removed before he was tied to the base of the Cross, much like a chicken going to market.

It had taken no more than five minutes and not a word was spoken as his punishment was completed.

At the foot of Lanark Brae the captain's good uniform, boots, and sword were flung over the bridge into the fast flowing Clyde. "Job done wi nae bother." Wull Cleland grinned in the dark. "Cudna happen tae a mair deservin man. An it's no as if he can name us for it wis pitch black, an we nivver spoke. In yon close we cud hae been onybody."

"Ah hope so," John said. "Ah hud tae dae somethin tae pay him back for Marion but ah dinna want the nicht causin ye ony bother."

When Crichton came to he was shivering, and very wet, with his hair plastered against his head, which was still pounding. He blinked and tried to see through the blur of driving rain. "Whaur am I? Whit happened?" He tried to move. Against his back he felt cold stone, and when he looked down he saw skin, his own skin, glistening in the faint, dawn light. "Chris almichty! Whaur's ma claes?" He struggled to escape and discovered a rope wound tight from his neck to his ankles. Any movement seemed to tighten the bonds, making them dig in further, almost choking him.

Suddenly he was reminded of a time six months ago in Lesmahagow, when he'd tried to best John Steel and ended up being lashed to his own horse then paraded down the main street in front of the whole village. Cold as he was he reddened at the memory. And then he thought of Marion Steel, of chasing after her. How she'd managed to hide, and then … this attack was down to John Steel.

Bessie Black, the garrison washerwoman, appeared at the top of the High Street. She was on her way to work and gasped when she saw the figure tied to the Mercat Cross. She hurried over and recognised the captain. "Mercy me. Whit's happened? An luk at ye, sir. No a stitch." She took off her shawl and held it out to Crichton.

"Ye need tae untie me first," Crichton snapped.

She did try but the knots were too many, and too tight. "Ah canna," she puffed. "Ye'll hae tae bide tied till ah fetch help. An here. This'll spare yer modesty." She draped the shawl over the captain's naked body then ran down the High Street chuckling.

Two hours later Crichton was summoned before the sheriff. Meiklejon glared at him. "Whit dae ye mean by this? Ye hae an uncanny knack o makin a fool o yersel. This time ye've surpassed yersel. Dain it in front o the hale toun."

"Ah wis overcome by ruffians," Crichton protested. " Ah had nae say in the maitter.

Meiklejon grunted. "Luk at ye. Whaur's yer uniform?"

"It wis stolen alang wi ma guid sword and a pair o new boots."

Meiklejon grunted again. "Nae maitter. Ye can explain it aw tae yer commander. I've sent for him. He'll be here afore lang. Meanwhile bide oot ma sicht till the great man arrives."

"My, my." Claverhouse smiled at his captain's discomfiture. "Whit a sicht for sair een."

"Sir." Crichton tried not to look as embarrassed as he felt. "Ah wis attacked last nicht, stripped, and tied tae the Mercat Cross till mornin."

"Jist a random attack?"

"No sir," Crichton answered. "Ah believe it wis John Steel, altho ithers helped him."

"Dae ye noo? And why wud that be?" Claverhouse's voice sharpened.

Crichton didn't dare answer.

Claverhouse sat up straight and stared at the captain. "And whit aboot ye disobeying orders tae bide awa frae Westermains Farm, and then taking it on yersel tae chase a pregnant wummin alang a river bank for nae guid reason ither than she's a rebel's wife? I heard the wummin ended up gien birth in the open and had tae be rescued by an auld shepherd. Tut, tut, sir. I'm a civilised man. That's no the kind o behaviour I expect frae ma men." Claverhouse shook his head. "Frae noo on I expect ye tae pin back thae big lugs and obey every order, or ye'll find yersel back in a corporal's uniform."

"Ay sir."

"As for this accusation against John Steel. Whit proof hae ye?"

Crichton hung his head.

"I thocht so. In that case dinna be trying onything on yer ain, if ye tak ma meaning."

Crichton nodded.

"Noo awa and see the supply officer and mak yersel luk respectable. As for anither sword, that comes oot this month's pay."

Crichton saluted and almost ran from the room. Behind him he could hear an amused chuckle. "Ane o thae days, John Steel," he muttered and clattered downstairs. "Ane o thae days."

# Chapter 14

Lucas Brotherstone hurried out of Trunks Close to merge with the heaving throng in the High Street. It was a relief to do this after weeks spent trailing behind Richard Cameron, visiting minister after minister, trying to persuade them of the need for field preaching as a way of countering the current repression.

Their answers were all the same. How could they contemplate such a thing so soon after Bothwell? The government win had been decisive. It would be wrong to invite further retaliation. Life was cruel enough, why make it worse? Pride had to be swallowed.

"And hoo aboot aw they men and women oot there?" was Ritchie's reply. "Can ye no see hoo they're longing for the Lord's word withoot aw thae fancy trappings the king has decreed? Danger or no, ye need tae be oot there telling them the truth frae the book itself."

Each minister's head shook.

He'd tried persuasion. He'd tried challenging their conscience by quoting scripture. It made no difference; whatever he said seemed to fall on deaf ears or increase the hostility towards Ritchie.

More than once Lucas dared to point this out.

"I'll no be put aff by a bunch o cowards," Ritchie refused to give way. "If us twa huv tae cairry the word forth on oor ain, so be it. Whitivver it taks we must behave lik the servants we are, and obey oor Lord's will. Ane way or anither his message will be heard. We'll send roond the parishes and tell folk tae gaither for an open-air meeting. If we get the response I'm hoping for we'll build on it, mibbe even start a regular preaching circuit."

"Dae we need tae wait a bit?" Lucas suggested. "It's ower early in the year for field meetings."

"Ay, ye're richt. But we can mak plans, decide whaur tae start. I wis thinkin aboot Glenlea."

"Whaur's that?"

"This side o Dumfries. I ken it weel. A guid place wi God fearin folk."

Lucas frowned. "C'mon man, dinna luk sae glum. Trust me. Ye'll no be disappointed."

Lucas flinched, but instead of confessing his fears he forced himself to nod and hoped Ritchie wouldn't guess the truth and disown him as another coward.

The next morning Lucas took the first of many long walks, needing time to himself to try and work out why he'd ever believed he could do this. But he must have. Why else had he abandoned his safe post in Utrecht to follow the likes of Richard Cameron back to Scotland? And for what? The questions rattled in his head, making him walk faster.

Tiring of the constant noise he turned onto the vennel steps and kept climbing till he was just below the steep roofs of the tight packed tenements with the fortress-like castle looming above, its outline proud against the sky. The thick walls spoke of defence, of strength, of being in control. What Ritchie was planning would be cruelly dealt with in there. He must know that after the way his father had been treated. The old man had been marched before a magistrate for not acknowledging the royal birthday, given a 100 merk fine, then thrown in prison when he refused to pay. He was still there, still refusing to pay.

Castle windows, like tiny eyes, stared down at the city. They seemed to be watching, noticing, recording. Lucas shuddered and wondered who might be behind those panes of glass, looking out, maybe seeing him. This made him turn and rattle back down the steps.

He walked on, trying not to think, increasing his pace then slowing again as he gave in to those thoughts which would inevitably take him back to that day he'd lost Bett in front of the whole village. She'd warned him about his defiance. He'd ignored her, thought he knew better. Being forced out of his parish for speaking against the king had been bad enough, but to put his wife in such danger? If only he'd listened, that terrible morning would never have happened. She'd never have been sitting high in the cart, obeying that bully of a lieutenant who lashed the horse and made it bolt down the street. She'd never have fallen off. Never have been – but she was, and nothing was worth that.

Gradually the streets petered out, and the cobbles gave way to a muddy track that led him past piles of jaggy rocks then up a steep hill. A few snowflakes fluttered down. He ignored them and kept going. By the time he reached the long, shoulder-like top, a white swirl surrounded him, cutting him off from the vast city below, making it seem like another world. This didn't bother him. It was nothing compared to the weight of Ritchie's expectation.

He stopped and waited. Gradually the snow eased then veered away. The sky cleared. He could see across the massive huddle of city with its roads and tracks leading outwards, past fields and villages, all the way to the Pentland hills.

The whole scene was transformed to simple black and white, for the moment pristine. To his fuddled mind it seemed like a clarification of what might lie ahead.

He stared a while then reluctantly began to retrace his steps.

As soon as Lucas stepped into the hall Ritchie called out, "Come awa thru. We hae visitors."

Lucas hesitated then came into the front room to meet three strangers.

Ritchie stood up. "Let me introduce Donald Cargill, a maist respected freend, here lik an answer tae my prayer for support."

Lucas blinked. An important visitor indeed. He gripped the offered hand. "Lucas Brotherstone. Guid tae meet ye sir. Yer preaching reputation goes afore ye."

The older man smiled. "Ye're ower generous, young man."

"Dinna be sae modest." Ritchie clapped him on the shoulder then turned to the two younger men. "Noo, let me introduce James Renwick and Thomas Douglas. Twa stalwarts for the cause."

Lucas nodded, shook hands, and waited for a fuller explanation.

Ritchie looked excited. "We're no on oor ane ony mair, Lucas. Oor ranks are swelled tae five. When my brither Michael arrives we'll be six. Miracles dae happen, ma freend."

"Indeed." Lucas tried to look pleased. "A guid response for the field preaching."

Cargill nodded. "That's why we're here. Ready and willing. The sooner the better."

The other two nodded and Lucas felt his throat tighten.

The landlady bustled in to say she'd set out a meal for everyone in the kitchen. The visitors followed Ritchie and Lucas through to the warm, friendly room to find the table laid with a large ashet pie, a tureen of steaming vegetables, and a basket filled with hunks of fresh baked bread.

They sat down, bowed their heads for grace then stared hungrily at the crusty topping of the pie. Cargill smiled. "This luks grand, and I'm sure it tastes grand, so serve me a portion and let me get started."

Ritchie obliged and handed round plates heaped with meat and a big slice of crisp pastry. After that little was said till every scrap was eaten and the gravy mopped up.

"Thank ye mistress." Cargill turned to the landlady who was clearing the plates. "Yer pie luked grand, and so it wis."

She blushed. "Nae bother sirs. Noo I'll leave ye tae it. Nae doubt ye've much tae discuss. I've banked up the fire so ye shud be comfortable for a guid while."

Thomas Douglas watched the little woman go then smiled across the table at Ritchie.

Ritchie smiled back, although Lucas noticed a slight coolness between them. Douglas seemed to sense it and turned to Lucas. "Noo Maister Brotherstone. I tak it ye're an ousted meenister as weel?"

Lucas nodded. "Ay. Frae Lesmahagow. It's a wee village, no far frae Lanark. Ye'll no hae heard o it."

"Ah but I did, frae a Mistress Gillon. She came ower frae Scotland tae tak up a post as cook in the college at Utrecht."

Lucas frowned. "I ken her fine. In fact I met the family when they came aff the *Marianne* at Rotterdam. We shared a carriage aw the way tae Utrecht and had a guid talk. Lesmahagow wis nivver mentioned. In fact I thocht they came frae Lanark."

"Naw, naw I had a few talks wi the guid lady. I'm shair she tellt me aboot livin in Lesmahagow afore comin tae Holland,."

"I dinna think so." Lucas shook his head. "It's only a wee village. I kent awbody, and them me."

"Weel that's whit she said. And no jist that, I heard aboot her man havin tae flee for his life aifter helping a local farmer who wis on the run aifter Bothwell."

Lucas gaped at Douglas. "Did she say ony mair? A name mibbe? Wis it Steel? John Steel by ony chance?"

"I canna richt mind."

Lucas sighed. "John Steel wis a guid freend tae me aifter I lost ma charge."

"We best get on wi the business at hand." Cargill stopped Lucas before he could ask any more

"Ay," James Renwick nodded. "But later on Douglas cud mibbe hae anither think aboot that name and set Lucas's mind at rest?"

Douglas said nothing and there was an awkward silence while Lucas looked at the four intent faces round the table. Not long ago he'd seen that expression in himself. Now it was gone. All these ministers he'd met over the past few weeks, all saying no to Ritchie, had affected him. Their arguments had begun to sound reasonable. Worse than that they'd reminded him of his own defiance, and how he'd ended up on a loaded cart, trying to hold back a terrified, bolting horse.

These men would have behaved differently. He could see that. They seemed prepared for anything, and they'd take him with them. He pushed back his chair and stood up. "Excuse me a minute." He made for the door.

"Must ye?" Ritchie sounded annoyed.

"Something I need tae dae." Lucas hurried from the room, well aware of three sets of eyes staring after him.

Once down the hall there was no alternative but leave the house to escape sitting through the planning about to take place. He stared at the brass doorhandle and hesitated. It seemed so cowardly to just disappear without explanation. But how could he explain what had been growing in his mind these past few weeks? What would Ritchie say? How would he react? The answer was no. He turned the handle and stumbled into the night air.

Once in the dark close Lucas stopped to take a deep breath. Ritchie obviously trusted him, relied on him to support his every word and yet he couldn't give it; not any more. He leant against the cold stonework and wished himself back in Utrecht, back to safety where his conscience could better cope with his troublesome thoughts and ever growing doubts about Ritchie's sense of the way forward. Preparing theological lectures and guiding students seemed another world to Ritchie's plans for field preaching throughout the country. This kind of action, expected action, never mind the consequences and danger it would bring, was terrifying. And for what? He'd asked himself this a hundred times, had almost convinced himself, and yet he couldn't bring himself to say a word, especially to Ritchie.

He stood there a long time then slunk back into the house and joined the other three round the table.

By now they were engrossed in their plans and simply nodded as he sat down. No one seemed bothered by his absence or even expected him to add anything to their conversation.

That night he spent a long time on his knees trying to pray. Finally he gave up and admitted he must still say nothing.

Winter held its grip for the next few weeks so Cargill and Douglas volunteered to use the time visiting a number of ministers in the hope of changing their minds about Ritchie's plan for field preaching. James Renwick, Ritchie and Lucas would study maps and find suitable spots for the meetings.

As the days passed, Lucas and James Renwick began to share their walks, plodding through slush and snow, talking and arguing over their pet theories from the Bible. During their private conversations Lucas dared to express his doubts about the way forward. James didn't round on him but tried to reassure. "Tak heart man. Doubts plague us aw. Wrestle wi them and ye'll come oot stronger. Trust me. Yer conscience will see ye richt."

"I hope so," Lucas said, expressing what was expected but thinking the opposite.

Douglas and Cargill came back with the same resounding no as Ritchie had experienced.

"Nae maitter," Ritchie dismissed their disappointment. "Nivver heed thae clerics. I believe the folk oot there will turn oot tae listen and support us."

A few days later the weather suddenly changed. Snow disappeared, the wind dropped, there were days of sunshine, the temperature rising as if spring had arrived.

"A sign." Ritchie would wait no longer and sent word south to Glenlea, inviting anyone from the surrounding parishes to come there on the following Sunday for an open air meeting. "We'll ride doon during the week and find somewhaur tae bide afore decidin hoo tae handle the service. If it gangs weel we'll double back by Lanark for a second ane and mak oor journey work for us. We'll dae the first twa thegither then we can split up and spread the word far and wide."

At the thought of the field preaching about to happen, Lucas did try to confess how scared he was, only to discover he was more afraid of being honest. Once again he simply nodded and tried to look pleased.

That afternoon James Renwick and Lucas took their usual walk. They were both unusually quiet, neither mentioning any of the earlier discussion. They'd gone a fair distance before James gripped Lucas's arm. "Can we talk aboot next Sunday?" He looked uncomfortable. "I've something I need tae say. Ye micht no like it."

Lucas half turned towards James. "Oot wi it. Liking it or no maks nae difference."

"As ye wish." James looked more uncomfortable. "I jist want tae warn ye aboot yer doubts. Dinna let them tak ower. Jist mind whitivver happens is mair important than oorsels."

Lucas coloured. "I ken." All his fine talk and arguing over theory had hidden nothing from this young man. "I'll dae my best."

"Jist watch Ritchie, and learn, and ye'll be fine."

"I hope so. But whit aboot yersel?"

"I've nivver been mair sure. We need tae dae this." James smiled at Lucas's strained face. "I can see ye're unsure. Whiles ye luk desperate. Hardly surprising aifter whit happened tae yer wife. Sic a loss must mak ye wonder aboot the richts o it aw, mibbe even blame yersel. But guilt isna the answer ma freend. Dinna go there."

"Ay. I've been ower it time aifter time, asking masel if whit I'm daing is worth it."

"Trust me, it will be. Maist o aw trust oor Holy Maister and dae his biddin. Ye've still a way tae go afore ye're there. Jist work at it ma freend." James squeezed Lucas's arm again then they walked on in silence.

On a fine, almost warm February morning Lucas stood in a field by Glenlea and studied a sea of expectant faces, quietly waiting for Richard Cameron to begin his sermon. The generosity of such a welcome wasn't lost on him. Neither was the fact that this first meeting was taking place only a mile from the mansion of a man appointed to enforce the law against conventicles. Lucas had stressed this, tried to make Ritchie see this was an unwise choice.

"Not at aw." Ritchie had laughed. "Nae problem."

"But he's Sir Robert Dalziel, a weel kent member o parliament, and nae doubt acquaint wi the Privy Council. They say he gangs tae great lengths tae put doon onything Presbyterian."

"Richt noo he's no at hame. I hae it on guid authority he's awa in Edinburgh meeting his maisters. Oor meeting will be past and us lang gone afore Sir Robert comes back. Whit he disna ken aboot will dae nae harm. And jist luk at the turnoot. Mair than I ever expected. Anither miracle, is it no?"

"So it is," Lucas agreed and said no more.

As he bent his head for the first prayer the sun shone on his head. He felt its warmth, and for the first time since that fateful day of losing Bett he felt comforted. It was a strange feeling, so strong his doubts seemed to disappear. Suddenly he knew it was all about giving, not taking. Was this what James Renwick had meant? He blinked, then smiled, as Ritchie began with his favourite line from Psalm 46:10 'Be still and know that I am God.'

The crowd also smiled and seemed reassured till Ritchie added, "He is the same God yesterday, today and forever. Yet how often our own thoughts change of Him."

Everyone seemed to stiffen, to listen more closely. Ritchie's every word seemed to confirm his authority as the mouthpiece of truth; as if the Lord had sanctioned him to say such things. Next came the strong urging that spiritual warfare by prayer and witness was the only way forward, so well delivered and explained that few were left unmoved.

Lucas's certainty grew. It was a privilege to be part of such a swell of support. And when they headed back to Clydesdale for the second meeting at Tinto Hill by Lanark the crowd was even greater, even more appreciative of Richard Cameron's preaching.

That's when Lucas realised that the authorities must be aware of all this. And yet there was no sign of any reaction, no troopers, no arrests, no reprisals. He tried to guess why. It began to worry him and as he worried his certainty began to slip away again.

# Chapter 15

William Steel's scared face peered round the kitchen door. "Pa, ah can hear horses comin up the track tae the hoose."

"Ay son, ah hear them." John jumped up from the rocking chair by the fire.

Marion squealed and dropped her mending.

John was already in the dark hall, pulling jackets from the long line of pegs. "Dinna worry. In oor ane hoose ah'd hae nae chance but here ah've a guid hidey hole jist waitin." His hand felt along the wood panelled wall searching for a tiny hole about half way up. He stuck a finger in and pulled. Part of the panel swung towards him. He quickly stepped into the dark space and disappeared when he pulled the panel back against the wall.

Marion gaped at what seemed like the wall again then realising what this meant, she hung the jackets back on the pegs.

There was a loud rap at the door, then another.

She called out, "Whae's there?"

"Open up in the name o the king."

"Whit dae ye want?"

"Jist open up."

"No withoot kennin whae ye are, an whit ye're aifter."

"Captain Crichton. Here on Commander Claverhoose's orders tae arrest John Steel."

"He's no here."

Something hard battered against the door. It shook. "Mistress Steel. Open up or we'll break it doon."

Marion pulled back the heavy bolt, turned the key, then jumped to the side as several troopers barged past and into her kitchen.

Crichton stood on the doorstep, holding a lantern, and looking pleased. "Search ivvery room, ivvery corner and bring Steel oot."

Marion glared at him and tried to sound braver than she felt. "This is ma faither-in-law's hoose. Ah've the richt tae be here. Ah canna say the same for ye or yer men."

Crichton came into the hall. He swung the lantern close to Marion's face. "Is that so? Weel hoo aboot yer man bein a named felon wi a thousand merks on his heid? We believe he's hidin here and we mean tae tak him awa for a wee taste o the justice he deserves."

"Ah'm tellin ye he's no here. Why wud he when yon great earl hunted him ontae the moor months ago?"

Crichton ignored her and marched into the kitchen. Minutes passed. The troopers came back to report, "Naethin sir. Nae sign o the man."

"Tak anither luk."

The men obeyed. Still nothing.

"Byre, sheds, oothooses. Check them aw." Crichton spat out the order.

More minutes passed with Marion now on the doorstep watching shadowy figures dart about the yard, in and out of buildings to find no John.

Eventually Crichton roared, "Leave aff!" He marched back to the house. "No this time, mistress. But he'll no git awa. We'll be back, ivvery day if need be till we git him. And then – " He left the rest unsaid, climbed onto his horse and signalled the off.

The platoon thundered past Marion into the dark but she stayed where she was listening till the sound of hooves faded and the night grew still again. She looked up at the stars twinkling down on the troopers who'd be galloping towards the village empty-handed. The thought of what might have happened almost took over and she quickly stepped inside to lock and bolt the door. Her hands shook and tears came as she stared at the length of wood panelling along one side of the hall.

The strange little door opened a fraction. It pushed against the hanging jackets. John peered out. "Ah've been expectin a visit. But comin late at nicht lik that near caught me oot."

Marion lifted off the jackets. The door swung further and John jumped out beside her. He gave her a reassuring hug and she whispered, "Ah'd nae idea. Thank God for that hidey hole."

"Faither made it years ago tae please mither. Thur wis a recess in the wa an Ma wis aye on aboot it bein unsightly. Aifter a while faither gied in an panelled the fu length o the wa tae please her. He made a door ower the recess wi hinges on the inside an insteid o a haundle he made a wee hole for yer finger tae grip an pu the door open or shut. Aifter that he fixed a row o pegs jist above the tap edge o the door. The door uprichts lined up wi the panellin lines so it wis hard tae see whit it really wis. Aince the jackets were hung ower it became a secret. Mither wis a keen beekeeper an she kept her honey jars in there, in the dark."

"Yer faither wis richt clever."

"Ay. An ah dinna suppose he ivver thocht his piece o work wud some day save ma life."

Marion burst into tears again. "It wis close."

"Ower close." John hugged her even tighter. "But it's by wi. An nae harm done."

"Ay." Slowly she pulled away and went down the hall to the boys' room to find them both asleep after all the excitement. Her tiny daughter was the same. The noise and chaos hadn't disturbed her. Marion sighed and looked relieved. She turned, came back towards John, then passed him, on into the kitchen where the candles were still guttering, the fire now a dull glow. Her mending lay where she'd dropped it. She bent to pick it up then sat down as if to continue where she'd left off.

John almost protested. How could she see for such close work? And why now? Her tense shape, the way she seemed to be only just holding together had him joining her, to sit and wait.

Neither spoke as the big needle slid back and forward, each wool strand gradually closing the gap in the stocking heel. Once this was done the needle turned, weaving over and under, creating a new, solid heel to last a few more days.

The steady movement seemed to have a calming effect. The tight bend in her back eased. Finally the needle stopped. She studied her piece of darning then looked up at the face opposite. "The money ye spoke aboot. Yer inheritance. If it's as much as ye say we cud dae onythin, go onywhaur, mak a fresh start, an leave aw this ahint."

John frowned. He'd just turned down such a chance. It was hard to defend. He hesitated then he heard himself say, "Ah wis born here. Ah belang here. Ah'm no goin onywhaur. If ah did ah'd jist end up comin back."

"Whit if Crichton had gotten haud o ye the nicht?"

"But he didna. Ah'm here, still free, wi nae intention o bein caught by him or onybody else. Ah ken ah shudna hae gotten intae the cause sae deep, an ah'm sorry for the pain it's brocht. Frae noo on ah mean tae go ma ain way an keep ma nose clean."

"Ah've heard somethin lik this afore."

John shrugged. "Mibbe so. At least we've noo got some money tae help us, money ah didna expect nor ken aboot. James McAvoy gied me a 1000 merks awa wi me an thur's mair tae come."

"That's guid tae ken. But richt noo ah'd raither think aboot bed."

"If ye say so."

They both smiled as John lifted her from the chair and gently guided her along the dark hall towards their bedroom.

John Graham of Claverhouse sat behind Sheriff Meiklejon's breakfast table and smiled at his uneasy looking captain. "Yer report, sir?"

Crichton shuffled his feet and stared at the floor. "Steel wisna at the farm, sir. Only his wife an bairns. We searched high an low. Nae sign."

"I see." Clavers smile tightened.

"Sir, ah dae believe he wisna ther."

"So ye say captain. So whit aboot mair effort afore my patience runs oot?"

"Ay sir." Crichton clicked his heels, saluted, and made his escape.

John Brown from Priesthill arrived at Westermains next morning. He looked excited. "Ah'm on ma way tae Crawfordjohn. Richard Cameron is hain a field meetin there the morn. He's had twa successful anes aready wi a richt guid turnout. The last ane wis by Tinto Hill an ah wis tellt it wis a big event. Ah'm a great respecter o the man an want tae hear whit he has tae say aboot oor sad situation."

John frowned.

"Whit's up?" John Brown asked. "Ye dinna luk very pleased. An here's me aboot tae ask ye if ye'll come wi me."

"Ah'd raither no." John shook his head. "Attendin field preachin got me intae trouble afore. An since Bothwell ah've a price on ma heid. Last nicht troopers wur here lukin for me, so bein amang a crowd's only askin tae be recognised, an then whit?"

"Ye'll be amang like minded folk. Safer than onywhaur. C'mon, it's ower guid a chance tae miss.

Marion listened to this discussion with a knowing expression while she prepared breakfast.

The two Johns set out early in the morning and were in sight of Crawfordjohn before ten o'clock. The weather was still fine, the air fresh, almost spring like, and they both enjoyed the journey.

Just before the village John Brown turned his horse to the left. "Ah've a guid idea whaur Cameron micht be. He has a freend an supporter in Anna Hamilton at Gilkersgleuch Hoose. He'll likely be there."

"Hoo dae ye ken aw this?" John asked.

"Ah'm aw ower the place as a carrier an it's wunnerfu whit ye learn alang the way."

They found Richard Cameron sitting at the big table in Anna Hamilton's kitchen. He looked far from happy although he did stand to welcome the two visitors.

John Steel was surprised how young Cameron appeared, after all he'd heard about the man and his fearsome reputation as a preacher.

Anna Hamilton seemed to know John Brown and warmly welcomed him before turning to the other John. "And ye are?"

"John Steel. A freend o John here."

"Steel. Captain John frae Lesmahagow?"

John nodded.

Anna Hamilton smiled. "Yer fame goes afore ye. Yer wee incident wi yon auld earl."

John blushed. "Ah'd raither it hudna happened. Ah ended up wi a price on ma heid."

"And the need tae be careful." Anna sounded sympathetic. "But dinna worry, the folk hereaboots will see ye safe enough. An ye'll no be disappointed when ye hear Ritchie speak."

John said nothing.

Anna went on, "Ritchie's in poor spirits this mornin. He had news earlier that's worried him."

"Ah'm sorry tae hear that," John Brown looked at Richard Cameron's set face. "Can we dae onythin tae help?"

"Naw, naw. I wis thinking aboot ma freend Donald Cargill nearly getting captured the ither day."

"Did it happen near by?" John Brown stepped closer. "Cud ye be in danger?"

"Not at aw. Donald wis left in Boness, working on a draft paper tae mak oor intentions public. We agreed he'd dae that while I kept on wi field preaching.

"It wis aw going fine till the meenister at Boness spied Donald. The traitor kens him, and cudna wait tae tell the captain at Blackness Castle. Aifter that the hunt wis up. Donald's on the wanted list, same as masel. The captain and twa men followed Donald tae Qeensferry whaur he wis due tae meet up wi a young advocate, Henry Hall. Henry had promised tae cast an ee ower Donald's proposal. They went intae an inn and sat in a quiet corner, and that's when the captain made his move. He wis fly enough tae go up tae them, kid on he wis freendly, talking aboot this and that while his men got intae position. That's when he announced they were under arrest. Donald and Henry forced their way by but the captain managed tae stab Donald and bring him tae his knees. Henry turned tae help when the innkeeper felled him wi a heavy tray. The hale place wis upside doon but somehoo Donald made it outside. He got awa. Henry wisna sae lucky. He ended up deid."

There was silence for a moment then Cameron shook his head. "There's mair. Ye see, Donald's case wi aw his papers in it wis still lying ablo the table. The powers that be hae it noo and are using it tae suit their ain evil ends."

"Evil?" John Steel blinked.

"Ay. They're trying tae mak us soond like mad men wi nae respect for the law which isna true. We only want whit's richt, tae bring this kingdom frae darkness and dae it withoot hurt tae ony ither than those that injure us." Ritchie was almost shouting. "Ane way or anither oor true intentions will be published. Aw I need is somewhaur quiet tae draft oot the words masel, get some signatures frae supporters, then mak the hale thing intae a public declaration aboot overturning the king."

"We tried that aready, an luk whit happened at Bothwell," John argued. "Ye ken that yersel."

"Next time we'll hae nae arguing, nae wasting time debating maitters o nae importance. We'll go furrit as ane."

John stared at the flushed face, the passion in the blue eyes.

"Ye're takin an almighty risk."

Cameron straightened then stared past him as if responding to something only he could see.

John almost groaned as he added, "Ye soond convinced."

"I am!" Ritchie thumped the table.

"Hoo aboot Priesthill?" John Brown butted in. "Ma farm is weel oot the way, fine an quiet for the work ye hae in mind."

Cameron's face lit up. "The very thing." He stepped forward and almost hugged John Brown. "Whit a generous offer. Thank ye. I'll gang back wi ye aifter this meeting." As he spoke the kitchen clock chimed twelve. Cameron glanced at it. "Time for oor field meeting." He went out of the kitchen and called upstairs, "Lucas. Time tae go."

Lucas Brotherstone appeared carrying Cameron's case and his big overcoat. He stopped at the sight of John Steel. "Why John, ye're a surprise."

John went forward, met Lucas at the foot of the stairs, and shook his hand. "Nae mair than yersel. Ah thocht ye wur safe in Holland."

"Ay. But I came back tae help Ritchie."

"C'mon. Ye can talk later." Cameron sounded impatient. "We hae a crowd waiting."

John's thoughts whirled as they walked to the meeting place, what with the story he'd just heard, the passion he'd seen in Cameron, John Brown's surprise offer, and now the sight of Lucas Brotherstone. Coming here seemed wrong. And he'd promised Marion, yet she seemed to know him better than he knew himself.

A sizeable crowd was waiting in the field beyond the farmhouse. Cameron smiled his approval and took his place before them. "Thank ye my friends. The effort ye've made tae be here will be noted and approved by oor Maister, as is the risk ye're prepared tae tak for yer ain freedom." He opened his Bible and held it aloft. "In Isaiah 6:8 the Lord asks this prophet, 'Is there anyone I can send? Will someone go for us?' We aw ken Isaiah's answer. 'I'll go. Send me.' He didna hesitate. We've read it often enough. But if this same question was asked the day hoo wud we answer?"

Everyone stiffened at the challenge. An hour later they were still listening to the why and the wherefore, even nodding in agreement as this skillful preacher warmed to his argument with Revelation 12:12, 'The devil is come down unto you.' Thereafter he listed the consequences of doing nothing against the dark cloak of apostasy now settling across the land. It was stirring stuff. Few misunderstood his references to king and government and few faces showed disapproval or seemed unmoved by his challenge.

John felt desperate. Why had it to be like this? He seemed the only one who wanted to shake his head. Once or twice he glanced at Lucas Brotherstone standing there in silent support of his colleague, still the same in spite of his own sacrifice.

When the crowd began to leave John walked over to Lucas. Neither spoke for a moment then John said, "Yer freend speaks weel. Aw they ears listenin seemed tae like whit he said, seemed convinced he's richt tae challenge the king and government. It's jist, weel, he soonds awfy determined, an no bothered aboot the consequences. Ah tak it ye're o the same mind?"

Lucas flinched and looked away.

"Ah didna mean tae offend ye," John said. "Ah jist wunnered."

"Ye didna offend me," Lucas admitted. "Ye hit hame. Noo I shudna say this, me that's here as Ritchie's freend and supporter, but tae tell the truth the man scares me. No jist for masel, but for aw thae folk listening an agreeing. For weeks he's been trailing the country, arguing wi meenister aifter meenister, tryin tae mak them agree wi him. Nane did. They aw said compromise wis the only way tae survive, that we need tae sit this oot or the suffering will only get worse. He wudna listen and named them for cowards. But as I heard the meenisters' words ower and ower I cud hear the richt in whit they said."

"Hae ye tellt him?" John asked.

"Hoo can I? I started oot believing and agreeing wi every word he uttered. He trusts me."

"Wud it no be best tae try afore it's too late?"

"It's aready too late," Lucas insisted. "Noo, if ye'll excuse me." He turned and hurried after Richard Cameron.

# Chapter 16

Richard Cameron took up residence in John Brown's front room. Apart from meals and going late to bed, he remained behind the closed door, scratching away on sheet after sheet of paper. Days passed and the Browns could hear the voice within, rising and falling, sometimes arguing, sometimes persuading, as if trying to clarify a difficult point of principle. John Brown was tempted to interrupt, to offer help, but his wife shook her head. "It soonds lik a sair fecht but Maister Cameron strikes me as a man that has tae gang his ain way. Whitivver it is ye best leave him alane."

Eventually Cameron seemed to be satisfied. He emerged with his papers along with a list of names and addresses for John Brown. "When ye're oot and aboot on yer business wi the cart ye cud mibbe visit some o the folk on this list, show them my proposal, and ask if they'll add their name ahint mine as support?"

"Nae bother." By the end of the week John Brown had almost twenty signatures to confirm the support Cameron was after. "A few mair days an ah'll hae a wheen mair."

"Excellent." Cameron shook John's hand. "Thank ye. Noo whaur can I find the nearest printer? I need a guid ane tae mak this document luk richt."

"Lanark. Ah dinna ken the man weel but he's pleasant enough, an aye busy. Ah suppose that's a guid sign."

Cameron nodded. "But will he be prepared tae print whit I want and say naething aboot it? I dinna want word getting oot afore I've everything in place.

"Ah'll find oot. Dinna worry, ah'll ask discreet like." Next day John Brown went to Lanark and came back with the right news. "The printer has agreed tae everythin ye asked. If ah tak yer papers in the morn he'll print the stuff oot at nicht when naebody's aboot. He guarantees discretion. It's aw goin jist fine, sir."

Once Cameron had the printed papers he sent word to all who'd signed the declaration to meet him at 10 o'clock, in a week's time, on the outskirts of the little town of Sanquhar.

"Then whit?" John Brown asked.

Cameron looked triumphant. "We mak history. When this is read across the land it'll shake the throne itsel." It was then he remembered that his closest colleague had not been there to sign the paper, would not see his name as part of this historical event. Lucas had accompanied him back from Crawfordjohn, stayed overnight at John Brown's farm then set out with John Steel, saying he wanted to visit Lesmahagow, particularly his wife's grave. This was understandable. But why had he stayed away and not returned to be involved as he always was?

Lucas and John went to the churchyard late in the evening to avoid meeting any villagers. That way no explanations would be necessary.

Back at last: Lucas stared down at the small boulder which marked Bett's resting place. A small rowan had been planted alongside. He smiled at the circles of white blossom drooping from the fine branches and thought about the significance and superstition associated with such a tree. Most of all there was kindness in the gesture.

John waited by the boundary wall and watched Lucas's torment till he could stand it no longer. Striding across the grass he touched the bowed back.

Lucas jumped as if stung.

"Enough, sir." John shook his head. "Ye're no solvin onythin blamin yersel ower an ower. Respectfu memory is aw very weel. But no this. Wud it no be best tae let the mistress lie in peace?"

"But if I hadna been sae bloody minded."

"An wrang heided if ye want the truth." John sounded impatient. "But it's by wi. Ye need tae accept that fact an try tae move on. But this time dinna jist dae whit's expected. Mind the auld sayin – tae thine ane self be true."

Lucas flushed and turned away.

Neither spoke on the way back to the farm. This was followed by an equally silent supper before Lucas excused himself and crept away to bed.

"Wis his visit too much?" Marion asked.

"Ay." John left it at that.

After breakfast Lucas announced, "I need tae get back tae

Priesthill and see if Ritchie has feenished his writing."

"Ah'll come wi ye," John replied.

"Nae need. I ken the way noo."

"Ah'm comin onyway." John went into the hall and took his jacket from the end peg.

Lucas shrugged, thanked Marion for her kindness then followed John out, across the yard, and on towards the moor.

Marion watched them go. "Dear o me." She shook her head. "Ane as bad as the ither."

Richard Cameron stood on the doorstep of Priesthill farmhouse and watched two dark figures coming across the moor. As they came closer he recognised them and hurried forward with a welcome.

Lucas saw Ritchie's happy expression and guessed he must have completed his declaration. He forced a smile. "It's gone weel then?"

Cameron nodded. "Ay. Paper feenished, signed by twenty, copies printed, and an invite sent oot for next week. I'm expecting the twenty signatories tae turn up alang wi a wheen mair o like mind then we'll mak a public declaration in Sanquhar. I chose the anniversary o Bothwell. Maks it mair significant."

Lucas glanced at John who was glaring at Cameron.

Cameron didn't seem to notice and ushered them both indoors. "Come thru tae the kitchen and I'll fetch the paper. Ye can still sign it."

"If ye dinna mind, Ritchie, I'd like a read at it first."

Cameron stared at him. "Dae ye need tae? Ye kent my intentions."

"That's why I need tae tak a luk."

Cameron shrugged and went through to the front room, brought out the paper, and smacked it down on the table. "Tak yer time." He stood back and watched Lucas bend over the printed paper.

Lucas's finger traced the words then suddenly stopped. He read out, "We disown Charles Stuart for his breach of the covenant and usurpation of the Kirk's rights." He looked up. "It's still treason then?"

Cameron's jaw tightened. "Tyranny in a ruler is just ground for disclaiming allegiance. Think aboot it, nae man can be supreme above religion as he at London noo pretends."

Lucas read on. "We declare war against this king." He read it again then stepped back from the table.

"Kirk and state are distinct yet complementary." Cameron's voice rose. "Spiritual rights cannot be separated frae the rights o the people. Whit choice hae we but disown Charles Stuart for his perjury and breaking o the covenant wi God and his church?"

"But this is war. Whit back up huv ye? The likes o that needs mair than twenty men, nae matter hoo keen. Whit aboot arms, ammunition?" He shook his head. "Ritchie, this is madness for yersel and ony ye persuade tae follow ye."

"Ye were ane no so very lang ago." Cameron turned to John Steel who was standing behind him. "Whit aboot ye? Dae ye want tae read the paper as weel?"

John stiffened. " Ah dinna need tae. Ah heard whit Lucas said an agree wi him."

Cameron swung back to Lucas. "Whit's happening? Ye were staunch enough afore. Ye came back frae Holland tae help. Ye kent my views, whit I intended. We've shared mony a mile tae get here."

Lucas hesitated then said, "Aw they meenisters whae said naw tae yer plans worried me. I've wrestled wi that, tried tae put their words and criticisms aside but I canna. And when I see they folk in the fields, tramping miles tae come and listen tae yer clever words aboot whit the Lord requires I can only see darkness aheid for them aw if they accept yer challenge. The mair they agree wi ye the mair I worry aboot the consequences. And when I stood by my wife's grave I kent I cudna pretend onymair."

"Pretend!" Cameron spat the word. "I nivver thocht tae hear ye sae sic a thing. Ye're a sad disappointment."

John Steel gripped Cameron's arm. "Apart frae onythin else if ye go aheid wi this it'll be the death o ye. Dae ye really want ta end up as a martyr?"

"It wud be an honour."

John sighed and released his grip. "Maister Cameron, ye're a fine preacher. Folk respect ye. Think aboot that an the responsibility that brings. Ye say Lucas is a disappointment. Whit aboot yersel? Aw ah can see is a deluded man eaten up wi his ain selfish ambition."

"Hoo dare ye?" Cameron raised his hand as if to strike John.

They stared at each other before Cameron wheeled round, marched in to the front room, and slammed the door behind him.

"That's it then." John looked at the white faced Lucas. "Ah'm for hame noo. Ye're welcome tae come."

Cameron looked out the farmhouse window and watched the two figures walk away onto the moor. For a brief moment he felt a twinge of regret and a tiny shiver of uncertainty.

On Tuesday 22nd June the quiet little town of Sanquhar had an unwelcome shock when a long line of armed strangers rode in single file along its main street.

The provost was standing in the baker's doorway and immediately guessed something was amiss. He ducked back as they passed then peered round the door to see what would happen next.

As he watched, the horses circled the market cross and waited while a single figure dismounted to stand there with a big paper in his hand.

"Whit's goin on?" The baker tried to push past the provost. "Did ye ken aboot it? Luks a bit rebellious tae me. Shud ye no be oot there puttin a stop tae it? Aifter aw, ye huv the authority."

"An whit cud the likes o me dae against a crowd o armed men?"

"Ah'm jist sayin." The baker was about to argue when the circle of men began to sing a familiar psalm. "Oh dear," he repeated, "ah dinna like this."

Just then the figure with the paper began to read out what sounded like an official declaration. On and on he went, the clear voice carrying in the still air. People began to gather, to listen; no one interrupted. And what the baker and provost heard convinced them that this was indeed a serious happening.

Once the announcement was finished the figure fastened the paper to the base of the stone cross and remounted his horse before one of the others, a young, fair-headed man, led the group in a long prayer.

The watchers bowed their heads, seeming to join in.

"This'll no dae. No dae at aw. The eedjits dinna realise whit thur dain." The provost sounded more worried than angry.

"Thur jist bein respectfu," the baker said.

"Respectfu? Dinna be daft. Hoo can ye be respectfu aifter listenin tae a rebel announcin war against the king?"

There was no answer to that and the two men fell silent as the group lined up, one behind the other, and began their procession back along the main street in an orderly fashion.

As the line of horses passed the baker's shop the provost whispered, "Yon fair heided ane is Cameron the rebel preacher." He said no more till the last horse had gone then he turned and grabbed the baker's arm. "Wur done for. If the Privy Cooncil gets wind o this they'll think we're in wi them."

The baker shook himself free. "No if ye tell them first. An let them ken braw plain we nivver invited them, nor wantit them here, an we certainly dinna approve o thur rebellious cairry on."

"Ay." The provost agreed. "Ah'll get ma clerk tae draft a letter. We'll send a fast rider aff tae Edinburgh this aifternoon tae deliver it personal like."

"Mind an tell thur lordships that it wis Cameron leadin the band. An ye best tak that paper doon frae the cross an send it along wi yer letter."


John Maitland, first and last Duke of Lauderdale, sat at the head of a huge, polished table and glared at the great and the good he'd summoned to this extraordinary meeting of the Privy Council.

"Guid day yer lordships. A maist serious matter has necessitated yer attendance this morning. We need tae – "

"Hae a discussion," Lord Ross dared to interrupt.

"No sir. I simply require yer agreement for whit I'm aboot tae propose."

"Naethin's chainged then." Lord Ross pulled a face and sat back in his chair.

Lauderdale ignored the jibe. "On the 22nd June a band o armed rebels rode intae the wee toun o Sanquhar and declared war on their king and government, aw because they dinna agree wi hoo the country's bein run."

Lord Ross blinked. "Why Sanquhar? I thought it wis a quiet kinda place."

"No on that day it wisna wi twenty horsemen taking ower the main street withoot a by yer leave and pasting up a treasonous declaration against his Majesty. No content wi that they dared tae read it oot then sing a psalm afore leaving again."

Lord Ross shook his head. "Sounds lik the ravings and antics o a group o fanatics opposed tae public peace. That we canna have."

"Indeed." Lauderdale nodded. "Yon renegade preacher Cameron wis at the heid o the band. God kens whit he's planning nixt. Afore he maks anither move we need tae stop him aince and for aw."

Their lordships murmured approval.

"The provost at Sanquhar has been guid enough tae send me a fu description, alang wi the so cawed declaration, and the reassurance that the toun denounces whit happened in the strongest terms. He seems tae think we're on the brink o rebellion, and I tend tae agree wi him."

The murmuring grew louder.

Lauderdale nodded. "For a start I propose we put a guid price on Cameron's heid, five thoosand merks deid or alive."

"Whit aboot the ithers?" Lord Ross asked.

"Three thoosand on the main players. A thoosand on each follower. Wi a bit o investigation and persuasion we'll get their names. I've also sent word tae General Dalziel at Langside tae heid oot wi his contingent and scour the area. Airlie's back doon frae the north and billeted at Ayr. His lot can come in frae the ither end. That way we'll hae Cameron squeezed in the middle. Naewhaur tae run or hide. Clavers kens aboot it. Even as I speak he's on the move."

"As Lord Advocate dare I ask whit His Majesty is saying aboot the situation?" Lord Mackenzie of Rosehaugh joined in. "I tak it he kens aboot this unfortunate development?"

Lauderdale's bushy eyebrows almost met, his normally red face growing darker as he spat out his reaction. "The Crown trusts me as his secretary o state tae judge whit's the best way forward in sic matters. He'll hear aboot the successful result and read a fu report when the deed's done. Does that satisfy ye, my lord?"

The elegant wig nodded. Mackenzie smiled but said nothing.

"Richt." Lauderdale waved an impatient hand at the other lords. "Can we get on? Hae I yer approval?"

Every head nodded.

Lauderdale's great bulk rose from the table. "In that case sirs, I'll awa tae my dinner afore it gets cauld. Aifter that I'll sign the orders on behalf o us aw." He stomped off, followed by his young clerk clutching all the relevant papers.

# Chapter 17

Donald Cargill and Richard Cameron stood by the Kype Water and watched a long line of men, women and children making their way downstream towards Lesmahagow. Cameron's sermon had gone well but now he was frowning.

Cargill glanced at him and shook his head.

"Ay weel," Cameron's frown deepened, "Lucas went awa wi yon farmer John Steel frae near here. I did wonder if he'd mibbe show his face at this meeting. Mibbe even admit he wis wrang. His lack o faith wis a sair let doon. Mair than that, I thocht he wis a freend."

"He's young," Cargill said.

"So am I," Cameron snapped.

"Ye're similar in years. In nae ither way," Cargill insisted. "I ken Lucas turning awa wis a sair blow. In truth I worry aboot his belief and hoo it can affect his commitment. He reminds me o my ain desperation. Mair important it maks me grateful hoo it wis turned roond. As a young man my ain sense o worthlessness gripped me that bad I wanted tae gie up the struggle; tae tak my ain life. Sinful as it was that thocht taen ower. I ended up searching oot an abandoned mineworking, tae stand on the edge o an open shaft."

"Whit?" Cameron gaped at his old friend.

"Weel micht ye luk but it's true and wonderful in its ain way for even as I stood there wanting tae jump the Lord's voice spoke and tellt me my sins were forgiven. In that meenit I understood and felt at peace. Withoot hesitation I accepted His word and stepped back frae that edge tae face my future. Aw they years later I still feel the same. Redemption and reassurance is mine and I pray yon young man will be blessed wi the same afore his mind gies way. He seems sair troubled and I feel for him. It's no as if he intends ony hurt. It's fear that's gotten the better o him."

"Ay weel." Cameron nodded. "Whit happened tae yersel wis a miracle but I wudna haud oot the same for Lucas."

"If ye feel he's caused a set back tae yer plans treat it as anither challenge and concentrate on the big picture. God has directed us tae be fishers o men, tae bring them the truth, so trust in Him

160

and dae whit's richt."

"Ay. That's whit maitters. Cameron sounded happier. "Oor support's growing wi ivvery meetin. If ye preach across the upper districts while I cover the south we'll soon bring the cause tae the fore again. The loss o Lucas is neither here nor there."

Later that day Gavin Weir appeared at Westermains farm with an armed stranger. He left the man in the yard and went into the house to look for John.

"He's no here," Marion said. "Whit's yon stranger aifter?"

"He's desperate tae reach Priesthill. He seems tae think Richard Cameron's ther."

Lucas appeared in the kitchen doorway. "I'll see tae him." He went out to the yard and spoke to the stranger.

Just then John came round the end of the byre. He stopped short and stared at the stranger. "Hackston?"

The man nodded. "Ay. An ah mind ye tae, John Steel."

"Whit are ye dain here?"

"Lukin tae find Richard Cameron an help keep him safe as he gangs roond the country preachin."

Lucas stepped forward. "I've said I'll tak Maister Hackston tae Priesthill. If Ritchie's no there John Brown will ken whaur he's gone."

"Please yersel." John turned and walked away.

After Lucas and Hackston had gone John hurried into the kitchen to find Gavin. He glared at him. "Why did ye bring that man here?"

Gavin shrugged. "He wis ootside the village inn, askin questions. Ah thocht it best tae git him awa afore ower mony folk saw him an mibbe guessed whae he wis."

"Ye ken then?"

"Ay. Ah saw him at Drumclog an Bothwell. Hackston's no the kind o man ye're likely tae forget. He tellt me he wis aff a boat frae Holland, sent by some committee in Utrecht tae help Cameron in his work. He said thur's a letter comin wi important instructions for Cameron. He thinks it micht be a chainge o plan. He hung aboot Glesca till the next boat cam in. There wis nae letter so he decided tae heid on by himsel."

"Soonds like him," John agreed. "Aye impatient."

"He's aifter findin Priesthill. Ah thocht ye cud help him on his way."

John frowned. "If ye ken it's Hackston ye ken he wis amang the yins that murdered Archbishop Sharpe at Saint Andrews. Ah'd nae love o yon prelate but killin an auld man lik that – " John shook his head. "Hackston's trouble. Aye wis. Ah'd raither bide oot his road."

"Ye dinna need tae," Marion cut in. "Ye ken fine he's awa wi Maister Brotherstone."

"Much guid may it dae him." John's voice rose. "If Cameron's attractin the likes o Hackston the troopers are no far ahint."

Claverhouse sat in sheriff Meiklejon's overheated garrison room and glared at Crichton. "Whit's this supposed tae be?" He flung the captain's report across the table. "It says Cameron's followers hae likely disbanded. Whaur did ye hear this nonsense?"

"We had it on guid authority frae mair than ane source. Naebody's seen the man or his supporters."

"Ye wudna ken the truth if it hit ye on the nose," Clavers snapped. "As far as nae sign o the man whit ye're really sayin is, he's gied ye the slip."

"Airlie and Dalziel havena seen ony trace either," Crichton protested.

"Useless. The lot o ye." Clavers crumpled the piece of paper and hurled it at Crichton's red cheeks. "Ye're supposed tae be professional, trained tae comb ivvery inch o the land, tae hunt and find ony runaway or rebel. And here ye are, back wi a useless report and nae sign o ony captive. In case ye've forgotten it's three weeks since that declaration at Sanquhar. The Privy Council are no pleased at the lack o progress. The maitter needs tae be dealt wi. We need an arrest, followed by a court hearing, and then a public hanging. It needs tae happen."

"A few mair days micht dae it, an then we'll hae him, sir."

"Mak sure ye dae." Clavers waved Crichton away and poured himself another glass of Meiklejon's good wine.

It was dark before Lucas returned from Priesthill. He seemed agitated.

"Whit's wrang noo?" John asked.

"Hackston tellt me aboot a letter that's comin frae Holland. He thinks it's frae some important college committee. I ken that committee. It's made up o sincere and honest men. They'll hae heard whit's happening ower here. Mibbe they're worried aboot the way it's developing and want Ritchie tae dae things different afore it's too late. Hackston left word for the letter tae be sent on tae the village. I said I'd watch oot and bring it tae him."

"Wis that wise?" John sounded surprised. "Why wud it come here? An hoo dae ye intend watchin oot? A man that disna dare gang intae the village," John sneered. "God sakes Maister Brotherstone, use yer heid."

"I am, John. I'm thinking aboot whit's likely tae happen next and I'm terrified. Luk at me. I wisna lik Ritchie, stravaiging aboot the country, declaring war on king and government. I only spoke oot aince, in my ain kirk, and I nivver said a word aboot war, and I still got flung oot o hoose and hame, and banished frae the parish. Worst o aw, my pair wife wis killed that day."

"Ah ken." John sighed. "Ah wis there."

Lucas flushed. "I believe that letter cud mak a difference. It micht stop Ritchie afore aw hell's let loose and we aw suffer. Please John."

John sighed again. "If ye're that sure ah'll ask Gavin tae watch for yer precious letter. Will that dae?"

Lucas looked relieved.

"Richt then, supper, an nae mair aboot it."


That night Lucas Brotherstone couldn't sleep. Wrapped in the darkness he thought about his own weakness, which seemed determined to follow him wherever he went, a constant reminder of how everything he did seemed to go wrong. Not like Richard Cameron, the most confident person he'd ever met, with an unswerving faith. When he shared it, his listeners believed every word and carried it away with them.

Once upon a time Lucas had been one of them, convinced enough to leave the safety of Utrecht, to come back and be part of Cameron's campaign to carry the faith forward. Except he wasn't anymore. He'd walked away. He'd had to. That moment by Bett's grave had made him admit his own insincerity for what it was. That felt more terrifying than knowing how Richard

Cameron's field preaching was reaching more and more willing ears; ears that might soon pay the price for their listening.

He jumped out of bed, stumbling across the floor to pull back the heavy shutters and press his brow against the cold glass. Bathed in soft moonlight he felt the dark recede a little. Gradually he began to feel calmer. He thought about that letter on its way from Holland. Maybe it would come soon.

Not many miles away, Richard Cameron was also having a difficult night even though he was a welcome guest in a fine house, with a kind host who'd provided a good supper and a comfortable bed while his supporters were left to sleep rough, with little to eat and no comfort to ease their weariness after a long walk across the moors.

The numbers around Cameron had swelled to over twenty riders, plus forty on foot, following him wherever he went. So many armed men were difficult to hide in open country but so far they'd avoided any confrontation with government troops.

Ritchie knew this couldn't last. And then what? His band would be outnumbered, probably wiped out. In the quiet dark he almost welcomed this thought. Tonight he felt exhausted, longed for his work to be over, to lay the responsibility on other shoulders. He'd been field preaching since February. Now it was 21st of July. A long time to be travelling far and wide, always trying to avoid those troopers who were searching for him, and all the time preparing more sermons to make sure his preaching was the best it could be. And he'd done that, spreading the word, cajoling and challenging those with other opinions. He'd defied both king and government in the most open and dangerous way. Soon they'd come for him. When they did, and he gave his all, his example would endure till the cause eventually reached its goal. He nodded to himself and felt comforted.

And then he thought about Lucas, that moment when his friend had said he couldn't pretend any more and walked away. Last night Thomas Douglas had also walked away. This time it was down to Hackston, the original firebrand, but loyal and focused on the cause. As soon as he'd joined Ritchie's group, he'd tackled Douglas over some previous disagreement. It went on and on with neither backing down. Finally Ritchie had suggested they both apologise.

"Nivver," Hackston had insisted.

Douglas had said nothing. He'd turned, touched Ritchie's shoulder then went to the stable, called for his horse, saddled up, and left with neither a wave nor a backward look.

Ritchie had been stunned. He was still shocked. First Lucas, now Thomas Douglas. It felt like a knife wound, forcing him to rise from his comfortable bed and pace the floor. Come morning he was still pacing, but his conviction held.

That night John Steel was another who couldn't sleep. Resentment kept him awake and tormented him as he stared into the dark. Eventually he got up to open the shutters.

"Whit's wrang?" Marion stirred and peered at the faint outline by the window.

John turned towards the voice in the bed. "Ah didna mean tae wake ye."

"Ye didna. Ah've been listenin tae yer huffin an puffin for hoors."

"Ah wish this wis aw by wi."

Marion sighed. "Come back tae bed an tell me aboot it."

John climbed into bed and leant against the headboard.

"C'mon," Marion said gently, "ah'm listenin."

"It wis yon meetin ah went tae wi John Brown. If ah hudna gone we wudna hae the meenister back wi us again. An ah wudna be feelin sae angry."

"Whit aboot? Ah thocht ye an the meenister seemed freendly enough."

"It's mair than that. Maistly ah'm ragin at Richard Cameron an the way he's hell bent on bringin disaster doon on us aw."

"Surely no."

"Think aboot it. Aw the support he's gaitherin will force the government's haund. Aifter Bothwell they canna let it go. Ah think they'll tak a harder line than afore. Whit's comin will be a hunner times worse."

"Ye soond lik a prophet o doom."

"Ah feel lik ane. As for the meenister, ah cud shake the eedjit. Jist imagine. He gits the chance o escapin tae Holland, a chance tae pit his past ahint him. When he goes ther he lands a job in some college, teachin meenisters, dain whit he's guid at, talkin in riddles aboot the Bible. Ye'd think that wud be enough, but naw, he alloos himsel tae git cairried awa wi Richard Cameron's talk aboot takin the faith furrit. Nixt thing he gies everythin up an trails back here aifter Cameron, tae help wi the grand plan. Except he disna. His conscience gits the better o him, forces him tae chainge his mind an tell Cameron he canna pretend ony mair. An here he is. Back wi me. Ah seem tae be stuck wi him an dinna ken whit tae dae."

"Ither than shake some sense intae him," Marion suggested. "Maister Brotherstone aye seems mair oot the world than in it. No that he can help hoo he is. Ah doubt if he'll ivver chainge."

John laughed. "Ah can jist imagine his face if he hears that truth.

"So can ah." Marion giggled. "But wheesht. He's sleepin next door."


Gavin arrived next morning with the letter from Holland. "Ah think this is whit ye're waitin for." He handed a little packet to Lucas.

"Thank ye." Lucas smiled until he saw the sender's scrawl across the back of the packet.

Gavin looked puzzled. "Ah thocht ye'd be pleased."

Lucas laid the packet down on the table. He turned as if to leave the room.

John grabbed his sleeve. "No ye'll no. No afore ye explain whit's wrang. The ither nicht ye wur desperate for that letter tae arrive."

Lucas seemed about to push past.

John didn't move.

Lucas pointed at the little packet. "Read the name on the back."

Gavin lifted it. "It's frae a Maister MacWard. Whit's the problem?"

Lucas looked uncomfortable. "MacWard's the problem. He's the meenister who encouraged Ritchie tae come back and tak the cause furrit. He's desperate tae tak on the government."

"Frae the safety o Holland?" John sounded annoyed. "As a man wi a price on ma heid ah've enough problems withoot ony mair bein added."

"I'm sorry." Lucas seemed embarrassed. "Truly I am."

"Ay weel. Ah'm jist sayin." John scuffed his feet then glanced up at Lucas. "Whit dae ye want tae dae aboot the letter?"

"Burn it," Lucas replied. "It'll be ordering Ritchie tae tak maitters further."

"Ye promised tae deliver it." John spoke slowly.

"Ay."

Gavin looked from one to the other. "So whit? Ah'd git rid o it. If it's as bad as ye think naebody wud blame ye. But please yersel. Ah've done ma bit." He made for the door.

John stared after Gavin then picked up the packet and turned it in his hand. "Mibbe it's no as bad as aw that."

Lucas shook his head. "Maister MacWard disna dae hauding back."

"The mair ah hear aboot this man the less ah like." John's voice hardened.

"He's a guid meenister. A highly respected, and sincere man, jist impatient for the cause tae succeed. He was flung oot his parish and then banished frae the country. That's hoo he ended up in Holland."

"Is that so?"

Neither spoke for several minutes then John said, "Ye best git on wi yer delivery."

Lucas picked up the packet and stuffed it inside his jacket. "I'll head for John Brown's and tak it frae there."

"Haud on a meenit till ah tell Marion. Ah'm comin wi ye." John went into the hall and lifted his jacket from the end peg.

Before breakfast Ritchie shaved and washed with the utmost care, brushed his jacket and breeches, tied back his fair hair, then looked in the mirror and forced a smile. And when he went out to meet the men waiting in the yard he seemed as cheerful as any other morning. "Morning freends." He managed another smile. "Today we'll head for Muirkirk where I'll prepare for anither meeting. Oor success is ever widening and the government is set on stopping us so we best tak care and stick tae open country raither than the roads. Wi that in mind we'll cut across Airds Moss. It'll tak mair time but dinna worry, we'll mak a stop aboot halfway, hae a bite tae eat, a sit doon, and a prayer tae refresh us."

Three hours later they stopped in the midst of a bleak stretch of moorland. They could see for miles. It seemed as good as anywhere to rest. Several of the men stretched out on the heather, closed their eyes, and were about to doze off when a figure appeared in the distance, running fast towards them. As it came closer those watching could see the arms waving like a madman. Soon they could hear wild shouts.

"Whae's that?" Hackston pointed towards the figure.

One of the men sat up and stared at the flailing arms. "It's auld Davie. He's a shepherd, kens the moor lik the back o his haund."

Suddenly they all heard, "Sir, sir! They ken whaur ye are!" The figure stopped running and turned to point at dark dots moving in the distance. "See. They ken ye're here. Thur comin aifter ye."

Ritchie studied the dots. They were growing in size with every minute. "Whit noo?" He turned to his friends.

Every voice said, "We fight. Tae the last if need be."

"So be it." Ritchie raised his hands and whispered, "We're ready, Lord. Tak the ripe and spare the green."

Hackston looked round. They needed something to aid their defence. A few yards off was a stretch of boggy ground. He pointed towards it. "Tak up yer position ahint yon stretch o swamp. That way the mounted troopers canna gallop amang us. They'll need tae stop an gie us the chance tae fire first. If oor aim's guid we'll tak some doon afore they ken whit's happenin. We need aw the help we can git. But God willing, we'll gie them a taste o hell."

Andrew Bruce of Earlshall, who was leading the government troops, drove his horse towards the waiting group of armed men. Years before, he'd been a childhood friend of the man he was hunting down. Now a sworn enemy, he was determined to stop Cameron and any other who resisted.

The ragbag of defiance ahead looked ridiculous. The idiots had chosen to stay and fight. With so few against so many, the outcome was assured. He smiled at this thought. In a few minutes he'd be the man to end the government's frustration over Cameron and his challenge against law and order. Best of all, he'd be the hero of the day.

As they arrived he shouted out, "The man in the centre wi the fair hair is Cameron. We want him deid or alive." He waved an arm at twenty dragoons behind him. "Aff tae the left. Attack Cameron's flank and create a distraction while the rest advance."

Hackston saw this and ordered those on foot to the left, then signalled the horsemen to stay put and meet the main advance. He waited till the mounted attack reached the edge of the bog and roared, "Fire!"

Several of the government cavalry fell. Others stumbled on. Unused to military discipline, the men beside Hackston couldn't resist the temptation and lurched forward. Soon both sets of horses were floundering in the swamp. Hackston abandoned his horse. "Dismount! Follow me!" He jumped from tussock to tussock. "This way. Attack! Attack!"

Swords clashed around Ritchie as his men did their best to protect him, not that he cared nor wanted protecting. He was on his own crusade, swiping at every flash of red jacket or metal breastplate.

The fury of it all seemed to work until a horse came in from behind. Its rider's sword hovered above the fair head before plunging down. Even as Ritchie screamed, "For Christ and the Covenant!" Captain Crichton was calling out, "Got ye!"

Those closest to Ritchie hesitated, which was all it took to provide an opening for more troopers to swarm in.

Those who saw Ritchie fall seemed to realise it was their turn next. As one they jumped sidewards, ploughed back through the swamp and kept running. Behind them lay Ritchie and eight others, along with twenty-eight troopers shot dead or badly wounded. Four, including Hackston, were taken prisoner.

Bruce stared at the carnage and shook his head. "Only a handfu o men and luk at the damage they did." He turned to the nearest soldier. "A guinea if ye cut aff Cameron's heid and haunds. We need them as proof for the Privy Council."

The man grabbed Ritchie's mangled body, turned it round, and began to saw at the neck.

Crichton pushed the man aside, lifted his sword and sliced through the slim neck with one swipe. "See? Nae problem." He swung the head back and forth by the long hair. "Weel micht ye luk a me." He grinned at the piercing blue eyes that seemed to stare at him.

Bruce watched and smiled at Crichton's antics. "Aifter yer fun captain, wud ye dae the same for the haunds?"

"Nae problem." Crichton swung the head one more time before chopping off both hands.

A man ran forward to bag the Privy Council evidence, then handed the sack to Crichton who hung it beside his saddlebag.

The men lined up. Bruce moved to the front and signalled for Crichton to join him. "We'll tak the prisoners tae Douglas and see tae their wounds."

"Why bother?" Crichton asked.

Bruce smiled again. "And let the beggars die afore reaching Edinburgh? Naw, naw. We dinna want them tae miss the special treat that's waiting for them."

"This is a surprise." John Brown smiled at his two unexpected visitors.

Lucas spoke first. "I need tae find Ritchie. I hae a letter for him."

"Whaur frae?" John Brown looked puzzled.

"Frae Holland," John cut in. "Seems important. Dae ye ken whaur Cameron micht be?"

"He wis at Meadowheid farm by Sorn the ither day. But he's preachin near Muirkirk come Sunday. Wull Semple at Douglas cud pit ye richt. He's been advisin Ritchie aboot the best way tae go on his journeys. Thur's mair than sixty followin him these days an it's no easy tae bide oot o sicht wi a crowd trailin ahint ye."

"Douglas. Thank ye." Lucas turned to leave.

"Haud on," John Brown called out. "A pony wud git ye there quicker."

Lucas and John waited while John Brown brought two rough haired ponies from his stable. He saddled them up then handed over the reins. "Richt. On ye go, an be carefu."

John Steel nodded and took two large bunnets from his pocket. He pulled one on then gave the other to Lucas. "Tak aff yer meenister's black hat an leave it here afore ye pu this bunnet weel doon ower yer een. Richt doon tae bide oot o sicht."

Lucas seemed about to argue, but John's expression stopped him. Bunnets on, they led the ponies across the yard towards the moorland path.

It was early evening before John and Lucas saw hazy smoke rising from Douglas village chimneys. Neither had said a word since leaving Priesthill. Eventually John could stand it no longer. "Haud on a meenit." He leant over, took the reins of Lucas's pony, and forced the beast to stop. "Can ah jist say, aince that letter's delivered we turn roond and come richt back. Nae discussion. Nae arguin wi Cameron or onybody else."

Lucas nodded. "I've made my decision aboot Ritchie and his intention for the cause. He kens hoo I feel. He'll no try tae persuade me itherwise. Even if he does I'll no chainge my mind noo."

John looked away. "It's no that. Ah'm thinkin aboot whit next. When we're back at the farm ye need tae sit doon an hae a proper think aboot yersel an the best way tae move on."

Lucas stiffened. "I understand. And I will. But first things first."

John let go of the reins. "Noo mind, we need tae tak care in the village. Ah'm a wantit felon an hae nae wish tae be arrested."

"Of course. That's the last thing I'd want. Dae ye ken whaur tae find this Maister Semple?"

John clicked the pony forward. "No. But ma cousin Tam works fur the Duke an bides on the Douglas estate. He'll pit us richt."

Half an hour later the ponies were safe in Tam's tiny stable while Lucas and John walked on towards the village. When they reached the first row of houses John pointed to the left. "Tam said that Maister Semple's hoose is in the Loanin, at the far end o the Main Street, we can skirt roond by Saint Bride's kirkyard. If we gang in by the back gate naebody's likely tae notice. If we nip oot at the front gate wur straight ontae the Main Street wi only a yard or twa further tae go."

They were just rounding the old church building when a trumpet sounded. John stopped. "Soonds lik the military."

They both listened. Now they could hear many hooves rattling steadily along the stone cobbles. Along with this came the tread of heavy, marching feet.

"Troopers, dragoons. Somethin's up."

"Dae ye think...?" Lucas didn't finish the question and John didn't answer. He looked worried, unsure about going any further. Equally unsure, Lucas waited by his side. Finally John pulled his bunnet further over his face. "Aince ah open the gate here keep ticht beside me till we see whit's goin on."

On the Main Street they found groups of villagers hurrying along, necks craning, trying to discover what the commotion was about. No one gave the strangers a second glance as they mingled with the crowd.

More people appeared. The noise increased. Further along they could see the heads of many horses, the flash of red from uniforms, and sense a growing excitement. "The military are by the Sun Inn. Somethin's definitely up." John nudged Lucas towards the back of the crowd.

Horsemen and dragoons had stopped in front of the village inn where the street almost widened into a small square. Rows of upper windows were flung open as many faces leant out to stare at the unexpected spectacle. At the front of this impressive line-up John saw a smug looking Crichton holding a horse with an unconscious, bloodied figure slumped against the beast's neck.

John's heart sank. It was Hackston.

Three prisoners were tied to other horses. Each seemed more dead than alive.

There was no sign of Richard Cameron.

Lucas whispered, "He's no there."

"So it seems." John edged further through the crowd.

The trumpet sounded again. Muskets at the ready the military stood to attention as the leading rider wheeled round to face the crowd. "We bring proof o what happens to ony who dare defy His Majesty or the law." He signalled to Crichton who leant to the side and loosened the strings of a rough sack dangling beside his saddle. The watching faces strained forward as a head was yanked from the sack. There was a loud gasp as those at the front drew back. Some turned away or closed their eyes, others kept staring, mesmerised by the battered remains of this so-called leader of the kirk hanging by long strands of matted, fair hair.

Crichton's horse was directly below the inn sign. The golden sign, much brighter than the faded hair, winked in the setting sun, and gently swayed in the same way as the captain now began to swing the head. "Here's yer prophet, yer preacher. Tak a guid luk. He's no sic a great man noo."

Lucas blinked. "It's Ritchie." He stumbled. His fingers dug into John's arm.

"Shh." John leant against the trembling figure. "Dinna draw attention."

The head swung back and forth. The eyes, still wide open, as blue and piercing as ever, seemed to know Lucas was in the crowd, seemed determined to accuse him again for the fraud he was.

Silently he mouthed forgive me. It made no difference. The swing continued. Held by the movement he kept staring while his conscience, like that bloody head, swung further and further, taking him beyond his promise to John, his insistence that he knew his own mind.

The crowd around him began to mutter. Their words seemed like accusations; not at the proud soldier enjoying his moment, but meant for Lucas Brotherstone. These people seemed to know who he was, how he'd abandoned his friend to this terrible fate. Panic took over. His breathing quickened. His heart raced. His chest felt fit to burst. The muttering grew louder. He could smell the animosity. Helpless to defend his guilt, he tried to swallow it. It stuck in his throat. He tried again. This time he choked, began to retch. Why was this happening? If only he could close his eyes against that swinging head and stop his shame being exposed before it was too late.

Ritchie's grand plan had gone wrong. More wrong than he'd ever imagined. Without his driving force, insistence on the word, the way he explained the need to resist the king and all he stood for, who'd dare take that truth forward? No one. *If only?* The question was there. The message was plain in those staring, accusing eyes. Confused, terrified, humiliated, Lucas turned to push his way through the crowd, lurching into the open space beyond, beginning to run.

John followed but only caught up with the fleeing figure at the end of the street. "Keep goin," he gasped. "Back the way we came. Twa meenits mair an wur thru the castle gates, then mak fur Tam's stable."

Tam gaped at the two red faces rushing into his stable. "My God. Ye luk as if yer tails are on fire." He hurried to saddle up the two ponies. "If it's that bad ye best tak the auld castle path awa frae the village. Gang past the castle gardens, alang the edge o the wood, richt tae the far end o Stable Lake then cut across the river beyond. The water's shallow ther, an it's a quiet spot. Wi aw that fuss in the village naebody'll see ye. If onybody comes askin ye wur nivver here."

"Thank ye."

"Ay weel. Jist git goin."

Two riders hurried along by the shelter of the estate wood, crossed the river, and began the climb to the moor. Neither man looked back. Neither spoke as they picked their way through the heather, into the fading light and welcoming dark, each step taking them further away from Richard Cameron.

# END

# Historical Figures appearing in Dark Times

**John Graham of Claverhouse, Viscount Dundee 1648-1689:** Stout supporter of Stuart Kings who relied heavily on his ability to keep order in South-West Scotland. One of the most successful Scottish soldiers of his time. Considered a ruthless opponent by Covenanters, earned title Bluidy Clavers. Administered justice throughout Southern Scotland, captain of King's Royal Regiment, member of the Privy Council, created Viscount in 1688. Killed at Battle of Killiecrankie 17th June 1689 where his men were successful.

**George McKenzie of Rosehaugh 1636-1691:** King's advocate. Main member of Scottish Privy Council. Sentenced many Covenanters to death. After what was known as the Glorious Revolution he wrote two books justifying his acts. A power-hungry man.

**John Maitland, 1st Duke of Lauderdale 1610-1682:** Secretary of State for Scotland. One of King Charles's advisers. Power hungry and unethical man. Fierce prosecutor of Covenanters.

**Thomas Dalyell of the Binns 1602-1685:** Long serving royalist. Earlier in career was Lieutenant General in Russian Army. Very individual, fierce, eccentric character. Raised regiment known as the Royal Scots Greys, paid for it from his own purse. Determined persecutor of Covenanters. Member of Scottish Privy Council

**Lieutenant John Crichton or Creichton, dates not verified:** Served in His Majesty's Regiment of Dragoons. He did rise to rank of captain. Well known for his brutality to prisoners or any rebel on the run. One of his infamous incidents involves the shooting of David Steel of Skellyhill on 20th December 1686. Imprisoned in Edinburgh Tolbooth for a time after change of government. He is remembered for Jonathan Swift's book in 1731 titled 'Memoirs of Lieutenant John Creichton' where the account of his exploits are somewhat at odds with recorded fact.

**David Hackston of Rathillet, time line not verified:** Present at Archbishop Sharp's murder. Fought at Drumclog, Bothwell Bridge, Airds Moss where he was captured, tortured then hanged, drawn and quartered in Edinburgh's Grassmarket on 30th July 1680.

**Reverend Alexander Peden 1626-1686:** One of the most significant Covenanter ministers. Inspirational preacher. Ousted from his parish at New Luce in Wigtonshire he spent most of his life living rough and taking secret religious meetings. Famous for wearing a leather mask. Credited with second sight and described as Peden the prophet. Ambushed in June 1672, sent to the Bass Rock for four years then ordered aboard the St Michael for transportation to America. The ship put in at Gravesend in England where the captain set all the prisoners free. Returned home then wandered between Scotland and Northern Ireland. Died at his brother's house 26th January 1686 aged sixty. After burial troops dug up the corpse with intention of staging a hanging. Local laird intervened and corpse was buried at foot of the gallows.

**Reverend Donald Cargill 1610-1681:** One of the main ministers and rebel preachers of the Covenant. Minister of Barony Parish Glasgow till 1662 when he was expelled for refusing to celebrate the king's birthday. He was a colleague and stout supporter of Richard Cameron. Fought at Bothwell Bridge. Long career of rebel preaching. 5000 merks reward for his capture. Caught at Covington Mill near Biggar on 12th July 1681, tried and hanged at Edinburgh Grassmarket 27th July 1681.

**Henry Hall of Haughshead, birth date not verified but killed in 1680:** Friend and colleague of Donald Cargill. Involved in writing the Queensferry paper against the government. Caught, papers fell into government hands then used against Covenanters. Hall badly wounded during this event and died soon afterwards.

**Reverend Richard Cameron 1648-1680:** Radical Covenanter. Ordained in Holland before returning to Scotland to try and revive resistance. Known as the Lion of the Covenant. Great preacher. Fearless against the government. Drew up the Sanquhar Declaration denouncing the king. 5000 merks reward for his capture dead or alive. Killed during skirmish at Airds Moss near Cumnock four weeks later. Had a short but eventful ministry. The 26th or Cameronian Regiment named in his memory.

**Andrew Bruce of Earlshall, birth date not verified:** Military man on royalist side. Led troops at Airds Moss and killed Richard Cameron in 1680. Appointed Claverhouse's lieutenant in 1682. Very active in pursuing Covenanters throughout south-west Scotland. Not the most trustworthy of men.

**James Ogilvie Earl of Airlie and Strathmore 1615-1703:** Stout royalist supporter. Cavalry leader at Bothwell Bridge. During final stage of battle he tried to capture John Steel. John Steel fought back, knocked Airlie off his horse then escaped. Airlie then tried to hunt down Steel. Unsuccessful. In revenge he claimed the Steel farm and land then forced John Steel's wife and family onto the moor to live rough.

**Sir Robert Hamilton of Preston and Fingalton 1656-1701:** A poor leader of the Covenanter army at Bothwell Bridge. Almost first to leave the field and flee to the safety of Holland where he continued to try and influence happenings in Scotland. Returned to Scotland after 1688. A difficult and self-opinionated man.

**John Steel, time line not verified:** Bonnet laird with three farms. Lived at Logan Waterhead near Lesmahagow. Fought at Drumclog and Bothwell Bridge. As a consequence he was declared a rebel with 1000 merks reward for his capture. Lost his property and spent ten years on the run. Was never caught. Captain in Cameronian Regiment in 1689 to oversee ousting of English curates without bloodshed. Buried in Lesmahagow Old Parish Kirkyard under a plain thruchstane. Date unknown but after 1707.

**Marion Steel, time line not verified:** John Steel's wife. As a rebel's wife she was forced to live rough on the moor with her family after Bothwell Bridge. Bravely endured ill treatment from government troops. Eventually returned to her farm.

**Robert Steel, birth date not verified:** John Steel's father. Disappeared near Bothwell on day of battle 1679. Fate unknown but assumed to have been killed by government troopers.

**David Steel, birth date not verified:** Cousin of John Steel. Lived at Skellyhill farm near Lesmahagow. Fought at Drumclog and Bothwell Bridge. Fugitive till 1686 when he was caught and shot by Captain Crichton.

**Thomas Steel time line not verified :** Father of David Steel. Killed at Drumclog in 1679. Named as a hero of the battle.

**James Renwick 1662-1688:** One of most inspiring Covenanting ministers. Last martyr at age of 26. Supporter of Richard Cameron. Ordained in Holland. Involved in Lanark Declaration 12th January1682 and 2nd Sanquhar Declaration 28th May 1685.

# About the Author

## Ethyl Smith

Ethyl Smith is a graduate of Glasgow School of Art and a Fellow of Manchester School of Advanced Studies. She is also a graduate of the University of Strathclyde Novel Writing course and the Stirling University M.Litt. Creative Writing course.

Ethyl followed a career in illustrating and design lecturing, before following an interest in holistic therapy & hypnotherapy, which she now teaches.

Her short stories have appeared in a range of magazines including Scottish Field, Gutter, Scottish Memories, Mistaken Identities (edited by James Robertson), Mixing the Colours Anthology, and Scottish Book Trust Anthology.

Her interest in Scottish language and history, particularly 17th century, has led to a series of novels based on covenanting times, where greed, power, and religion created a dangerous mix. Changed Times is the first in that series.

## Also from Ethyl Smith
## Changed Times
### ISBN: 978-1-910946-09-1 (eBook)
### ISBN: 978-1-910946-08-4 (Paperback)

1679 – The Killing Times: Charles II is on the throne, the Episcopacy has been restored, and southern Scotland is in ferment.

The King is demanding superiority over all things spiritual and temporal and rebellious Ministers are being ousted from their parishes for refusing to bend the knee.

When John Steel steps in to help one such Minister in his home village of Lesmahagow he finds himself caught up in events that reverberate not just through the parish, but throughout the whole of southern Scotland.

From the Battle of Drumclog to the Battle of Bothwell Bridge, John's platoon of farmers and villagers find themselves in the heart of the action over that fateful summer where the people fight the King for their religion, their freedom, and their lives.

Set amid the tumult and intrigue of Scotland's Killing Times, John Steele's story powerfully reflects the changes that took place across 17th century Scotland, and stunningly brings this period of history to life.

**'Smith writes with a fine ear for Scots speech, and with a sensitive awareness to the different ways in which history intrudes upon the lives of men and women, soldiers and civilians, adults and children' – James Robertson**

# More Books From
# ThunderPoint Publishing Ltd.

## The Oystercatcher Girl
### Gabrielle Barnby
### ISBN: 978-1-910946-17-6 (eBook)
### ISBN: 978-1-910946-15-2 (Paperback)

In the medieval splendour of St Magnus Cathedral, three women gather to mourn the untimely passing of Robbie: Robbie's widow, Tessa; Tessa's old childhood friend, Christine, and Christine's unstable and unreliable sister, Lindsay.

But all is not as it seems: what is the relationship between the three women, and Robbie? What secrets do they hide? And who has really betrayed who?

Set amidst the spectacular scenery of the Orkney Islands, Gabrielle Barnby's skilfully plotted first novel is a beautifully understated story of deception and forgiveness, love and redemption.

With poetic and precise language Barnby draws you in to the lives, loves and losses of the characters till you feel a part of the story.

**'The Oystercatcher Girl is a wonderfully evocative and deftly woven story' – Sara Bailey**

# The False Men
## Mhairead MacLeod
ISBN: 978-1-910946-27-5 (eBook)
ISBN: 978-1-910946-25-1 (Paperback)

North Uist, Outer Hebrides, 1848

Jess MacKay has led a privileged life as the daughter of a local landowner, sheltered from the harsher aspects of life. Courted by the eligible Patrick Cooper, the Laird's new commissioner, Jess's future is mapped out, until Lachlan Macdonald arrives on North Uist, amid rumours of forced evictions on islands just to the south.

As the uncompromising brutality of the Clearances reaches the islands, and Jess sees her friends ripped from their homes, she must decide where her heart, and her loyalties, truly lie.

Set against the evocative backdrop of the Hebrides and inspired by a true story, *The False Men* is a compelling tale of love in a turbulent past that resonates with the upheavals of the modern world.

# Dead Cat Bounce
## Kevin Scott
### ISBN: 978-1-910946-17-6 (eBook)
### ISBN: 978-1-910946-15-2 (Paperback)

*"Well, either way, you'll have to speak to your brother today because...unless I get my money by tomorrow morning there's not going to be a funeral."*

When your 11 year old brother has been tragically killed in a car accident, you might think that organising his funeral would take priority. But when Nicky's coffin, complete with Nicky's body, goes missing, deadbeat loser Matt has only 26 hours in which to find the £20,000 he owes a Glasgow gangster or explain to his grieving mother why there's not going to be a funeral.

Enter middle brother, Pete, successful City trader with an expensive wife, expensive children, and an expensive villa in Tuscany. Pete's watches cost £20,000, but he has his own problems, and Matt doesn't want his help anyway.

Seething with old resentments, the betrayals of the past and the double-dealings of the present, the two brothers must find a way to work together to retrieve Nicky's body, discovering along the way that they are not so different after all.

**'Underplaying the comic potential to highlight the troubled relationship between the equally flawed brothers. It's one of those books that keep the reader hooked right to the end' – The Herald**

# The Wrong Box
## Andrew C Ferguson
### ISBN: 978-1-910946-14-5 (Paperback)
### ISBN: 978-1-910946-16-9 (eBook)

*All I know is, I'm in exile in Scotland, and there's a dead Scouser businessman in my bath. With his toe up the tap.*

Meet Simon English, corporate lawyer, heavy drinker and Scotophobe, banished from London after being caught misbehaving with one of the young associates on the corporate desk. As if that wasn't bad enough, English finds himself acting for a spiralling money laundering racket that could put not just his career, but his life, on the line.

Enter Karen Clamp, an 18 stone, well-read wann be couturier from the Auchendrossan sink estate, with an encyclopedic knowledge of Council misdeeds and 19th century Scottish fiction. With no one to trust but each other, this mismatched pair must work together to investigate a series of apparently unrelated frauds and discover how everything connects to the mysterious Wrong Box.

Manically funny, *The Wrong Box* is a chaotic story of lust, money, power and greed, and the importance of being able to sew a really good hem.

**'...the makings of a new Caledonian Comic Noir genre: Rebus with jokes, Val McDiarmid with buddha belly laughs, or Trainspotting for the professional classes'**

## The House with the Lilac Shutters:
### Gabrielle Barnby
ISBN: 978-1-910946-02-2 (eBook)
ISBN: 978-0-9929768-8-0 (Paperback)

Irma Lagrasse has taught piano to three generations of villagers, whilst slowly twisting the knife of vengeance; Nico knows a secret; and M. Lenoir has discovered a suppressed and dangerous passion.

Revolving around the Café Rose, opposite The House with the Lilac Shutters, this collection of contemporary short stories links a small town in France with a small town in England, traces the unexpected connections between the people of both places and explores the unpredictable influences that the past can have on the present.

Characters weave in and out of each other's stories, secrets are concealed and new connections are made.

With a keenly observant eye, Barnby illustrates the everyday tragedies, sorrows, hopes and joys of ordinary people in this vividly understated and unsentimental collection.

**'The more I read, and the more descriptions I encountered, the more I was put in mind of one of my all time favourite texts – Dylan Thomas' Under Milk Wood' – lindasbookbag.com**

## The Bogeyman Chronicles
### Craig Watson
### ISBN: 978-1-910946-11-4 (eBook)
### ISBN: 978-1-910946-10-7 (Paperback)

In 14th Century Scotland, amidst the wars of independence, hatred, murder and betrayal are commonplace. People are driven to extraordinary lengths to survive, whilst those with power exercise it with cruel pleasure.

Royal Prince Alexander Stewart, son of King Robert II and plagued by rumours of his illegitimacy, becomes infamous as the Wolf of Badenoch, while young Andrew Christie commits an unforgivable sin and lay Brother Brodie Affleck in the Restenneth Priory pieces together the mystery that links them all together.

From the horror of the times and the changing fortunes of the characters, the legend of the Bogeyman is born and Craig Watson cleverly weaves together the disparate lives of the characters into a compelling historical mystery that will keep you gripped throughout.

Over 80 years the lives of three men are inextricably entwined, and through their hatreds, murders and betrayals the legend of Christie Cleek, the bogeyman, is born.

**'The Bogeyman Chronicles haunted our imagination long after we finished it' – iScot Magazine**

# Mule Train
## Huw Francis
## ISBN: 978-0-9575689-0-7 (eBook)
## ISBN: 978-0-9575689-1-4 (Paperback)

Four lives come together in the remote and spectacular mountains bordering Afghanistan and explode in a deadly cocktail of treachery, betrayal and violence.

Written with a deep love of Pakistan and the Pakistani people, Mule Train will sweep you from Karachi in the south to the Shandur Pass in the north, through the dangerous borderland alongside Afghanistan, in an adventure that will keep you gripped throughout.

**'Stunningly captures the feel of Pakistan, from Karachi to the hills' – tripfiction.com**

# QueerBashing
## Tim Morriosn
## ISBN: 978-1-910946-06-0 (eBook)
## ISBN: 978-0-9929768-9-7 (Paperback)

*The first queerbasher McGillivray ever met was in the mirror.*

From the revivalist churches of Orkney in the 1970s, to the gay bars of London and Northern England in the 90s, via the divinity school at Aberdeen, this is the story of McGillivray, a self-centred, promiscuous hypocrite, failed Church of Scotland minister, and his own worst enemy.

Determined to live life on his own terms, McGillivray's grasp on reality slides into psychosis and a sense of his own invulnerability, resulting in a brutal attack ending life as he knows it.

Raw and uncompromising, this is a viciously funny but ultimately moving account of one man's desire to come to terms with himself and live his life as he sees fit.

## '…an arresting novel of pain and self-discovery' – Alastair Mabbott (The Herald)

# A Good Death
## Helen Davis
## ISBN: 978-0-9575689-7-6 (eBook)
## ISBN: 978-0-9575689-6-9 (Paperback)

'*A good death is better than a bad conscience,*' said Sophie.

1983 – Georgie, Theo, Sophie and Helena, four disparate young Cambridge undergraduates, set out to scale Ausangate, one of the highest and most sacred peaks in the Andes.

Seduced into employing the handsome and enigmatic Wamani as a guide, the four women are initiated into the mystically dangerous side of Peru, Wamani and themselves as they travel from Cuzco to the mountain, a journey that will shape their lives forever.

2013 – though the women are still close, the secrets and betrayals of Ausangate chafe at the friendship.

A girls' weekend at a lonely Fenland farmhouse descends into conflict with the insensitive inclusion of an overbearing young academic toyboy brought along by Theo. Sparked by his unexpected presence, pent up petty jealousies, recriminations and bitterness finally explode the truth of Ausangate, setting the women on a new and dangerous path.

Sharply observant and darkly comic, Helen Davis's début novel is an elegant tale of murder, seduction, vengeance, and the value of a good friendship.

**'The prose is crisp, adept, and emotionally evocative' – Lesbrary.com**

# The Birds That Never Flew
## Margot McCuaig
### Shortlisted for the Dundee International Book Prize 2012
### Longlisted for the Polari First Book Prize 2014
### ISBN: 978-0-9929768-5-9 (eBook)
### ISBN: 978-0-9929768-4-2 (Paperback)

*'Have you got a light hen? I'm totally gaspin.'*

Battered and bruised, Elizabeth has taken her daughter and left her abusive husband Patrick. Again. In the bleak and impersonal Glasgow housing office Elizabeth meets the provocatively intriguing drug addict Sadie, who is desperate to get her own life back on track.

The two women forge a fierce and interdependent relationship as they try to rebuild their shattered lives, but despite their bold, and sometimes illegal attempts it seems impossible to escape from the abuse they have always known, and tragedy strikes.

More than a decade later Elizabeth has started to implement her perfect revenge – until a surreal Glaswegian Virgin Mary steps in with imperfect timing and a less than divine attitude to stick a spoke in the wheel of retribution.

Tragic, darkly funny and irreverent, *The Birds That Never Flew* ushers in a new and vibrant voice in Scottish literature.

## '...dark, beautiful and moving, I wholeheartedly recommend' scanoir.co.uk

# Toxic
## Jackie McLean
### Shortlisted for the Yeovil Book Prize 2011
### ISBN: 978-0-9575689-8-3 (eBook)
### ISBN: 978-0-9575689-9-0 (Paperback)

The recklessly brilliant DI Donna Davenport, struggling to hide a secret from police colleagues and get over the break-up with her partner, has been suspended from duty for a fiery and inappropriate outburst to the press.

DI Evanton, an old-fashioned, hard-living misogynistic copper has been newly demoted for thumping a suspect, and transferred to Dundee with a final warning ringing in his ears and a reputation that precedes him.

And in the peaceful, rolling Tayside farmland a deadly store of MIC, the toxin that devastated Bhopal, is being illegally stored by a criminal gang smuggling the valuable substance necessary for making cheap pesticides.

An anonymous tip-off starts a desperate search for the MIC that is complicated by the uneasy partnership between Davenport and Evanton and their growing mistrust of each others actions.

Compelling and authentic, Toxic is a tense and fast paced crime thriller.

**'...a humdinger of a plot that is as realistic as it is frightening' – crimefictionlover.com**

# In The Shadow Of The Hill
## Helen Forbes
## ISBN: 978-0-9929768-1-1 (eBook)
## ISBN: 978-0-9929768-0-4 (Paperback)

An elderly woman is found battered to death in the common stairwell of an Inverness block of flats.

Detective Sergeant Joe Galbraith starts what seems like one more depressing investigation of the untimely death of a poor unfortunate who was in the wrong place, at the wrong time.

As the investigation spreads across Scotland it reaches into a past that Joe has tried to forget, and takes him back to the Hebridean island of Harris, where he spent his childhood.

Among the mountains and the stunning landscape of religiously conservative Harris, in the shadow of Ceapabhal, long buried events and a tragic story are slowly uncovered, and the investigation takes on an altogether more sinister aspect.

In The Shadow Of The Hill skilfully captures the intricacies and malevolence of the underbelly of Highland and Island life, bringing tragedy and vengeance to the magical beauty of the Outer Hebrides.

**'...our first real home-grown sample of modern Highland noir' – Roger Hutchison; West Highland Free Press**

## Over Here
### Jane Taylor
### ISBN: 978-0-9929768-3-5 (eBook)
### ISBN: 978-0-9929768-2-8 (Paperback)

*It's coming up to twenty-four hours since the boy stepped down from the big passenger liner – it must be, he reckons foggily – because morning has come around once more with the awful irrevocability of time destined to lead nowhere in this worrying new situation. His temporary minder on board – last spotted heading for the bar some while before the lumbering process of docking got underway – seems to have vanished for good. Where does that leave him now? All on his own in a new country: that's where it leaves him. He is just nine years old.*

An eloquently written novel tracing the social transformations of a century where possibilities were opened up by two world wars that saw millions of men move around the world to fight, and mass migration to the new worlds of Canada and Australia by tens of thousands of people looking for a better life.

Through the eyes of three generations of women, the tragic story of the nine year old boy on Liverpool docks is brought to life in saddeningly evocative prose.

**'...a sweeping haunting first novel that spans four generations and two continents...' – Cristina Odone/Catholic Herald**

# The Bonnie Road
## Suzanne d'Corsey
### ISBN: 978-1-910946-01-5 (eBook)
### ISBN: 978-0-9929768-6-6 (Paperback)

*My grandmother passed me in transit. She was leaving, I was coming into this world, our spirits meeting at the door to my mother's womb, as she bent over the bed to close the thin crinkled lids of her own mother's eyes.*

The women of Morag's family have been the keepers of tradition for generations, their skills and knowledge passed down from woman to woman, kept close and hidden from public view, official condemnation and religious suppression.

In late 1970s St. Andrews, demand for Morag's services are still there, but requested as stealthily as ever, for even in 20th century Scotland witchcraft is a dangerous Art to practise.

When newly widowed Rosalind arrives from California to tend her ailing uncle, she is drawn unsuspecting into a new world she never knew existed, one in which everyone seems to have a secret, but that offers greater opportunities than she dreamt of – if she only has the courage to open her heart to it.

Richly detailed, dark and compelling, d'Corsey magically transposes the old ways of Scotland into the 20th Century and brings to life the ancient traditions and beliefs that still dance just below the surface of the modern world.

**'…successfully portrays rich characters in compelling plots, interwoven with atmospheric Scottish settings & history and coloured with witchcraft & romance' – poppypeacockpens.com**

# Talk of the Toun
## Helen MacKinven
### ISBN: 978-1-910946-00-8 (eBook)
### ISBN: 978-0-9929768-7-3 (Paperback)

*She was greetin' again. But there's no need for Lorraine to be feart, since the first day of primary school, Angela has always been there to mop up her tears and snotters.*

An uplifting black comedy of love, family life and friendship, Talk of the Toun is a bittersweet coming-of-age tale set in the summer of 1985, in working class, central belt Scotland.

Lifelong friends Angela and Lorraine are two very different girls, with a growing divide in their aspirations and ambitions putting their friendship under increasing strain.

Artistically gifted Angela has her sights set on art school, but lassies like Angela, from a small town council scheme, are expected to settle for a nice wee secretarial job at the local factory. Her only ally is her gallus gran, Senga, the pet psychic, who firmly believes that her granddaughter can be whatever she wants.

Though Lorraine's ambitions are focused closer to home Angela has plans for her too, and a caravan holiday to Filey with Angela's family tests the dynamics of their relationship and has lifelong consequences for them both.

Effortlessly capturing the religious and social intricacies of 1980s Scotland, Talk of the Toun is the perfect mix of pathos and humour as the two girls wrestle with the complications of growing up and exploring who they really are.

**'Fresh, fierce and funny…a sharp and poignant study of growing up in 1980s Scotland. You'll laugh, you'll cry…you'll cringe' – KAREN CAMPBELL**

Lightning Source UK Ltd.
Milton Keynes UK
UKHW02f0802030518
322049UK00010B/259/P